RIVERSTAR

TESS THOMPSON

Booktrope Editions
Seattle WA 2013

Copyright 2013 Tess Thompson

This work is licensed under a Creative Commons Attribution-Noncommercial-No Derivative Works 3.0 Unported License.

Attribution — You must attribute the work in the manner specified by the author or licensor (but not in any way that suggests that they endorse you or your use of the work).

Noncommercial — You may not use this work for commercial purposes.

No Derivative Works — You may not alter, transform, or build upon this work.

Inquiries about additional permissions should be directed to: info@booktrope.com

Cover Design by Greg Simanson
Edited by Jennifer D. Munro

This is a work of fiction. Names, characters, places, brands, media, and incidents are either the product of the author's imagination or are used fictitiously. Any resemblance to similarly named places or to persons living or deceased is unintentional.

PRINT ISBN 978-1-62015-146-4
EPUB ISBN 978-1-62015-242-3

For further information regarding permissions, please contact info@booktrope.com.

Library of Congress Control Number: 2013914983

*For my beautiful and talented
star in the making, Ella Caroline.*

ACKNOWLEDGMENTS

First and foremost, thank you to my editor Jennifer D. Munro for her careful and insightful guidance. Greg Simanson for the beautiful cover; it is perfect, as they always are. My daughters, Ella and Emerson, for being more mature than you should have to be, for all the times you entertain yourselves while I work, and for your tenacity and resilience during this painful year. To Jesse James Freeman, Marni Mann, Steven Luna, and Tracey Frazier for helping me fight this war of words. To Katherine Sears for making sure my stories make it out of the drawer. And to Heather Ludviksson for your unflappable belief in me. To Ronald and Alex Gallacher for spreading love despite your unimaginable loss—Ella is forever changed by your extraordinary gesture on an ordinary day. Finally, to my readers, thank you for the letters and notes and requests for more books. You are beacons of light on dark and lonely days. I write for you, always.

Prologue

IT WAS THE GIRL'S AGE that crawled under Bella Webber's skin like an unseen but insufferable rash. Not the fact that the girl was attached to Ben Fleck in a python grip. No, it was that she was a girl, barely legal, and had no right to even be here. The wedding of her brother Drake and Annie was a small affair, intimate, not for strangers. One had only to look at the white chairs, rented for this simple outdoor wedding on the lawn of Drake's house, to know this. There were only a dozen, three on each side, arranged in two rows for the bride's close circle of friends—Annie's *gang of misfits*. Ben should have had the common decency, at least, to know this. He was an insensitive womanizer. That was all there was to it. What had Bella seen in him, anyway? Lust. That was all. It was nothing real, despite the fact that two months ago he'd so expertly made love to her for sixteen hours that she'd temporarily forgotten everything about her real life, including her married lover lingering in California with empty promises that he would someday leave his wife.

Stop, she told herself, hearing the voice of her therapist in her mind. *Just stop trying to mask your pain by telling yourself lies or making excuses.* This condemnation of Ben Fleck was not the truth. Surely she'd learned enough in her copious visits to the therapist to admit this to herself. Her feelings for Ben were more than lust. He was a good man, a man to be trusted and to trust. It was her fault he was not sitting next to her now, with his strong arm draped around her shoulders, sheltering her from any storm that might come her way and from the thoughts of the past that haunted her.

She'd created this chasm between them. This was the undeniable truth.

And why? Graham Rouse: movie producer, power broker, dealmaker in the inexplicable world of Hollywood. They'd met on the set of one of his movies three years ago; Bella was the makeup artist for two of the main actresses in the film, and Graham was the head producer. With his polished looks and smooth tongue, he'd made it his mission to get Bella to fall for him. Unfortunately, she had, despite his situation: married with two little boys. *I just need a little more time,* he said, time and time again. Or, *I can't leave now because of my boys. Soon. Next month. After the holidays. Just one more birthday.* There were three years of lies she'd clung to during endless dark nights, asking God why and how and please, all the while knowing this was not the life He wanted for her or envisioned for her when He created her from nothing. Finally, she said, *enough.* One afternoon last spring, during a walk through her Westwood neighborhood in Los Angeles, she'd stumbled into an empty Catholic church that smelled of incense and candle wax and roses. She'd gone down on her knees to pray. *I'm on my knees, Lord. I need help.* And the answer had come, swift and clear, like a voice in her head. *Go north.*

So she did. North to Oregon. North to her older brother. North to Drake's enormous, chalet-like home perched on the side of a mountain, with the river below that curved and flowed in its natural cycles until it emptied, finally, into the sea. Yes, it was the river that had reminded her of her name, forgotten for three years in the embrace of a liar. *I must start a new life,* was her daily mantra, as she hiked the mountain and swam in the current and watched the stars from Drake's deck. And slowly, she thought less and less of Graham, in a way she couldn't have if she'd stayed in Los Angeles. Indeed, all through June and July she'd grown and healed, basking in the Oregon sun and submerging all the pain and heartbreak in the water of the river until she was ready to let go of the past and move forward into the life she dreamt of—one she was just learning to believe she deserved.

And then one night that summer there was Ben at her brother's dinner table—just there, out of nowhere, visiting from Seattle on business—lean and blond with green eyes that looked as if he were about to burst into laughter at any moment. She'd fallen for him, quickly and without provocation. But Graham had shown up in almost the next moment, confessing his devotion, saying her disappearance had awakened him to what he really wanted and needed—her. And although her heart had been forever changed in the moments with Ben, she was compelled to explore, at least, if Graham was telling her the truth. Or, perhaps, just to have final closure.

Of course, as it turned out, he was still a liar. He hadn't left his wife. It took only two days home in Los Angeles to understand it was yet another empty promise from a man who lied without apology as only a narcissist could. So she'd ended it once and for all. When she'd emptied her apartment of everything Graham had ever given her, she called Ben, apologizing, explaining that Graham had shown up unexpectedly and she'd had to figure it out without Ben's influence, without him making her crazy in bed. He'd listened silently, and then, finally, just this: "My dance card's full. I'm sorry."

Dance card? Surely, she thought now, he hadn't meant this child clinging to his arm? Who was she, anyway? Amanda, hostess at Riversong, the restaurant where Annie was head chef. Some trust-fund baby exploring her inner artist by moving to southern Oregon or some other equally ridiculous nonsense. Yes, she told herself again, it was the girl's age that bothered her. Not that she herself was dateless, sitting alone across the aisle as beautiful Annie exchanged rings with Drake.

Annie's ten-year-old son, Alder, stood with his mother and soon-to-be stepfather, included in a union that bonded them as a new family. The sun was low in the sky, casting everything in an orange tinge. A slight breeze rustled in the firs surrounding the yard. The wooden swing tied to a thick branch of the large oak swayed slightly.

Bella crossed and uncrossed her legs, skirting her eyes just slightly to the right, stealing a glance at Ben, who sat across from her in the other aisle. And there it was. He was looking at her legs. Indeed, *her* legs, not the child's legs. That was something, at least.

What had he said about her that night? The night? *Power in a tiny package*, referring to her petite but tight and muscular body. He'd splayed his fingers through her dark curls, worn short so they fell over her forehead and dangled just below her ears. He'd kissed the dimples on the sides of her mouth and traced his fingers along her heart-shaped jawline. *So beautiful,* he'd whispered with his mouth at her neck. *So very beautiful.*

Now she shook her head, as if that would dispel the memories. The vows were done; Annie's dear friend Linus was pronouncing them Mr. and Mrs. Drake Webber. Alder clapped his hands together and let out a shout. The rest of them all jumped to their feet and clapped and cheered as well.

Then, as it sometimes did, out of nowhere, Bella remembered her little niece, Chloe, and Drake's first wife, Esther, now buried side by side in the family plot. On the tombstone: *Always in our hearts.* Bella's heart ached; tears came to her eyes. *Esther,* she said silently, *he's happy with Annie and Alder but we'll always love you. There's room enough in our hearts to love you all.*

The next thought was of her mother, gone since Bella was sixteen. How she would have loved to see this day. But they were all in heaven now; perhaps her mother was frolicking through a rose garden holding Chloe's hand. She reached into the small purse wrapped around her wrist and took out a tissue, dabbing at her eyes.

Drake and Annie were coming down the aisle, both beaming. Bella turned slightly and her eyes met Ben's. For a split second, before he made them dull and unreadable, she'd seen sympathy, as if he knew what was on her mind. The night they'd spent together, she'd talked of her niece and sister-in-law; it had given her comfort to know he'd known them as well, because of his long relationship with Drake. She'd confessed to a deep emptiness since their deaths that she couldn't rid herself of, despite all the ways she tried to fill the caverns of grief with friends and booze and intense sports. The only thing she hadn't confessed to Ben? Graham Rouse. She'd tried to fill the grief with Graham, as well. But he brought further grief, time and time again. Those days were done, at least. Yes, at least there was that.

* * *

After the ceremony, she stood with Drake and Annie on the corner of the deck. She held Annie tightly for a moment before taking her hands in her own. Annie's skin was so fair and pink against her own olive complexion, tanned from California sunshine. "Does this mean we're officially sisters?" asked Bella.

"Yes, it does," said Annie. "I'm so happy." She lowered her voice. "Are you all right? I mean, with Ben here?"

"I'm fine. But really? Did he have to bring a child to the wedding?"

"Alder has to have a little friend too," said Annie, laughing.

Drake glanced over at where Amanda was standing with Ben, laughing at something he must have said. "She's not that young."

"Spoken like a man," said Bella.

Annie wrapped her arm around Drake's waist. "You stay away from her."

"You know I only have eyes for you," said Drake, reaching down and kissing Annie on the mouth. He looked up at Bella. "This is my wife. Can you believe it?"

"It's wonderful," she answered. "Truly."

Annie leaned closer to her, whispering, "Just tell him you miss him. I can see the way he still looks at you."

"I don't know. I already did that when I called him on the phone a couple of months ago. I blew it, Annie. He's not going to give me another chance."

"Put yourself out there. What can it hurt?"

Bella shrugged and glanced over at Ben, his dark blond hair shining in the last rays of September sun. She was flooded with it then—the wanting of him. Why had she ever let him slip through her hands? *Because you're an idiot,* she told herself. *Always have been.*

"It could hurt my pride," said Bella in answer to Annie's question.

"Who cares?" said Annie.

"You know, you're right. It deserves at least another try. Men are so cowardly when it comes to this kind of thing. Right?"

"Just don't get all sassy and mean," said her brother. "And maybe you'll have a chance to make amends."

"I'm not mean," said Bella, instantly annoyed. Why did her brother always have to point out all her flaws?

"Drake, that wasn't helpful." Annie poked him in the stomach. "You two aren't allowed to fight on my wedding day."

"Sorry, sweetheart," said Drake.

"Yeah, sorry, Annie. We'll be good. Can we have cake now?"

"As soon as we get the photos taken" Annie laughed. "Billy made an extra large cake so you can have as many pieces as you want."

She did love cake. Not exactly a substitute for the hot sex she had with Ben two months ago but it would have to do. For now.

* * *

Later, Bella sat on the wooden swing under the oak with a piece of cake. It was handmade by Billy, Annie's assistant chef at Riversong, and was white with raspberry filling and butter cream frosting, the bride's favorite. Bella ate it slowly, savoring the creamy frosting, especially. She was finishing the last crumb when she looked up to see Ben striding across the yard toward her, carrying two flutes of champagne. He'd taken off his suit jacket and rolled up the sleeves of his button-down shirt, revealing his ropy forearms. She stood, her high-heeled sandals sinking slightly in the soft lawn, holding onto the rope handles of the swing in one hand, her empty plate in the other.

"Annie said you might want this." He handed her a glass.

"Thanks." She met his gaze for a moment before taking a sip. His eyes were the same color as the pale tufts of new grass at her feet. When she'd met him two months ago, he'd seemed always on the verge of laughing. Now, his face was set, guarded, unreadable. She'd done this to him, she thought, filling with regret. Why hadn't she handled their parting better?

"Only you could wear a tight red dress to a wedding and get away with it." He gestured toward her body with his champagne glass.

She smiled, letting her eyes twinkle at him. "Is that a compliment, Benjamin Fleck?"

He shrugged, his eyes cold. "Sure. I guess."

How different he was than their first meeting, when he'd flirted with her without hesitation, teasing her about wearing her bikini on the deck of Drake's house.

"How you been?" he asked. *Uncharacteristically nonchalant*, she thought.

She matched his tone. "Fine. Busy with work."

"Yeah. Me too. The building's almost done. They put it up in record time." Ben's company, Hylink, had sent him to River Valley to open a new call center. According to Drake, it would bring hundreds of new jobs to the town.

"Just finished a shoot in Los Angeles. High budget thriller with Stefan Spencer."

"Big fan of his."

"I remember."

"You between gigs, then?" He took a sip of his champagne, his gaze constant on her face, unflinching, but there was something else, too. Distrust?

"For a few days. I have a film starting next week back in Los Angeles. And then I'm coming up here in October. I don't know if Annie told you but Graham chose River Valley for the film's location."

"She told me. Yes." His expression was dark. He shoved his free hand into the pocket of his slacks.

"It's a love triangle set in a logging town, so this place is perfect." It sounded cheesy to Bella but what did she know? She just painted the actors' and actresses' faces to be as pretty as possible despite the harshness of HD film. "Gennie's starring in it so I couldn't say no."

"Genevieve Banks. Movie star by day. Bella Webber's best friend by night."

She smiled. "You remember?"

"I remember everything." His eyes pierced into her.

"Me too." She said this softly, peering into her champagne glass. "Stefan Spencer's the male lead in it. He and Gennie have never worked together so I'm excited."

"It's still weird you know these people."

"That's what Annie says too." She shifted her weight to one leg, lifting the toes of her left foot out of her sandal and letting it dangle for a second or two, before turning her gaze to his face, wanting nothing more than to look upon him for the remainder of the evening as she slipped her foot back into place. "How are your nieces?"

His eyes lit up for a moment. "They're good. Both just had their birthdays. Seven and ten now. Hard to believe."

"Did your older brother find a new job yet?"

"Yeah. Like a month ago."

"Oh, good. So they're fine?"

"Is Gennie the only reason you couldn't say no?" asked Ben, his voice sounding pinched and as if he hadn't heard her last question.

She looked up, aggravated in an instant, knowing his implication, but wanting him to say it. "What do you mean?"

"Graham's the producer of the film. Which means he'll be here. Isn't that right?"

She flushed and turned her gaze back to the glass in her hands. "Unfortunately, that's right. He doesn't mean anything to me anymore. That's the truth, Ben."

"Okay."

She took a sip of her drink, watching him over the rim of the glass. "I'll be staying here at Drake's."

"I figured." His eyes widened slightly.

She smiled and used her saucy voice. "You can't get away from me even if you try." Damn him, anyway. There was no reason she couldn't flirt. Make him remember how hot it had been between them.

"Oh, is that how it's going to be?" He grimaced, rubbing under his eye with a circular motion.

"What?"

"All flirty and tempting before you disappear again with no warning?"

She took a step backward, gripping the side of the glass with her now damp palm. "Is that what you think I did?"

"Bella, it *is* what you did. And in the words of Maya Angelou, 'when people show you who they are, believe them the first time.'"

Her voice went higher, defensive. "That isn't who I am. I had some unfinished business."

"Yep. I get it. You weren't available. Too busy giving it all up for a married man. Brilliant move."

His anger surprised her but she felt it too, hot in her chest. What gave him the right to judge her? "Glass houses, huh, Ben? Must be nice to be so morally superior. If I remember right, you weren't exactly holding back that night in your pursuit of me. And you didn't exactly ask my situation."

"Guess I figured you were free when you fell into bed without pause. Especially given everything else we talked about that night. You know, our dreams for the future, your business idea, my love of fly-fishing. The difficult relationship I have with my distant yet controlling father. My flaky younger brother who smokes too much pot. My engagement that ended abruptly. Your grief over your niece and sister-in-law. How much you still miss your mom. Your fear of heights. Jesus, Bella, you told me every detail about your idiot father hanging you over the side of a building when you were three but you couldn't tell me about the long affair you'd just ended with a married man? It's not like we just talked about frivolous, meaningless stuff, Bella. I thought it meant something to you. I thought you were free."

She stared at him, the anger in her throat now. "It did. I was. Free that is. Crap, Ben, it was complicated. I'm sorry I didn't tell you. I should have. I see that now."

His question came fast, like he was spewing without thought. "Bella, what were you doing with him? Three years?"

"It was a mistake."

"A long one." His face was pink. He pulled at the collar of his shirt.

"I've beaten myself up enough over this. No need for you to do it, too." Her voice caught; a lump had formed at the back of her throat.

"I have a low tolerance for cheaters. And you deserve better," he added, softer.

"I know that."

"Do you?" He cocked his head to the side, staring at her with what could only be described as skepticism. "Will you remember that while you're seeing him every day on set?"

"I've been doing the work, Ben."

"The work?"

"Therapy."

"Good for you."

He sounded so bitter, she almost gasped. "It's no coincidence I fell for Graham three months after Chloe and Esther were killed. I'm sure you can imagine how this might happen."

"Yes," he said, his face transforming into something less shielded but more pained.

Neither said anything for a long moment. The light was fading now and a breeze had come to the mountain, bringing the scent of Drake's late September roses. The scent of roses had been there the first time Ben had kissed her. Did he remember? "Where's your date?" asked Bella, both as a way to break the silence and to keep herself from asking him about the roses.

"In the house." He leaned against the tree, taking another swallow of his champagne. "She's not really a date."

"What does that mean?"

"I'm not dating her. She's just my date here. For the wedding," he added, as if that weren't implied.

"How old is she, anyway?"

He smiled for the first time. "That bugging you? You hate it because you're not the most attractive woman at the party?" Despite the smile, there was more than just a hint of spite.

"Wow. That wasn't nice," she said, fighting tears as she swallowed the last of her champagne. She needed another glass. Pronto. And it was true. The girl was pretty, even though she looked remarkably like a Barbie doll, and it bothered Bella. A lot.

His face softened. "I'm sorry. I didn't mean that." His voice sounded husky and tender now, like the night they'd spent together. "Anyway, you *are* the prettiest girl at this party. At any party."

Like she'd just been wrapped in a soft blanket, she went warm with pleasure. *Have the courage to tell the truth*, she instructed herself. "Ben, I'm finished with Graham. Have been since the moment I went back to Los Angeles. The truth is, you got under my skin. Big time. And I'm sorry for how we left things. It was my fault. Totally my fault. I was confused and, well, it was just bad timing. I'd love to try again." She paused, watching the bubbles in his glass of champagne. Even his hands were sexy: close cropped nails, thin tufts of dark blond hair on his wrists and knuckles. She shivered, remembering the way he'd moved his hands over her body, the way he'd gripped her hips, how lightly he'd touched her breasts. "I'm going to be here. Working on the film. We could start over." She moved her gaze to his face, hoping to see a clue to his thoughts, but he was looking toward the house with the same veiled look in his green eyes. "There was a real connection between us. Right? You felt it too?"

"I did." His voice was muffled, subdued. "Like nothing I'd felt before."

She filled with hope. Perhaps there was a chance. Annie was right. *Just be open, tell him the truth.* "I haven't stopped thinking about you."

He met her gaze then, reaching out and touching her bare arm with the tips of his fingers. There it was, the undeniable spark, like something alive between them. "I haven't stopped thinking about you either." He withdrew his hand, looking up at the sky and then back at her. "But Bella, you're bad news—a heartbreak waiting to happen. And I can't go through another one. I won't survive."

"Because of what happened with your fiancé?"

"Yes." He rolled his glass between his hands and spoke as if relaying someone else's story instead of his own. "I was engaged to her for three years. A week before the wedding I found out she was in love with my cousin, who was like a brother to me. We grew up together. Close. It wrecked my world. I couldn't function. Almost lost my job. If it hadn't been for your brother's grace I would've. I cannot possibly go through something like that again. I had a little taste of it that morning you left. Took me weeks to get past it and start breathing again. So, no, Bella. Just no."

With that he turned and strode across the grass to the deck.

Bella felt the pain in her chest, hard and bitter and hollow. She sat on the swing, fighting tears. *Well, screw you, Ben Fleck. If you're stupid enough to walk away from this, then it's just your loss.* But her bravado was only a trickle, a small glimmer of anything true. She wanted to bury her face in her hands and weep. But she would not. Not on this day, of all days. Her brother, finally, had found happiness with a sweet and beautiful girl. This was to be celebrated. She could weep later, alone in her room, like she'd done all her life.

Chapter One

ON A MID-AFTERNOON during the second week of October, Bella arrived in River Valley. As she entered the city limits she slowed her Mini Cooper, an extravagant thirty-first birthday gift from Gennie. The population sign still said 1420 but it didn't seem so today. Hollywood had invaded. The main street bustled with people. There was a new coffee shop two businesses up from Riversong and people milled about outside or sat in classic wooden Adirondack chairs lined up against the building, talking in the crisp autumn afternoon, steam rising from coffee cups. Linus's inn displayed a No Vacancy sign. In the distance, perched on the side of one of the mountains overlooking the river, was the River Valley Resort and Lodge. She could see from their full parking lot they were probably at full capacity as well. The grocery store, which only months before seemed almost empty with mostly canned goods and a row of limp produce, now had vegetables, fruit, and flowers in attractive displays outside the front entrance. Through the window she saw gourmet cheeses and a deli. Several women were gathering flowers in their arms.

The sidewalks were now red brick; old-fashioned street lamps lined the sidewalks; and every storefront was painted in light brown, with muted red trim and blue awnings. Hanging flowerpots spilling over with mums and other autumn foliage hung from doors and rafters. Benches were strategically placed on each block, and there was a fountain and a small park between two of the older buildings right in the middle of the main street.

She drove out of town and across the valley, passing barren fields, empty of their summer bounty, oaks and maples vibrant with autumn colors, until she reached the gate of her brother's home, perched on the side of a mountain. Using the gate code, she turned her car into Drake's long driveway and then parked in her usual spot near the guesthouse. Annie ran across the yard and had grabbed her into a tight hug before she could even close the car door.

"Bella, I'm so glad you're here. I've missed you so much."

"Me too." The two women held one another, jumping up and down for a few seconds before stepping back to observe the other. Annie, petite and fair with wild blond curls, didn't have her usual peach flush. There were gray smudges under her eyes. She wore no makeup.

Annie tugged on a strand of curls. "I'm sorry I look like such a mess. I didn't have time to clean up yet today. It's been a weird morning." She took Bella's hand, guiding her inside. "Drake went to fetch Alder from school but they'll be here in a bit. It'll give us time to get you settled."

Drake and Annie's home was something out of a magazine. Designed by Drake's late wife in the rustic ski lodge style, it blended into the mountain as if it had always been there despite being 9,200 square-feet, using rustic wood and river rock for the exterior. Inside it had the same American West feel combined with an urban refinement of muted designer furniture and sophisticated rugs and art.

They headed to the guest suite, which had been custom designed for Bella, Drake ever hopeful she might come live with him, as if she weren't an adult. "Is Ben still in the guest house?" Bella asked, keeping her voice casual.

Annie opened the curtains in the bedroom. The October light was soft in the room of tan and blue. "Yes. He's been in and out, working some weeks in Seattle and some here. I'm not sure when he'll be here next. Probably this week. The call center officially opened last week so we've barely seen him." She plumped a pillow on one of the easy chairs. Particles from the cotton pillow floated in the streaks of sunlight. "Are you going to be all right with him being here?"

"Of course. I'll be busy." She went to the window so Annie wouldn't see the hurt on her face. The ache of regret and loss and rejection was in her stomach, like physical pain. Each time it came like a wave she couldn't escape, washing over her, pulling her under, slamming her face into the sand.

"The call center's employing over two hundred people. Isn't that incredible?" asked Annie.

It was, of course. But here was the pang again. Ben had been here in River Valley without her, building the call center in a town she felt was her own and yet she didn't get to be part of his life. When they'd been together last summer he'd told her all about Hylink's strategy to build call centers in the U.S., targeting small towns with high unemployment rates as locations. Ben was a Vice President, in charge of finding appropriate locations and subsequently building the centers and hiring and training personnel. He and Drake had known one another for fifteen years, having worked together in Seattle, and when Ben had called to ask about River Valley as a possible location, Drake had immediately asked him to come for a visit. Once here, Ben quickly agreed it was the perfect location for the new call center.

"Have you thought any more about your makeup line?" Annie asked this a little too casually, following Bella to the window.

"I went to the chemistry company I told you about." Bella moved the curtain closer to the sill.

"And?"

"They're ready when I'm ready. I don't know if it's the right time."

"Drake will invest. You know that, right?"

"I know. But I have to be sure it won't fail before I let him do that."

Annie peered at her for a moment, her sweet face tilted to one side. But she left it alone. Bella was grateful for this small yet significant act of kindness. Sometimes a person needed to know when to talk and when to be quiet. Annie was someone who understood both. She turned away and opened the top drawer of the bureau. "Need help unpacking?"

"Sure." Bella opened the first of her suitcases and handed a stack of sweaters to Annie. She tossed panties and bras into the top drawer of the bureau, thinking of her dream to start her own makeup line. Covering the desk at her apartment in Venice were hundreds of sketches for her cosmetic line. She had entire collections based on different women's coloring, everything from the fairest blond to the darkest brunette. For the darker woman was "Venice Beach"—bright oranges and reds and blues inspired by the art sold along the boardwalk and graffiti on the walls of the buildings here. Her latest collection, called "Oregon," was well-suited to a woman with fair, peaches-and-cream skin like Annie—hues of greens and browns and the pinks and reds in Drake's rose garden. For Annie's friend Lee, a redhead with skin the color a porcelain plate, there was the "Malibu" collection—eye shadows in pale gray and various shades of tan and almost translucent pinks for the lips and cheeks.

Bella used pastels mixed with one another until she found just the right color. Someday she would give all of this to the chemist and they would create the actual product. When she was ready. If she was ever ready.

She sighed, tossing several pairs of shoes into the closet as Annie put her toiletries bag in the bathroom. Why couldn't she be more like Drake? He hadn't hesitated to develop his idea and now he was a billionaire. And her best friend Gennie? She'd pursued an acting career despite the incredible odds of making a living at it, let alone reaching the status she'd achieved. But they were different than she. They were fearless, undaunted by the odds.

During a moment of vulnerability in the first months of their heady affair, she'd confessed to Graham she might like to start her own makeup line. She'd done some research, she told him, and had chosen a chemical company that could make the products if she had the capital to invest. He'd encouraged her to ask her brother for the money. But what if it didn't work? she'd argued. Then she'd have wasted her brother's money over what was probably a ridiculous dream. How many makeup lines were there already? What would make hers any better?

When she'd broken it off with Graham, he'd gone into attack mode, bringing up one of the sorest discussion points between them: her business idea. "It's like you never grew up from the scared, sad little girl your own father hung over the side of a building. Always in limbo like you were that day. You can't go back and you can't jump. You're a scared little girl, Bella, who puts makeup on women's faces for a living. Is this really all you want to be?"

In an act of the utmost maturity, she'd flipped him the finger and stormed out of his office.

Now, Annie interrupted her thoughts. "Well, I can't wait to meet Genevieve. Drake says she's lovely."

"She is. I've missed her so much. After her divorce from Moody she decided to take that job filming in Colombia for six months. I was worried she was going to get carried away by some wild animal or something." Genevieve Banks was one of the highest paid actresses in the business but she was also just a regular girl. Sweet Gennie was a small-town girl from Wisconsin, raised by a single mother, as Bella and Drake had been. Despite her fame, she was the type of girl who understood how to be a girlfriend; she didn't judge or lecture or try to steal your boyfriend even though she could have. They'd bonded immediately during their first jobs in the business ten years earlier. Adults raised poor could smell it in others, like a secret club. *Oh, yes, I know what it's like to do without, to wear shoes until your toes poked through, to never see your mother buy herself a new dress, to carry your house key in your backpack because your mother was at work and you had to let yourself in, the thrill when you found a pair of jeans that look like new on the rack at Goodwill.*

The miniseries they worked on was an awful piece; they'd laughed recently about the terrible script. And the actors? Some of the worst Bella had ever seen before or since. "Only good part was the costumes," Genevieve had said as they walked arm-in-arm on the beach. "And meeting you, Bellie." Regardless, it had given them both an entry into an almost impossible business. And now, Genevieve was an Oscar-nominated actress.

Annie closed the top drawer of the bureau. "Linus is hell bent on keeping them sheltered from the press while they're here. He has the back entry all set up for her and Stefan."

"I heard. And that's so Linus." Bella went to the closet and pulled out several wooden hangers.

Annie yawned and then brushed a stray feather, which had broken loose from the down comforter, from her jeans. "I have a surprise for you."

"You do?"

"Linus is bringing both Stefan and Genevieve for dinner tonight here at the house."

"Really? Wait, don't you have to work?"

"Billy and our other two assistants are going to take over tonight. I've been having them take more and more shifts without me. They do great." Annie fiddled with the pocket of her jeans, yawning. "I'm going to scale back a bit, take another night or two off every week."

"That doesn't sound like you." Bella peered at her. Annie was pale; it wasn't just the lack of makeup. She'd yawned twice in the last few minutes. Was she sick? Was it cancer? *Please, God, do not let her be sick. Not when we just found her.* She said it out loud, tension tight in her stomach. "Annie, what is it? Are you sick?"

Annie smiled her gentle smile. "No, goose, I'm pregnant."

Bella's legs felt weak with relief. She stumbled back, sitting on one of the two easy chairs. "Oh, thank God. I thought you had cancer."

Annie shook her head and wrinkled her brow, peering at her like she had lost the last of her sanity. "What are you talking about? Cancer? That's where your mind went?"

Bella put her hands together like she might pray, staring at her sister-in-law. "Drake and I keep losing people we love. I'm scared all the time it will happen again."

Annie crossed the room and sat next to her in the other chair, taking her hand. "I understand. But I'm healthy as can be. Other than that I can't keep any food down. It's terrible. I wasn't like this with Alder. Maybe it'll be a little girl."

A little girl. There would be a baby, a niece or nephew to join Alder. "Oh, Annie, a baby. A baby. I'm so happy." She glanced toward the hallway. "What do the boys think of this?"

"We haven't told Alder yet. I want to wait until the first trimester is over before we tell him, you know, just in case."

"Sure. What about Drake?" She couldn't be certain. Would he be excited for another child or would it bring the loss of his first child to the surface? Would the old, unimaginable grief spill into the joy of this new life?

Annie's eyes misted over. "He cried when I told him."

"Cried?"

"Sobbed." Annie wiped a stray tear from the corner of her eye. "It was heart-wrenching. He was happy and yet, well, you know."

"Right. Of course."

Bella stood, pulling Annie to her feet and hugging her. "Nothing will bring more happiness to all of us than a baby."

They heard a car turning into the long driveway from the road. "That'll be Drake and Alder," said Annie. "Let's go the kitchen. I'll make you all a snack."

"You know I love your snacks."

"I have a new truffle oil popcorn with Parmesan cheese I want you to try."

"Is it strips of Parmesan like you do with the Caesar salads at Riversong?" Bella's mouth watered.

"Exactly. I toss it all together. Everyone loves it so far. I have to hold my nose though. The stinky cheese makes me totally sick."

"You're so pregnant."

Annie giggled, taking Bella's arm as they headed down the hall. "I really am."

* * *

But it was not Drake and Alder coming up the drive. It was Benjamin Fleck in his sports car. No mistaking the flash of red between the trees.

"Crap." Bella looked down at her skinny jeans and riding boots splashed with mud. She fluffed her curls. And she needed a fresh coat of lipstick.

"You look fine. Beautiful, in fact."

"Whatever. I don't care."

"Sure you don't," said Annie, smiling as she left the kitchen.

A few minutes later Annie reappeared with Ben in the doorway of the kitchen. He wore a pair of khakis, wrinkled from sitting in the car on the long drive from Seattle, Bella assumed, and a blue silk T-shirt with a leather jacket over it. He flinched when he saw Bella. Yes, flinched, like someone had thrown a ball at his face without warning. "Hey, Bella."

"Hey," Bella mumbled, turning away as she sat at the counter on the stool closest to the wall.

Annie went to the stove and poured popcorn kernels into hot vegetable oil.

"You just get into town, Bella?" he asked, leaning against the counter with his forearms.

"Just now, yes." Her voice felt strangled, like she couldn't get enough air. She caught a whiff of his cologne and that was enough, she was back in the guesthouse with him like it was last night instead of three months ago. He'd held onto her hips, his thighs against her backside, pushing her up the stairs, stopping half way and turning her around, kissing her until she pulled away. She'd taken his hand and led him the rest of the way into the small sitting area of the guest house and then through to the bedroom. She'd wanted him like she'd never wanted anyone before, yanking at his belt, kissing him, his hands under the skirt of her sundress, tugging at her panties. He'd lifted her, wrapping her legs around him, and they'd fallen on the bed, not laughing or playful but almost ferocious in the way they'd attacked one another's mouths and bodies.

Annie was saying something to her. "I'm sorry, what?" Bella swallowed hard.

"I asked when you had to report for work." The sounds of kernels popping grew faster and faster. Annie shook the pan, twice in rapid succession. The room filled with the particular aroma of vegetable oil and popped corn.

"First thing in the morning. We have an all-hands meeting. Richard likes to give an opening-day talk for inspiration and to set the vision."

"Who's Richard?" Ben took off his jacket and hung it over the back of the stool, watching her like he knew what she'd been thinking. His eyes were almost amused but there was something else too. Hurt? Longing? Regret? *Don't go there*, she thought. He made it clear he didn't want anything to do with her. She must remain strong and distant.

"Our director." His jacket smelled of his cologne and leather. *Damn you, Ben Fleck.*

He slid onto the stool next to her. His cologne, again, was in her nose. Did he have to sit so near? His thigh muscles were evident under his khakis. She averted her eyes.

The popping slowed. Annie took the pan from the stove and set it on a hotplate. She then scooped two cups of the popped corn into small bowls and sprinkled them with truffle oil and shaved pieces of Parmesan.

She'd felt hungry, but now, with the aroma of the popcorn intermingled with the smell of Ben's leather jacket and his cologne, it was nothing but longing in the pit of her stomach. Her hands itched to touch the sides of his face. Or even to just put her nose into the folds of his leather jacket and breathe in his essence like oxygen.

"Annie, did you get my message I was coming down today?" asked Ben.

Annie shook her head, her face blank and innocent. "I didn't."

She's lying, thought Bella. *She didn't want me to know he was coming. She planned this little meeting.* Annie was more devious than she appeared.

"Sorry to arrive unexpectedly. Something came up down here that I have to take care of tomorrow."

"It's no problem. You know this is your home for however long you need it," said Annie, bringing her hand to her mouth, looking greener than the moment before. Was she feeling sick again? "How was your fishing trip to the Smith River?"

Ben grinned. "Really good. Used some Bivisible flies that worked great. Love that river."

Bella shuddered and pulled her sweater tighter, thinking of the skinny, curvy highway that ran above the Smith River in northern California. When she'd driven it earlier that day she'd gripped the steering wheel tightly and told herself over and over: *Don't look down. Don't look down.*

Ben glanced at her. "You okay?" Had he noticed her shudder?

She shifted in her chair, picking up a piece of popcorn. The kernel had exploded into four petals, like a lucky clover. "Yeah. Drove that highway this morning. It was terrifying. Just like the last time." The popcorn smelled of dank soil and mildew from the truffle oil.

"Takes courage to do something that makes you that afraid, Bella," he said, his eyes soft.

"I guess," she said.

She looked up. Annie's watchful eyes were perceptive, almost shrewd. *She sees what's between us*, thought Bella. *It's not just me.*

There was the sound of another car coming up the driveway. "That'll be my boys," said Annie, filling two more bowls with popcorn.

Neither Ben nor Bella had eaten. Annie's eyes darted to the full bowls but she didn't say anything.

Alder and Drake arrived in the kitchen. "Aunt Bella and Ben are here," shouted Alder, his ten-year-old face as round and sweet as the last time she'd seen. He gave Bella a hug and bumped shoulders with Ben. "Can you believe they're filming a movie here, Ben?" His big brown eyes sparkled with excitement. *Oh, to be ten again,* thought Bella.

"No, I really can't. Makes Hylink look like nothing big." He smiled and ruffled Alder's hair. "You been practicing your blackjack and poker face while I was gone?"

"Totally." Alder made his face blank. "Can you read me now?"

Ben laughed. "I'm not sure what that face means, actually."

Drake kissed Bella on the cheek. "Good to have you home, little sister. You get settled already?"

"Yep. Unpacked and everything."

Alder gave his mother a high-five before digging into the popcorn. "Thanks, Mom, I was hoping you'd make this today." He looked over at Bella. "Truffle oil. I mean, seriously, how cool is my mom?"

"The coolest," said Bella, smiling.

"Take that into your room and get your homework out of the way," said Annie to her son. "We have guests coming for dinner."

"Suddenly you're not as cool," said Alder with a sigh. He picked up his bowl. "What guests? Ben and Bella?"

"Ben, you're invited to dinner, of course. That goes without saying." Annie tapped the counter with one finger, looking at Alder with a slight smile. "Some friends of Aunt Bella's."

"Like movie friends?" asked Alder, smacking his hand against his forehead. "Please say it's who I think it is."

"Genevieve and, yes, Stefan Spencer."

"No way. Stefan Spencer is coming to our house. He's only the coolest cat on the planet." He looked over at Drake. "Dad, he's the one in that badass motorcycle movie we watched the other night."

"I know who he is," said Drake drily. "And that movie was God awful, not badass."

Alder threw up his arms, a look of utter amazement on his face. "Sometimes I don't even know who you are."

Drake chuckled and pointed at the door. "Get your homework done and then you can tell him how much you liked his movie."

After Alder left, Drake put his arm around Annie. "You feeling any better?"

She rested her head against his shoulder. "I threw up again after you left but I had an apple with peanut butter and that's staying down. For the moment, anyway."

Ben looked over at Annie with a concerned look on his face. "Have you had the flu?"

She shook her head. "More of the nine-month variety."

His face went from concern to delight. "What? Really?" He jumped from the stool and went to where they stood on the other side of the counter. "You guys, that's awesome." He shook Drake's hand and hugged Annie. But when he turned back toward Bella she saw the sting of envy pass over his handsome features. He wanted a family of his own. They'd talked of it that night, holding hands under the covers. "I want nothing more than to share my life with a woman I love and have a few children. I'm a simple guy, Bella, with simple dreams."

"Me too," she'd whispered into the dark.

Now, Drake motioned toward the back of the house. "Sweetheart, I want you to take a nap before tonight."

"My husband's so bossy," said Annie to Ben.

"Don't I know it," said Bella.

She expected Annie to protest about the nap but instead she nodded, following Drake out of the kitchen with a guilty glance back in their direction. "See you all later."

She was alone with Ben. Great. Now what?

"You're teaching him blackjack and poker?" It came out sounding like an accusation.

He raised one eyebrow, looking at her. "You have a problem with that?"

No. I don't. I think it's the coolest thing ever. And so are you.

She shrugged, pushing her popcorn bowl away. "What do you care what I think?"

His eyes skirted sideways. "I didn't mean to imply I did."

"Fine."

"Fine."

Her cheeks flamed. There was the blasted lump at the back of her throat again. "I'm his aunt now. I take that very seriously. Regardless of what you think of me."

"Bella." He said it quietly, almost under his breath.

She stared at the counter, fighting tears. "What? You have a few more digs? I'm too irresponsible to be a good aunt? I'm just a bitter single woman with no hope of having a child of my own and isn't that a blessing in disguise? Why don't you bring up Graham again? Anyone who had an affair with a married man doesn't get to have an opinion about what her nephew should or shouldn't do? Or how about telling me I'm just a stupid, frivolous makeup artist too chicken to do anything important with my life. Those are good ones."

He put up his hands. "Bella. Stop. I would never say those things to you. You've got me confused with someone else."

"Do I now? Aren't I just a heartbreak waiting to happen? Isn't that what you said?" The tears slid from her eyes onto her hot cheeks. She jumped from the stool, her foot catching in the bottom rung and causing her to lurch forward.

He stood, catching her in his arms. "Stop, just stop." He brought her close, leaning down, his mouth capturing hers, kissing her hard, pressing into her, tugging at her bottom lip with his own, his tongue flicking like a teasing flame. It took her breath away, this kiss that went on and on so the world ceased to be anything but Benjamin Fleck.

He pulled away, finally, setting her onto her stool as if she weighed nothing. It was intoxicating the way he tossed her about, handled her, touched her. "Bella, I'm sorry. I don't know what just happened." He raked his hand though his short blond hair. "I cannot be in the same house with you and not have this happen time and time again." His eyes were wild, like a trapped animal.

"Why don't you want it to happen time and time again?" she whispered. "Am I really that awful?"

"You're beautiful and smart and holy shit, the sexiest woman I've ever met but you scare me to death, Bella Webber." He said it sadly, as if resigned to his fear, knowing it paralyzed him but helpless to fight against it. Then, he turned away, marching out the door, leaving her alone in the kitchen. She picked up his bowl of popcorn and threw it against the wall. It shattered and splintered into a dozen pieces on the floor, the untouched popcorn intermingled with the broken china.

She put her head onto the counter. This was a mistake, this going north. She should have stayed by the beach where she belonged.

* * *

Bella ran along the path, breathing hard, the sun warm on the back of her neck, the crisp air filling her lungs. *Run, just run*, she told herself. *Don't think.* Her headphones blared Coldplay, the pounding music matching her pounding feet. The oak and maple leaves were red and orange and yellow, bright under the sun. The ground was damp and muddy as she trudged up the hill, the burn in her calves and thighs a welcome distraction from the ache of Ben's rejection. She stopped when she reached the top of the hill, leaning against a tree to catch her breath before running the rest of the way back to the house. Once there, she came in through the kitchen door from the deck. Drake was there, looking slightly panicked.

"Annie's exhausted. And puking again," said Drake. "Which means we have to cook."

"We?" She touched her chest with her index finger. "I think you mean you. I don't cook. I eat."

"Yeah, well, tonight you're cooking."

"How about take-out? Like Thai?"

"There's no Thai take-out here."

"Well, there should be."

"Dammit, Bella, this is serious."

She looked at him, crossing her arms over her chest. "How about we barbeque something? You used to do that in Seattle."

"Right, I did, didn't I? Before Annie started feeding me like a king. Like steaks and chicken? That would be acceptable, wouldn't it?"

"Sure. And salad. Yeah, I could make a salad. I guess. You just cut stuff up, right? How hard could that be?"

She showered and dressed in tight jeans and a light sweater, paying special attention to her makeup. If Ben chose to reject her she would at least remind him what he was missing.

Drake turned on the gas barbeque and tossed salt and pepper on the steak and chicken breasts while Bella chopped the vegetables she found in the refrigerator.

* * *

The weather was holding out; it was still clear skies and not yet dark when Linus, looking suave in a blue designer suit, arrived with two of the biggest movies stars in the world. Both Stefan and Genevieve were dressed casually and wore hats and sunglasses. They all lingered in the foyer, exchanging hugs. Stefan was holding a pink box with chocolate frosting smeared on the lid. Bella pointed at the box. "What's in there?"

"For you, Bellalicious. Cupcakes. I had them express-shipped from your favorite shop in L.A."

"You're the best." Bella knew and worked with a lot of beautiful people in her profession but Stefan had to be one of the most extraordinary. He had delicate features, a small nose and a slight but well-defined chin with full lips that gave his face a sultry and refined beauty. And yet, almost strangely, it did not deter from a raw and rugged manly quality conveyed through his vulnerable and almost wild dark green eyes. His eyes pulled you inside of him, both watching him onscreen and in real life. Over the years Bella had come to the conclusion that this way of portraying deep emotion and intellect through their eyes was a commonality amongst the great actors.

While Gennie was still shooting the film in Colombia and after Bella had left Oregon last summer, she'd worked with Stefan on a film in Los Angeles. They'd immediately bonded, quickly developing a gentle rapport like brother and sister. Despite often playing angry characters, Stefan was soft spoken and sensitive. He was also a man susceptible to predatory women because he simply couldn't fathom duplicity or manipulation and more than once had fallen for his female costars.

"Oh, I'm so happy," said Bella now, peering into the cupcake box. There were a dozen, in various flavors. "I call the Chocolate Velvet. Actually, I'll try one now."

"Before dinner?" asked Linus, raising his eyebrows as if he disapproved. "How scandalous."

"No one gets as excited about cupcakes as Bella," teased Gennie, her eyes on Stefan. "We might need to find her a support group."

Drake appeared from the front room, punching Bella lightly on the arm, before gesturing towards the kitchen. "Come in. As far as the cupcakes go, you best take one now before Bella eats them all."

Stefan closed the lid of the box as they all moved toward the kitchen. "Bella might be the only woman in Los Angeles who actually eats."

"Yeah," she said, glaring at Drake. "And that's a good thing. Right, Stefan?"

"Absolutely, Bellalicious," said Stefan.

Bella stuck her tongue out at Drake. He rolled his eyes.

"Did anyone bother you?" asked Bella of Genevieve, referring to the paparazzi.

"It's weird but I haven't seen one photographer since we arrived. I don't think they know we're filming here," said Gennie, taking off her baseball cap and letting her shiny brown hair fall loose about her shoulders. "And if the locals recognize us they're too polite to approach us so far."

Bella looked at Gennie. There was no question she was one of the most recognizable women in the world. Bella forgot this sometimes because Gennie was unpretentious and fun, just a regular girl. But it could not be denied that she was, quite simply, stunning. She was tall and slender with eyes the color of iced tea and full lips covering impossibly white, straight teeth. Her skin was fair for a brunette and glowed with health. "I should hate you for being so damn beautiful," Bella whispered to her as they linked arms and headed toward the large windows in the main sitting room.

"I'm a mess," Gennie whispered back. "I can't figure out how to do my makeup without you."

"The river's below," said Bella to Gennie and Stefan, pointing out the window. "Is Tiffany Archer here yet?" She turned away from the window and went to warm her legs by the stone fireplace. "They follow her everywhere."

"I didn't see any news people or paparazzi in town. We may have a few days of respite on that but they'll find us soon enough," said Gennie, following her to the fireplace. "They always do."

"I think you have it worse than I do," said Stefan with smile. "Must be because you're a huge movie star and I'm just some two-bit actor from Canada."

Gennie laughed. It was a real laugh, too, thought Bella. The kind that came from her chest; she hadn't heard it for a while. And Stefan was staring at her adoringly. Already? This is the way it was with Genevieve Banks. Everyone fell in love with her eventually.

Annie had come into the room, looking considerably better than she had that afternoon. Introductions were made and they all settled back into seats around the room.

"Who's Tiffany Archer?" asked Drake, picking up the thread of the earlier conversation.

"Jeez, Drake, do you know anything about my world?" Bella pretended to be annoyed. Did he live in a box here on the side of this mountain? "She's their costar. She's just out of rehab and the press are all over her twenty-four seven."

"Is she the one who shaved her head and put the photo on Twitter?" asked Drake.

Bella chuckled, getting up and going to the bar. She poured Annie a glass of sparkling water. "No, that was someone else. Tiffany just keeps driving her car high and drunk and getting arrested. This last stint in rehab was her fourth time, I think. I worked with her four or five years ago, before all the trouble was public. She's a sweet girl, actually, from what I remember. But wow, I had to do some major repair on her face a couple of times. Several days she came onto set with bruises on her face and arms, which I had to cover up with heavy makeup so we could get the shots we needed. The director was not happy. He made both of us cry, actually. But anyway, when I asked her where she got the bruises she made up some story about tripping outside a bar, but I got the feeling it was something more personal. Like maybe an abusive boyfriend."

Annie shivered as she sat on one of the couches with a worried look on her face. "Poor girl. I hope she's escaped him. That said, I also hope she doesn't ruin your film."

"Richard's taking a big risk but he believes everyone deserves a second chance," said Bella. "And he thinks she's talented. She was only seventeen when she did the film about the country singer and his rebellious daughter and she was spectacular."

"Richard's the director," Bella said to Drake, knowing he would have no idea.

"Wasn't she nominated for an Oscar for that one?" asked Annie.

"Oh, look at Annie, all up with the gossip," said Linus.

"I didn't know you cared about this kind of thing," said Bella to Annie.

Annie looked sheepish. "I don't really. But I was at the dentist last week and there was a big article about her in *People*. All about her career and rehab and everything. I feel bad for her. She has that look in her eyes of a lost little girl. I want to set her down at my kitchen table and give her a bowl of pasta and then send her to bed."

Bella laughed as she made a martini, up with two olives, for herself. "If anything could help her, it'd be one of your meals."

Linus pointed at Bella's martini. "Make one of those for me too."

Annie continued, serious about her subject. "Her parents were killed in a car accident, according to the article. When she was only sixteen or something. So sad."

"The girl's got chops," said Stefan. "Anyway, everyone deserves another go round in this business after they've made a few mistakes. She had fame come to her so fast and furious. One day she's a girl from some small town in Idaho and the next thing she knows she's on every billboard in the country and every magazine cover and nominated in the same category with Meryl Streep. It could cause anyone to go crazy."

Annie nodded, brushing back her unruly curls from her face. "That makes perfect sense. She was just a child when all that happened. It would take a strong person to get through without going a little crazy. Anyway, she's come to the right town for a second chance. Maybe some of our good vibes will rub off on her."

"Her twin sister goes everywhere with her," said Bella. "She tries to keep her on the right track but clearly it's a tough job." Sabrina Archer was Tiffany's manager and assistant. Nothing went to Tiffany without first going through her sister.

What wasn't said, but Bella knew only too well, given her job, was that Tiffany's looks had faded since her debut when she was eighteen. What had been exquisite, delicate beauty—she was fair skinned, a natural blond with piercing green eyes and a slightly crooked mouth that made her seem vulnerable and interesting—had faded with age and hard living into something more ordinary. She was no longer getting lead roles, not because of her reputation but because she wasn't pretty enough to carry a film. Now destined to be a character actress, more the quirky best friend roles or the psycho neighbor, or, as was the case in this film, the sister who doesn't get the man. It would be up to her now, in Bella's opinion, to act so well that no one could dispute her talent. There was honor in that. No matter the sharks posing as critics or the haters that posted cruel things about her on their blogs and tweets and Facebook pages.

"I think I saw her sister in town the other day." Annie set her drink on the coffee table. "I hope this doesn't sound callous but it freaked me out a little when I saw her. I thought it was Tiffany at first and then she turned and I saw her scar."

"It happens all the time. Sabrina hates it. She never goes to events or parties because of it," said Bella. Sabrina's scar was a skinny scarlet ribbon that ran from her left cheekbone to the corner of her mouth.

"Does anyone know what happened to her?" asked Stefan.

"No one I know," said Bella. It was one of those things no one could ask. Everyone knew about it and wondered how it happened but neither of the sisters talked about it.

The conversation continued but Bella wasn't fully listening. Where was Ben? Had he decided to skip dinner after what happened between them?

Drake had disappeared out back to grill the meat. Bella excused herself from the group and followed him, careful not to spill what was left of her martini. The light had faded by now; it was just an orange glow behind the trees. "Is Ben coming to dinner?" she asked her brother.

Drake, shutting the cover of his grill, looked at her sharply. "No. He decided he had something better to do, apparently."

She watched him. His light blue eyes were cold. "Are you mad at him?"

He set the spatula on the bench next to his grill. "You know, Bella, I am. I don't know what he thinks he's doing. Kissing you this afternoon and then running off like a coward."

"You know he kissed me?"

"Yes, unfortunately, I do." He walked over to the outside cooler where he kept drinks and grabbed a beer. "I happened to see you guys. I think I'm scarred for life." This was Drake's attempt at humor, she knew, but it didn't come out funny.

"I'm sorry." She took a big sip of her martini. It burned her throat. "It's my fault. I blew it with him and now he can't get past it."

"You know what? I call bullshit on that. You've done what you needed to do and you've let him know you're interested. If he can't get it together enough to give you guys another chance when he's clearly in love with you then that's just cowardly and not the man I thought he was."

She stared at her brother. He'd never taken her side before, especially when it came to her choices with men.

"You were brave, Bella, and that matters."

"I just did what Annie told me to do."

"That's what both of us should do at all times." He opened the grill, turned the meat and then closed the lid once more.

They were quiet for a moment, sipping their drinks and listening to the sizzle coming from the grill. "Drake, are you okay about the baby?"

His eyes were sad when he smiled. "I am. So very much. But it's hard, you know, because I miss Chloe so much. I almost feel guilty for being excited."

"What're you going to do about the two rooms you have shut off?"

He opened the grill again. Smoke came out in a puff. "I don't know."

"It's not fair to Annie."

"I know. She hasn't asked me to change them. Isn't that amazing?"

"It is. But it's also time." She paused, putting her hand on his arm. "I'll help you."

"Yeah. Good. Okay."

"Drake, I remembered something about Dad. About the day he dangled me over rooftop."

He turned away, taking a paper towel and wiping the platter free of the blood left from the raw meat. "What's that?" His voice was guarded. He hated to talk of it, she knew, but her need to tell him what she remembered outweighed any feelings of protectiveness.

"It was you who saved me. Did you know that?"

He looked at her, his eyes blinking five times fast. "I don't remember anything from that day. I don't know how you possibly could. You'd just started preschool."

"It was you, Drake. You pulled us back. You straddled him and beat on his face until the cops came. I remembered it in therapy."

He leaned against the wall, shaking his head, his face twisted in pain. "He was a monster, not a man. And you were such a sweet little girl. I remember that. Mom and I both adored you."

Bella's eyes filled. "I've carried it around for so long, you know, this idea that I was somehow bad enough to deserve what happened. I don't know if I even realized it fully but, well, it explains so much of what I do to mess up my life. Especially with men."

"I know, Bellybear. I know. And this is a great place for a second chance." He pulled her against his chest, kissing the top of her head. "Wish Mom could see how beautiful you are."

"Me too."

* * *

Bella and Gennie, wrapped in blankets, lay side by side on the lounge chairs on Drake's deck, staring up at the night sky. It was clear, the horizon almost blue and the stars millions of silver splintered lights, brighter than anywhere Bella had ever been.

Gennie, her gaze fixed upward, reached over and took Bella's hand. "I've been a lot of places and I've never seen stars like this."

"I was just thinking the same thing."

"This is why we're best friends," said Gennie, squeezing her hand. "Kindred spirits."

They were silent for a moment. Looking up at the stars was like standing next to the ocean, thought Bella. One felt insignificant and yet also omnificent, as if it were possible to steal the power displayed, for nourishment and strength, possibly even courage.

She turned to look at her friend just as Gennie swiped at her cheek with her hand.

"Are you all right?"

"It's been a year today that Moody moved out," said Gennie quietly. She dropped Bella's hand and shifted onto her side. "Everyone says it takes a year to recover from divorce."

"Do you feel recovered?"

"I'm broken, Bellie. I'll never be able to have a relationship that works. You know that." Gennie, regardless of her sensual performances, was unable to consummate any of her relationships. With Moody Gennie had believed there was a chance she would eventually soften and open to his touch, but it didn't happen and finally out of frustration he'd ended the marriage. Bella did not know why Gennie could not bear a man's touch. As close as they were, this was something Gennie refused to talk about.

So, now, Bella said only this, "You and me. Kindred spirits."

Again they were quiet, shifting on the chaise lounges to look back up at the sky. After a few moments, Gennie stirred. "I've been thinking about your cosmetic line."

"Yeah?"

"I'll invest 49% if you can come up with the 51%, and don't say you can't come up with that kind of money because I know Drake will give it to you. And think of it this way—it's actually a favor to me. I'll need some source of income after I retire, and all the other actresses have already invested in restaurants. Seriously, once I turn forty I'm dead in Hollywood and then what am I going to do? I need a backup plan."

Bella laughed, turning her head to look at her friend. "How long did it take you to come up with that argument?"

"There's more." Gennie met Bella's gaze, her eyes shining in the light from the house. "I'll do the ad campaign. My face can be the company's face."

"What did you just say?" Gennie never did any sort of advertising work, believing it compromised her image as a serious actress.

"You heard me. You know it's the sure way to make this work. Jeez, does that sound arrogant or what? I don't mean to sound that way."

Bella chuckled. "It's only arrogant if it isn't true, which in this case it is. But I don't know. It seems too big. I don't know anything about running a company."

"Don't be afraid to look stupid, Bella. That's the only difference between wildly successful people and those who think, 'what might have been?' I'll get us some T-shirts made that say, 'I'm with stupid.'"

"What if I make you look stupid too? I can't stand the thought of that."

"I, clearly, am not afraid to look stupid, given the shit I do on a daily basis in front of a camera."

Could Bella really pursue this dream she'd talked about for so long? Here was a chance, offered up out of pure generosity from her best friend. How many others would get a chance like this? And yet, there it was like another person on the remaining chaise lounge: the fear of failure. The fear of looking like a fool in a world that loved more than anything to pile upon failure like it was something life-giving to those too afraid to look stupid themselves. The haters. They were everywhere.

Bella's eyes were drawn back up to the sky. "Under the stars here, it gives me the same feeling as standing by the ocean."

Bella shivered, the night air penetrating through the blanket. "It's cold. We should go inside."

"Promise me you'll think about my offer."

"I promise."

Chapter Two

THE NEXT DAY the cast and crew of "Stone River" gathered on set, or "base-camp," as it was called in the business, for the first day of filming at a restored farmhouse. Surrounding the farmhouse were the grip, electric, props, and camera trucks, in addition to the "star-wagons" or trailers, for the director, Richard Greenwood, Gennie, Stefan, and Tiffany, all of whom were given the three-room variety. There was also a hair and makeup trailer, where Bella would do her work, along with the wardrobe truck that was like a huge walk-in closet.

The meeting was held in a "lunch-box," which was actually an enormous pop-out trailer with ten long tables and folding chairs. Members of the crew were there now, sipping coffee and eating breakfast. Pastries and coffee were laid out on a side table and Bella chose a cherry Danish but skipped the coffee, feeling wired from nervousness, given the proximity of Graham Rouse.

Yes, there he was, dressed in expensive slacks and a dress shirt, looking strangely out of place amongst the rest of the crew, all wearing jeans and sweaters. Stefan, talking quietly in the corner with one of the cameramen, wore work boots, jeans, and a fleece, seeming like a native to River Valley. Must be his Canadian roots, thought Bella. She made a mental note to tease him about it later.

Graham ambled over to her. His eyes skirted to the pastry and back to her face. He didn't need to say anything. She knew what he was thinking. But apparently he felt the urge to say it anyway. "You're not going to get away with eating like this forever."

"Doesn't seem to be catching up with me yet." She turned slightly so that he might catch a glimpse of her perky bottom and took a large bite of the pastry. He looked tired. There were bags under his eyes, like he hadn't slept. And his hair seemed more salt than pepper than the last time she saw him. She almost wished she cared enough to ask if he was all right. But she really didn't. It was liberating to no longer care. She was free. How had she cared for so long? Might she still be wrapped up in the dysfunction had it not been for meeting Ben? Ben. The familiar ache came back to her chest. Had she ever cared about Graham the way she did for Ben? Had he ever understood her the way Ben had seemed to? Had she ever been as attracted to him as she was to Ben? The answers were all no. Well, at least there is this, she thought. Ben had given her freedom even if he didn't want her any longer.

"How you been?" asked Graham. With the index finger and thumb of his right hand he twisted his wedding ring round and round. This unconscious habit had vexed Bella at one time. Now she noted it but it did not hurt her. But once? At one time it had bothered her beyond anything else, this physical manifestation of his marriage. They'd had a horrific argument over it one night. *Can't you at least take it off before you come to my house,* she'd screamed at him one evening.

She took another bite of pasty before answering. "Great." She wiped a stray bit of cherry filling from the side of her mouth with her middle finger. Why hadn't she grabbed a napkin?

"I hear you're single. Didn't work out with that Hylink guy, huh? He wasn't in your league anyway, Bel. You need someone from our world. Someone to challenge you."

"Don't see how that's your business. And I'm plenty challenged."

His eyes followed the movement of her finger. He had the same expression on his smug face before he took her to bed. "I miss you, Bel." He said this quietly, leaning into her. "You should come by my room later. We can catch up."

She matched his level of volume. "It'll be a cold day in hell if I ever visit you in the lodge or anywhere else."

His eyes were startled. "Then why are you here?"

Did he think she took the gig to be near him? So typical. Her hand twitched at her side. She stuffed it into the pocket of her jeans, digging her fingernails into the side of her thigh. "I'm here for Gennie. And because this is my town and I'm proud of it and want to be part of the film made here. I'm grateful we're filming here. It wouldn't have happened if you hadn't chased me up here. Other than that, I'm so far along the road I can't even see you in my rearview mirror."

Richard Greenwood was heading toward the front of the room. They both turned towards him. Richard was in his late fifties, short and slightly plump, with an air of a tenured English professor but without the tweed jacket. He wore his shock of thick white hair longer than was fashionable and a close-trimmed white beard, all of which gave the impression (Bella believed rightly so) of a man who cared little what others thought of him and had no regard for his appearance.

"You sound like a bitter old woman," said Graham out of the corner of his mouth.

"I may be bitter but I'm not old."

He touched her lower back with his fingertips. "You'll be back."

She spoke silently to him. *You wear too much cologne. And get your slimy hands off me. I just picked up this sweater at the dry cleaner.* She moved away from him to the pastry table and grabbed another large Danish.

Richard clapped his hands, looking around the room with a wide grin. "Welcome to the first day of what I hope will be a time of great creativity and collaboration. I've worked with most of you before and am honored and humbled you've agreed to be part of another project. There's not a day I don't shake my head in disbelief that people are actually willing to pay me for doing what I love. I've loved the movies since before I could speak, watching at my mother's feet the classic movies on television. It was a look of pure pleasure instead of the face of a woman who faced the hard physical work of cleaning rich people's houses every day. In those moments she escaped into the story, into the characters. She was Grace Kelly or Katharine Hepburn or Bette Davis. And I thought then, as I do now, what better way to spend my time than to create stories people can fall into and escape from the drudgery and difficulty of this hard life? And my sensibilities have never strayed. I choose scripts with happy endings. I aim to make films that make people feel good. Films they can escape into like my mother did all those years ago. I'm scorned sometimes by the critics, these cowardly men and women who hide behind computers and say my work is fluffy and unimportant, but who are unwilling to get into the ring, as Theodore Roosevelt so aptly put it in his famous speech. 'Another feel good movie from Richard Greenwood,' they'll say. There will be no Oscar nods my way." He gestured toward his stars before putting his hand over his heart for a moment. "Although the three talents we have on this film may break my streak. How I'd love that! Regardless, I don't care what they say about my films or me because this is who I am. The people who need our films, they come in droves. Every time. Because we give them comfort, escape, a moment away from their troubles, and there's honor in this.

"And now I will get off my proverbial soapbox with these last parting words. Do good work and people will notice. This is all we need to commit to, my friends, each and every day. It's the harder way. I know this. It's easier to cut corners, smudge the details, accept mediocrity. But this isn't why we're here on this earth. No, we're here to be something bigger and more beautiful than we think we can be. It's in the small choices, of integrity, of quality—working from our hearts and pushing ourselves a little harder than we think we can bear that adds up to something in the end. And that something is art. It's beauty."

Bella, in tears, glanced around the room. Many of the others were obviously feeling the same. The burly cameraman Stefan was talking to earlier wiped under his eyes. Tears streamed down Genevieve's face. Tiffany, holding an unlit cigarette in her hand, was staring at the ground, her cheeks flushed like two red apples. But Stefan was smiling, his hands clasped behind his back. A man content with himself, she thought. Both he and Richard were not only at the peak of their creative careers but also inhabited a tranquility, a peace about who they were and what they were doing with their lives.

It begged the question, was this true for her? What about for Genevieve? Certainly not for Tiffany.

Bella noticed Sabrina then, standing in the back. She was in the corner, jotting something in a notebook, pulling long blond hair over her angry scar, as she often did.

Graham was standing by Bella again. How long had he been there? He stuffed his hands in his pants pockets and spoke under his breath. "Where does Richard get this shit? Seriously."

She looked at him for a long moment. "People like you will never know."

* * *

Bella walked outside, slipping into her rain jacket, shivering in the cool air. They were to film at various locations around River Valley but the primary location was this farmhouse, perched on a small hill down one of the many country roads outside of town and owned by Lee Tucker, who owned Riversong, the restaurant where Annie was head chef. Annie told her Lee had it completely restored, but the original feel of the house remained, which made it perfect for a film set in the 1930s. Bella stood gazing at the house and felt transported to a place that felt familiar in a way she couldn't quite understand. She'd certainly never lived in a place like it when she was a child. No, it was cramped apartments with the sounds of traffic and people's voices in the various impoverished parts of Seattle she remembered from her childhood, not a cozy and sweet house such as this. It was painted white with black shutters and had a sweeping porch with several rocking chairs.

A week ago, the movie crew had begun work on the set. The grassy hillside was covered with trucks and equipment. The house had been stripped of its furniture and filled with set pieces, carefully selected by the set dresser from antique shops in Los Angeles, to reflect life in the late '30s in an Oregon logging town. Now it was expertly furnished with pieces from the era, including a wood stove and colored glassware.

Out of the corner of her eye, Bella saw Tiffany, smoking a cigarette, sitting on the wooden swing hanging from a large oak. She was dressed in an orange raincoat and black rain boots with white polka dots. Bella walked towards her. It had rained the night before and the ground was damp. Her rain boots sank into the wet grass.

"Hey Tiffany. You doing all right?"

Tiffany jumped. "Oh, hey Bella. Yeah, I'm fine. I guess." She took a deep drag from her cigarette and blew it out slowly. "It's just I can see them all looking at me, wondering if I'm going to mess up the film for all of them. Despite what people think, I'm not completely self-centered. I know they support families and if I misbehave it hurts them."

"So don't. Misbehave, that is."

Tiffany patted the end of her cigarette, the red tip falling in the mud. "Not as easy as it sounds, I guess. They told me at rehab to hire a sobriety coach. I'm like, that's the stupidest thing I ever heard of.

Plus, I have my sister so far up my ass it's pretty much like having one of those." She paused, taking another drag of her cigarette. "I used to be good, you know. People used to look at me with respect instead of fear or dread."

"You're still good. Richard wouldn't have hired you otherwise."

"Richard's speech made me feel like a loser."

It's because we're not at peace with ourselves and when you're in the light of someone who is, it makes you feel like you might fall farther into the abyss, she thought.

Tiffany tossed her cigarette into the mud under the swing, stomping it out with her boot. "It's beautiful here. Sabrina and I were raised in Idaho. It's pretty there too, except everyone's so bass-ackwards and redneck no one like us could stand to live there."

No one like us? What did she mean by that? "I like backwards. It's refreshing after living in L.A. for so long."

"You don't really think that, do you?" Tiffany's light eyes were piercing, watching, narrowed.

"Sure I do."

Tiffany took in a deep breath, squaring her shoulders for a second before slumping forward in the swing. "I'm glad you're here, Bella. It helps to have a friendly face. Someone I feel is on my side."

"Gennie and Stefan are on your side too. They believe in you. Both have told me how good they think you are."

"Really?" Tiffany's hard face relaxed slightly, making her appear young and vulnerable. "I didn't think either of them had an ounce of respect for me."

"They're good people. Not like so many we know in the business."

"Ain't that the truth?" She pulled out a pack of cigarettes from her raincoat pocket and lit another. "Can't seem to give up the smokes." The sun glistened on the dewy grass and the air smelled of Tiffany's cigarette. She swayed slightly on the swing, pushing at the ground with her foot. "Graham Rouse isn't worth it, you know."

"What did you say?" It was a jolt in Bella's stomach, like lightning on a clear day.

"He's not worth giving up your life in the hope he'll do the right thing."

"It's been over for months now."

Tiffany's knuckles were white, gripping the rope. "I'm glad to hear it."

"How did you know?"

"I can tell by the way he looks at you. He's in love with you." She took another drag from her cigarette, brought it into her lungs and blew out. "My mother said I noticed all the details about people. I still do. All my self-destructive ways haven't killed that part of me."

Bella was hot and her legs shaky; perspiration gathered on her nose despite the cool air. She put her hand on the tree's rough trunk, wishing she could erase the fact she'd ever been involved with him. And that people might know? It was too much. Why had she come here? *Gennie. Don't forget Gennie needs you.* Out loud, she said, "He's in love with himself and nothing else."

Tiffany looked at her directly then, with clear eyes. "Good, because you're way too good for him. You know that, right?"

"Tiffany, sometimes I don't know. I'm working on it. Self-love, that is. I know, it sounds so cheesy but it's true."

"Me too. But the demons are always there, telling me I suck."

"I know." She moved away from the tree, standing directly in front of Tiffany. "Prove to them you're back in the game for good."

"The demons or the cast and crew?"

Bella laughed. "Both."

Tiffany nodded, with a tremulous smile. "Yeah, okay."

"Screw the haters."

"Screw the haters."

Chapter Three

BELLA, AT THE END OF RIVERSONG'S BAR, nursed a dirty martini and let Tommy's beautiful voice and guitar-playing wash over her. Tommy was married to Lee, the owner of Riversong, and they had a beautiful little daughter, Ellie-Rose. His band, Los Fuegos, was rocking the joint, alternating between fast and slow tunes and reacting to the calls from patrons for this song or that. The restaurant turned into a bar after ten o'clock and tonight was at full capacity, the crowd mingling and dancing. Cindi, behind the bar, poured draft beers and made the occasional margarita, setting them on the end of the bar for the cocktail waitresses to carry out to waiting patrons.

"This here crowd's getting their buzz on like it's Friday, not Thursday," said Cindi during a momentary lull, sipping on a glass of water. "Never saw the place filled with so many strangers. We're not used to that, you know."

Bella smiled, lifting her drink in a mock toast. "Hollywood's invaded."

"Damn straight. Hey, they're a strange lot, that's for sure, but we're happy for their money." Cindi's base makeup was too dark for her skin and the mascara was applied too heavily and looked clumpy. The blue eye shadow? It had to go. If only there was an anonymous way to give people makeup tips.

Bella glanced toward the end of the bar. Was that Amanda? It was. Bella would know her bland Barbie-replica face anywhere. Who was she with? Fred. The town cop? They were huddled together, obviously talking intimately, her long blond hair like a curtain over their faces. Then they kissed. Just a light kiss but a kiss just the same.

Bella leaned back slightly to see under the bar. Fred's hand was on Amanda's thigh.

Just then Amanda looked over and waved. She and Fred slipped off their stools and came over. "Bella Webber, right?" said Amanda.

"Yes, nice to see you again, Amanda. And Fred, right?"

"That's right. Welcome back." Fred Hughes was unsophisticated and earnest, with skin the color of a baby pig and a receding hairline unfair for someone in his early twenties. Hapless, Drake called him, which Annie chastised him for. Annie didn't like any of her local friends mocked, especially by her new husband, who could be sarcastic and wry. According to Annie, Fred was fresh from the police academy and had the potential to be a great cop despite the fact he'd been worthless to help Annie when her abusive ex-boyfriend had threatened her life. "Never mind that," Annie had said to Drake. "Fred came through in the end."

"Annie told me you're working on the movie. That's so cool." Amanda smiled, her eyes blank. *The girl was guileless, sweet,* Bella thought. *Don't be such a meanie.* But, still, there was just nothing much between this girl's ears. "Did Annie tell you I'm opening a café?"

"A café?"

"Yeah, well, more like a diner. Just breakfast and lunch. My grandmother and Lee and Tommy are investing."

Amanda was opening a business? How was it possible a twelve-year-old was opening a business? But the town needed a good breakfast place, no question. "Will you have blueberry pancakes?" asked Bella.

"I guess." Amanda paused, wrinkling her brow. "Should I?"

"It's a must."

"Do you hear that, baby? Blueberry pancakes are a must."

Baby? Fred had more game than she thought.

"Anyway, we're on our way out," said Amanda, flushing as she put her arm through Fred's. "Just wanted to say hello."

They were headed out to have sex. Because that's what people in love did. Well, at least there was a chance Bella might get some blueberry pancakes while she was here. This was a consolation, at least. There was always cake, in its various forms.

A few minutes later Mike plopped on the bar stool next to her. "Bella, good to see you. How you been?" He sounded subdued, almost defeated. This wasn't like him. Mike looked like the Marlboro man and had the soul of Ghandi. When it came to River Valley and its residents, the town's honorary mayor would die trying to save it.

"I'm good," she answered. "Just got into town. Great to be here."

"You bring a little extra light to the place, that's for certain." He tapped the bar. "Cindi, I need a beer and a shot of whiskey."

Cindi looked at him with surprise. "Whiskey? Hard day?"

Mike rubbed his eyes. "One of the worst of my life."

Cindi poured him a shot from one of the whiskeys lining the shelf behind the bar and set it in front of him. "What happened? Is Sharon all right?" She tilted a pint glass under a draft, stopping the flow of the amber liquid just as it reached the top.

"Yeah, she's fine. On her way over here now, as a matter of fact. I told her she'll need to drive me home." He threw back the shot, wiping his mouth with the back of his hand. "I have to close the sawmill."

"What?" Cindi's face looked like he'd just told her someone close to them had died. "The sawmill?"

"It's been coming for a long time now. Just can't afford to keep it going with so many of the restrictions on timber. You know I've wondered for years how I'd keep it going and if it was possible to make it work, but it's just not. I only employ thirty people out there now, but still, that's thirty about to lose their jobs."

They spoke for a time about the logistics of stopping production and what he would do about telling the employees. Bella was listening absently because her mind was whirring. Could her makeup line be manufactured here? Could they turn Mike's mill into a factory that made cosmetics instead of lumber? She'd need at least thirty employees if not more if she were to do what she wanted to do.

"Mike," she said, without thinking first. "I have an idea for a business. I've been too scared to actually do it but I don't know, maybe the mill closing is a sign or something."

Mike's face went from defeated to interested. "I believe in signs. The vision for River Valley's resurrection came to me in a dream in the form of a talking fish."

"A talking fish?"

"Yep. You heard me. Never mind. I'll tell you later. Tell me your idea."

"I've wanted to start my own makeup line for years. I have a company that can put together the formulas for the products. I have funding. We could manufacture it here if we built a lab."

"Like where my mill is now?"

"Exactly. It could employ a lot of people."

"Holy shit, girl. Why haven't you done this before?"

"Too chicken."

He motioned for Cindi to pour him another shot. "Pour me another. A shot to toast the future, not mourn the past."

"Well, I'm still not sure." Amanda was starting a business. Dumb little Amanda. Surely she could do as much.

He looked her straight in the eyes. "Fear is the opposite of love, my dear. Just keep that in mind." He downed the shot and then tapped the surface of the bar with the tip of his finger. "Speaking of love, Ben Fleck was talking about you today. I left him a message about the mill closing to see if maybe he had work for any of my people. Instead of calling me back, he came by my office personally to see how he could help. So nice of him."

Her heart pounded hard in her chest. She pulled on her earring, trying to appear nonchalant. "He was asking about me?"

"Yep." Mike's eyes twinkled at her. "You heard me."

She sipped her martini, wanting to ask what he'd said but her pride kept her from it.

Mike lowered his voice. "Don't you tell him I said this but don't give up on him. He's been hurt and has some scar tissue but he fell for you hard. He'll be back. You mark my words on that."

Just then Gennie entered through the front door. Bella stood and motioned for her to come over. "Mike, you want to meet Gennie?"

"Oh, shoot, she won't want to meet me."

"Don't be silly. She's a regular girl."

"I want to meet her," said Cindi.

Mike's face was flushed, probably from the whiskey. "I'm starting to feel a hell of a lot better."

Genevieve was making her way toward them. The locals, interspersed with the movie folks who seemed not to notice her at all, stopped whatever they were doing and stared. Bella was used to this. Whenever the two of them went out in Los Angeles the same thing happened.

When Genevieve reached them, Mike immediately jumped from his stool as Bella introduced them.

"Mike's kinda the honorary mayor in town here," said Bella. "He and Tommy," she said, pointing toward the band, "have transformed this town from a dying meth factory to a tourist destination."

Cindi, grinning, reached her hand across the bar. "I'm Cindi. That's Cindi with an i."

Gennie returned Cindi's vigorous handshake. "So nice to meet you. Bella's told me so much about you. I hear you're quite the sharp shooter."

"Well, God don't care for a bragger but yeah, it's true," said Cindi. "Now do you want a cof a cuppa? I hear you actresses don't eat or drink."

"Miss Banks, please, take my seat," said Mike.

"Thank you so much." She smiled at him, revealing perfectly straight white teeth behind her full lips: the smile that made millions of fans, both men and women, swoon. "Actually, Cindi, I'm dying for a glass of wine." Before she slid onto the stool, Genevieve leaned over and kissed Bella on the cheek. "Sorry I'm so late. Richard had a bunch of notes for me." Genevieve's long brown hair was loose, falling glossy down her back. She wore only a touch of foundation, blush, mascara, and lip-gloss and was dressed in loose jeans and a light blue cashmere sweater. This was one woman who needed no makeover. She turned back to Mike.

"Now, tell me more about how you transformed River Valley. I'm from a little town very similar to this and I can't imagine how you did it."

Mike grinned. "Well, now, it's not entirely true that it was just Tommy and me. It started with this restaurant when Lee took it over, then her friend Linus opened the inn next door, and then the resort was built, and then Ben Fleck brought Hylink into town and now, Miss Banks, you and your beautiful people have come. And, as they say, the rest is history. But more importantly, Miss Banks, red or white?"

"White. Less calories and it won't stain my teeth." She rolled her large brown eyes. "Cindi's right. I can't eat or drink much, especially during filming. My trainer's been texting me to stay away from the craft table."

"Craft table?" asked Mike.

"The food table. My favorite place on set," said Bella. "Gennie's trainer is this forty-pound waif with the heart of a Nazi. I think it's because she's so hungry."

Genevieve's eyes went wide before she burst out laughing. "You know she gets results. But yes, she's a nasty little thing." She turned her attention to Mike, who hadn't taken his eyes off her during the entire conversation. "Bella's very protective of me. You should see how she acts before an awards show—like a little hummingbird, touching up my face every five minutes. She's Hollywood's most talented woman with paint and a brush."

Bella, flushing, shook her head dismissively. "That's my job, Mike. Don't listen to her."

"Well, Miss Banks, Bella didn't lie about you. No doubt about it." Mike's handsome, rugged face was soft with admiration.

Genevieve raised her eyebrows and cocked her head to the side. "Oh, really? What did she say? That I look like hell in the mornings before she fixes me up?"

"Miss Banks, I doubt you could ever look bad even on your worst day."

Genevieve smiled again, putting her hand on Mike's shoulder for a moment. "How kind of you to say."

Mike motioned to Cindi, who was talking with several of the cameramen at the other end of the bar. "Now, let me get you a glass of wine."

"Mike just got married," said Bella to Gennie.

"Yeah, old codgers like me can get a second chance. Never would've predicted it in a hundred years."

Gennie's face darkened for a moment, and she met Bella's eyes. "We're looking for a second chance, aren't we, Bella?"

"This is the place for them. Something in the water." Mike motioned for another shot.

Sharon had come in and was walking towards them. Mike stood, motioning to his wife to join them. "Oh, Miss Banks, my wife is your biggest fan. I'm warning you, she may gush."

Sharon made her way through the crowd and stared at Genevieve with an expression somewhere between seeing a ghost and Jesus. Or maybe the ghost of Jesus. As Bella introduced the women, the normally refined and unflappable Sharon flushed pink.

"Sorry, my hands are damp," said Sharon, shaking Genevieve's outstretched hand.

"We're just talking about second chances," said Genevieve.

"Ours in particular," said Mike, kissing his wife on the cheek.

Sharon, as if she were outside her body, began to stammer and babble. "Yes, right, we're second chanced. I mean, we had a second chance. Me widowed. Mike divorced. Both of us so lonely. And then, boom, there he was, all manly in his cowboy boots and jeans." She stopped, bringing her hand to her mouth. "I'm sorry. I don't normally talk this much."

Genevieve, her brown eyes warm, took a sip of wine. "No worries. It's nice to see two people so obviously in love."

Bella darted a quick glance at both Mike and Sharon. Did they know about Genevieve's recent divorce? Of course they did. It was impossible not to.

"Oh, Bella, Stefan just came in." Genevieve pointed at the front door. "He said he couldn't come out, that he had to study his lines for tomorrow."

Bella looked at her friend closely. Was there something in her voice that had changed with the mention of Stefan's name?

"I think I might faint," said Sharon. She put a hand up to her collar. "This is too much all in one night." She looked over at Genevieve. "I'm just such a fan of both of you."

"Oh my gosh, I understand," said Genevieve. "I've wanted to work with Stefan for a long time. Well, that and I loved the book. Have you read it?"

Sharon nodded. "Of course. You know the writer's from Oregon, right?"

"Yes, from a town just like this one, is my understanding," said Genevieve. "There's something so romantic about it."

Mike chuckled. "You know what Lee Tucker always says about small towns in Oregon?"

"What's that?" asked Bella.

"They all have Dairy Queens."

Genevieve laughed. "This is true. I wish I could have a Blizzard right this minute."

Bella nodded, stabbing an olive with a toothpick and pointing it at Genevieve. "Too bad it's not open this late or I would run and get one. I'm thinking cookie dough."

"Stop," said Genevieve. "My stomach's growling." She stood, waving to Stefan.

"Nicest guy in the business," said Bella to Sharon, eating her olive. "Easy on the eyes too."

"So true," said Sharon, her eyes following Stefan as he made his way across the room.

"Hey now, don't forget about how handsome I am in my cowboy boots," said Mike, his hand on Sharon's leg.

"Of course not, honey," said Sharon. "What's your name again?"

Stefan was stopped twice to sign autographs on beer-soaked napkins before he finally arrived at the bar. Cindi, as if he were no different than any of her local patrons, slapped a napkin on the counter. "What's your poison?"

"Draft beer? Something bitter?" he said before kissing his costar on the cheek. "Hi, Gennie. Hey Bellalicious." He tousled her curls.

"I thought you weren't coming out?" Genevieve was staring into her glass. Had her neck flushed when he said her name?

"I've got the lines nailed. Felt like spending some time with you might be good for our work tomorrow," said Stefan.

Genevieve went pale. Tomorrow was the filming of their steamy scene. Bella knew she dreaded them. But Stefan was sweet and thoughtful. Surely that would make it easier?

After a small break, Tommy and his band were back on stage. He greeted the crowd, who cheered and clapped, especially the locals. "Something slow to get this set started?"

A couple of the women whistled. "Hell yeah, Tommy."

"Who's this?" asked Stefan.

"Tommy. Local. Songwriter for Nashville," said Mike with pride in his voice. "And nicest guy you'll ever know."

"And an EMT," said Bella. "Hot, hot, hot EMT."

"You like him, Bellalicious?" asked Stefan, popping several peanuts into his mouth from the dish on the bar.

"God no," said Bella. "He's married to my sister-in-law's best friend, Lee." She made brief eye contact with Genevieve.

"We take care of our own here," said Mike to Gennie and Stefan. "You two let us know anything you need. And we'll keep those idiot photographers away from you if we have to."

Cindi, pouring another draft beer for Mike, said, "I have ways of getting people to cooperate. Oregon ways."

Sharon whispered to Gennie and Stefan, looking somewhat alarmed. "She's talking about a gun."

"I love this town," said Genevieve, smiling wide and taking another sip of her wine.

"I love the people in this town," said Bella.

"Couldn't be happier we're filming here," said Stefan. "Makes me miss my home in B.C. Maybe I'll buy a place here. What do you think, Bellalicious? Think I could meet a nice girl here, settle down?"

"And break every single woman's heart across the country?" teased Bella. "That's just cruel."

Tommy began to sing one of his originals, currently a hit on country radio for one of the biggest stars in Nashville. "He's fantastic," said Stefan. "Reminds me of some of the Canadian folk singers I grew up listening to."

Mike put his arm around Sharon. "Great to meet you folks but we should get on home. Big day tomorrow."

"Yes, right. So nice to meet you," said Sharon.

Both Bella and Genevieve slid from their barstools. There were hugs all around. This is how they did it in River Valley, thought Bella. Always hugging.

After they were gone, Bella was about to order a glass of red wine when she spotted Ben Fleck coming in the doorway.

"I don't believe it," she muttered.

"What?" asked Gennie.

"Tiffany just walked in. With Benjamin Fleck."

"I thought she promised Richard she'd stay clean and sober for the shoot," said Genevieve after glancing towards them.

Stefan turned to look and then shook his head sadly. "Clearly the deal's off. She's loaded."

He was right. Tiffany was hanging on Ben's arm and walking unsteadily. There were dark smudges of mascara under her eyes and her lipstick was smeared, making her look almost clown-like. Her hair was wet too. It must have started raining. What was Ben doing with her? Had they been out together? The idea of his hands on her made Bella physically ill. Her dinner churned. How could she get out of here without him seeing her?

Tommy began another song, a slow ballad. Most of the crowd danced, couples moving across the dance floor in various degrees of skill. Ben, with his arm around the drunk Tiffany Archer, headed towards them. *Dammit*, thought Bella, *no way to escape*.

"Hey everybody," Tiffany slurred.

"What the hell?" Bella asked before Ben could open his mouth. "She just got out of rehab. You really think getting her drunk was a good idea?"

Genevieve had slid from her stool and was now getting Tiffany situated in her place. Cindi, without anyone needing to say anything, set a coffee in front of her inebriated guest.

"I did not get her drunk," said Ben, emphasizing every word, his eyes snapping. "I happened to be driving into town when I saw her stumble out of Lefty's and head for her car. There were two men lurking in the parking lot, not to mention she's clearly in no shape to drive. I brought her in here knowing you were here, Bella, and thought you could help me."

"How did you know I was here?"

"Tommy texted me."

Tommy texted him? Why had he done that? She glanced at the stage. Tommy winked at her. She flipped him off behind her hand but he didn't seem to care. He simply grinned and said to the crowd, "Here's a song for all the love birds out there tonight."

Ben steadied Tiffany on the bar stool by putting both his hands on her shoulders. "Cindi, is there any food left in the kitchen?"

"I'll go see," said Cindi. "Just let me finish making these here drinks first."

"This is good of you, man," said Stefan to Ben. He held out his hand. "Good to meet you."

"You too," said Ben. "Big fan."

"Hey, thanks. Bella's told us a lot about you," said Stefan.

Bella twisted on her stool, suddenly finding the remaining olive on the toothpick enormously interesting.

"Don't believe all the bad things she says. I'm actually a good guy," said Ben.

"He rescued me," said Tiffany.

"Sweetie, where's your sister tonight?" Genevieve pushed the coffee closer to Tiffany. "Drink this. It'll help."

"We had a fight. She's mad at me," said Tiffany, shaking her head in refusal of the coffee.

"What happened?" asked Bella.

"Oh, just the usual," said Tiffany.

No one said anything, not knowing, of course, what "the usual" was. Although it wasn't too much of a leap to assume it was Tiffany's drinking. Still, this surprised Bella. She'd never seen the sisters fight. Sabrina was protective and supportive, always defending Tiffany even when she didn't deserve it, which was most of the time.

Just then, they saw Sabrina come in the front door, her eyes darting to where they all huddled around Tiffany. In long strides, she approached them, moving through the crowd, ignoring the stares that came her way.

"Tiff, what happened to you?" Her scar, running from her cheekbone to her mouth, was a scarlet line.

Tiffany put her face into her hands and began to cry. "Sorry, Sabrina."

Ben held out his hand to Sabrina. "I'm Ben Fleck. I saw her about to get into her car outside Lefty's and thought I'd bring her here to get some food in her."

Sabrina looked up at Ben, scrutinizing his face with a look of distrust. "That right? You just happened to see her coming out of the bar?"

Ben looked over at Bella, his eyes pleading with her to help him.

Bella put her hand on Sabrina's arm. "He's okay. He's a friend of mine."

Cindi came out of the kitchen carrying a bowl of soup and a dinner roll. "This here's all we have left from dinner." She set it next to the now cold coffee. "Come on, baby," she said to Tiffany. "No more crying. Just get a little food in you and you'll feel better."

Sabrina, watching her sister, rubbed her temples before looking over at Bella. "You know what? I've had enough for tonight. Can one of you just get her back to the lodge? We're in adjoining rooms, 502 and 501. She's in 501. I'd appreciate it if you didn't wake me when you come in."

"Sure, yeah, I'll get her back," said Ben. "We'll get her to eat."

Sabrina looked at Ben with less mistrust than the moment before, but it was there just the same. "What do you want out of this? How much will it take to get you to sell out to the first tabloid that calls you?"

"No, Sabrina, he's not like that," said Bella. "He's only trying to help. He probably saved her life tonight when he didn't let her get in that car. He and my brother go way back," she added by way of explanation.

"There were two men following me, sissy," said Tiffany, raising her head. Her mascara was streaked down both sides of her face. "I was trying to get away from them. They followed me when I came out of the bathroom, so I had to get to my car and get away from them."

"I saw them," said Ben to Sabrina. "I didn't recognize them but they didn't look like anyone you'd want around your sister." He paused, looking over at Bella for a moment before meeting Sabrina's gaze directly. "And I am most certainly not interested in selling a story to one of those morally bankrupt tabloids."

"That's what they all say," said Sabrina.

* * *

Bella walked Sabrina out to her car. It had stopped raining hard but there was a light mist that would make her hair curl up like a short bush on top of her head. *Ben.* Why did she have to care what he thought of her?

Sabrina leaned against the side of her car. "Bella, I'm so tired of this. I really thought she was different this time, thought she'd finally grown up." She took keys out of the bag over her shoulder. "How the hell am I going to get Richard and Graham to overlook this?"

"Maybe it's just a minor setback. People relapse all the time. She said you two had a fight."

Sabrina shook her head, a look of bafflement on her face. "That's ridiculous. We didn't have a fight. I don't know why she'd say that. We never fight. I left her in her room after dinner with her script and a hot bath running. I made sure they'd taken all the booze out of the minibar. I thought she was good."

"Listen, if it helps, I'll talk to Graham for you. And I know Richard believes in her. And, really, there's no reason they even have to know. Ben and I will get her back to her room and settled in. Maybe this can just blow over. Okay?"

"I guess. Regardless, I need to get to bed. Tomorrow's going to be rough either way. Sometimes I don't know what's worse, drunk Tiffany or shamed, hung-over Tiffany."

"It'll be all right. Just get her to me in the morning and I'll fix her so she looks like she had that bath and went to bed early."

"Bella, thank you." Sabrina's eyes filled with tears. "You have no idea how important it is that she keep this job."

"What do you mean?" asked Bella softly.

"We're broke. Dead broke. Most of what she's made she's blown on bad investments and snorting it up her nose. If this doesn't work, I don't know what will happen to us."

"Surely it isn't that bad?"

"Yeah, Bella, it is. We're up against it here."

"Well, we just have to make sure she keeps this job then." She hugged Sabrina. "It'll be all right."

After Sabrina drove away, Bella went back inside Riversong. It was almost eleven o'clock and Tommy's band was putting away their instruments. The place had emptied of almost all the patrons except for a few tables finishing drinks. Her friends and Ben were where she'd left them at the bar. Tiffany, Bella was glad to see, was eating her soup with Ben sitting next to her. Cindi was putting clean glasses on the shelves behind the bar. Genevieve and Stefan were huddled together, talking quietly.

Ben looked up at her when she slid onto the barstool next to him. "Everything okay?"

She nodded, still processing what Sabrina had just told her. "Yeah."

"I have to go to the bathroom," said Tiffany, still slurring her words. She had broccoli bisque on the side of her face.

"I'll take her," said Genevieve. "I need to go too. And then I should get out of here and get some beauty sleep." She said this last part to Stefan.

"Don't oversleep, then," said Stefan, smiling at her. "The world can't take it if you're any more beautiful."

Genevieve laughed, blushing. "You're just getting me buttered up for our scene tomorrow."

He sobered. "Don't worry. Like I said, it'll be okay. I'll take care of you."

Genevieve put her hands on both of her cheeks, gazing at him, her brown eyes warm. "You're sweet." She steadied herself on the back of Stefan's barstool. "Jeez, I think I'm a little drunk, too."

"After two glasses? Cheap date, huh?" Stefan held out his hand to her, a little too eagerly. Another man falling for Genevieve. Poor bastard wouldn't know what hit him. "I'll get you back to the hotel." He looked over at Ben and Bella. "As long as you two can get Tiffany home?"

"We're on it," said Ben, exchanging a look with Stefan that could only be described as man code for, *I got you covered, man, I know what you're up to here.*

Genevieve turned to Tiffany. "Come on, doll, let's get you to the bathroom and home to sleep it off."

"I'm fine," said Tiffany, stumbling as she slid from the barstool.

Genevieve put her arm around Tiffany. "I know. But I'll hold onto you just in case."

"I'm going to hit the restroom as well," said Stefan. "And thanks, man, for letting me get Gennie home."

Bella put her hand on Stefan's shoulder. "Be careful with her. She's more fragile than she looks."

He nodded, his eyes soft. "I know. I get that."

Stefan headed towards the men's room, leaving Ben and Bella alone at the bar. She let her gaze slide to him. He was watching her. "What?"

"You're beautiful."

Her heart skipped and fluttered. "Not compared to this group I hang with."

He shook his head. "I disagree. You're still the prettiest girl at the party."

"Ben. Don't."

He looked at her, long and hard, the evasiveness gone from his eyes. "I think of you more than I should. I came out tonight knowing you were here."

"You did?"

"Yeah. Then I saw Tiffany."

"Most men wouldn't have wanted to get their hands dirty, unless they thought they could get laid, which obviously isn't what you wanted or you wouldn't have come here."

"There was no way I was leaving her in that parking lot with those guys obviously following her. And I have no interest in sleeping with her. As a matter of fact, she repulses me." He glanced towards the bathroom and lowered his voice. "What a screwed up girl. She was telling me some crazy stuff in the car on the way over here."

"Like what?"

But before he could answer, Genevieve and Tiffany were coming towards them. Ben stood, reaching for Tiffany's jacket and helping her into it. By then, Stefan was there as well.

"Gennie, you all set?" asked Stefan, with a covert wink at Ben, offering his arm to his costar.

"I am." She kissed Bella on the cheek. "Be ready to make me beautiful first thing tomorrow."

"You know it," said Bella.

"I'll steal you a couple of donuts from the buffet at the lodge."

"Cherry Danish if they have them," said Bella. "This is serious."

"I know." Gennie leaned close and whispered in her ear. "Be careful with Ben."

"I will," she whispered back.

"But not too careful either."

Gennie and Stefan walked away, arm in arm.

Tiffany looked as if she might fall asleep on her feet. Ben put his arm around her and pointed her toward the door. "Come on, slugger, let's get you into bed." Tiffany turned suddenly and wrapped her arms around his neck before planting a wet kiss on his mouth. "What's your name again?"

Bella looked away, her stomach turning. *Get your hands off him,* she screamed silently. *He's supposed to be mine.*

Ben tucked Tiffany's head against his chest, making eye contact with Bella. "I'm sorry. Didn't see that coming."

"Maybe I should get her back to the hotel," Bella said. No telling what might happen if Ben Fleck was alone in a hotel room with Tiffany Archer: drunk and promiscuous and aggressive.

Ben lifted Tiffany and plopped her onto a barstool. "Just sit here for a minute while I talk to Bella."

"Okay, hurry though." Tiffany, her eyes unfocused, wrapped an arm around the back of the stool as if her life depended on it.

Cindi, looking thoroughly disgusted, set a fresh glass of water in front of Tiffany. "Oh, girl, you're just a hot mess."

Ben took Bella's hand, leading her over near the entrance to the kitchen where it was quieter. "Honestly, I don't know if you're capable of getting her back to her room. I have a feeling I may need to carry her upstairs. You go back to Drake's and wait for me in the guesthouse. We'll talk." He leaned over and kissed her lightly on the mouth and then harder, pulling her close.

"I've missed this," she whispered against his mouth. "So much."

"Me too. I've tried to stay away from you but after I saw you at the wedding you're all I can think of."

"Ben, I won't break your heart. I promise."

He smiled, his eyes dancing the way they did the first time she met him. "I don't know if that's true but I guess it's worth the risk."

"Just take a chance with me, Ben. I won't disappear on you ever again."

He kissed her, this time pressing her against the wall before pulling away. "Wait for me. I'll do this as fast as I can."

Chapter Four

BELLA LET HERSELF into the guesthouse. The ground level was set up as a home gym, but above were a fully furnished sitting room, bedroom, bathroom, and small kitchen, all beautifully decorated in the same rustic and modern fusion as the main house. Since she'd been here last, the sitting room had a lived-in quality. There were a half-dozen fly-fishing magazines, a copy of a James Patterson novel and a copy of one of Ralph Waldo Emerson's book of essays on the coffee table. The decorative throw pillows were piled on one end of the couch like they'd recently been used for a nap. The small desk in the corner was scattered with various fly-fishing ties and Ben's tying equipment: tweezers, floss in various colors, several types of pliers, razorblades. A vise attached to the table held a tie with a shiny silver quill. She yawned, resisting the urge to rub her eyes. Ben better hurry or she wasn't going to be able to stay awake. But she wasn't due on set until eleven o'clock the next morning so she could sleep in, although she didn't want to be late. Tiffany needed her; it might take longer than usual to cover up the night of drinking. She curled up on the black leather couch, resting her head on the softest of the throw pillows.

She woke to the sound of footsteps coming up the stairs. Opening her eyes, she peeked up over the back of the couch. It was Ben, his eyes red from fatigue. The front of his shirt was wet, like something had spilled on it.

"Sorry it took me so long," he said. "She started vomiting the minute I got her into the room. I've never seen a girl that small puke that much."

"What time is it?"

"A little after midnight."

"Good God, she's a pain in the ass."

"I was dying to get back here to you but I couldn't leave her to choke on her own vomit. Finally she stopped and I was able to get her into bed." He offered his hand and pulled her gently to her feet. "Come to bed."

"Do you have a toothbrush?" asked Bella.

"Yeah, there's an extra one under the sink."

She followed him into the bathroom. He handed her a new toothbrush and toothpaste. Behind her, Ben turned on the shower. "Need to get the smell of drunk girl off me," he said. "I'll just be a minute. Get into bed."

"I love it when you boss me around."

He laughed. She brushed her teeth, listening to him lather his body with soap. From the mirror, she saw his hand reach for the shampoo from a hanging basket around the showerhead.

After her mouth felt clean, she went into the bedroom, stripping down to nothing and sliding between the cool sheets. She was on her side, facing the wall and trying not to drift off to sleep when he pulled back the covers and got in with her. "You still awake?" he asked against her neck, his fingers on her hips and then trailing up to her breast. His hair was wet on her skin, his body warm and damp. She rolled onto her back and slipped her arms around his neck. His breath smelled of peppermint, his neck of his cologne. She sighed, awake now, wanting him. He kissed her, searching her mouth with his tongue until she was breathless.

"We should probably talk first," he whispered, his mouth trailing down her neck to her breasts.

"Probably."

But it was too late by then. They were lost to it, this attraction between them stronger than any rational thought. Like two teenagers in the backseat of a car, she thought, wrapping her legs around him. Before she could think of what was happening next, he was inside her, thrusting hard, both of them unable to slow down, her hands on the backs of his legs, his holding her hips. She climaxed hard and fast, crying out; in the next instant he joined her, letting out a small groan.

Afterward, they lay together like two spoons in a drawer, their bodies damp with sweat. Bella's heart still pounded as she snuggled closer. "Not one day's gone by I haven't thought of you. You have no idea how much I regretted how I handled things. I'm an idiot."

He turned her so she faced him and then stroked the side of her face so tenderly it brought tears to her eyes. "Bella, I've been in love with you since the moment I met you. I know it's crazy but when you know, you know."

"I feel the same."

He smiled; the area around his eyes crinkled. "That said, I'm scared out of my mind."

"Me too."

"When this thing happened with my fiancée I vowed never to let myself be vulnerable again. I'd turn myself into a player, you know, and not have to feel anything again. But it didn't work. Because at the end of that vow was you, walking around in your bikini on Drake's deck. I told Annie that night I was a goner over you."

"What did she say?"

"Same thing as everyone else. Stay away from Bella Webber."

She couldn't help but feel a little hurt over this information "Why would Annie say that?"

"Because Annie knows I have a tender heart. That's how it is between two tender hearts. We recognize the each other."

"I have a tender heart too," she said, husky, feeling defensive.

He kissed her, soft and searching. "I know you do. All this sass is just an act to hide how you really are. I knew that after the night we spent together last summer. But when you ran away, every red flag in my baggage-laden brain went crazy."

"I understand that, actually." How good his body felt next to her. Familiar, like they'd been together all their lives. "Everyone has so many hurts, just piled up one on top of another until all we are is those hurts instead of the way we begin, open and willing and ready to love one another." She kissed the side of his face gently. "How did you find out about your fiancée?"

She felt him stiffen. "I don't want to talk about that now, okay? It's done. In the past. That drawer is shut."

"Okay."

"Bella, we have to see this thing through—meet it head on instead of running away."

"You make it sound like a combat sport," she teased, reaching up to run her fingers through his hair.

"The physical part kind of is," he whispered into her ear. "You won't run away. Will you?"

"Not this time." She nestled into him, yawning. "I wonder if Annie and Drake will notice I'm not in my room in the morning?"

"Not if you show up at breakfast demanding a meal big enough for a lumber jack."

"Hey, I'm very hungry. What can I say?"

He chuckled, kissing the top of her head. "I remember."

And for the second time in her life, everything felt right. This was the man she'd waited for, a man to be trusted and who deserved to be repaid for that trust with truth and loyalty and bravery. She drifted off to sleep. Happy.

* * *

Bella dreamt. Her father smelled of body odor and stale booze and old cigarette smoke. His eyes were wild and unfocused, with small red stripes. He sat with his feet dangling over the edge of the building and held her with both hands around her waist. She knew not to kick or wriggle because it might send them both over. "Mommy, Mommy, Mommy." She screamed, shifting her eyes without moving her head to see her mother standing. Her hands were clasped together. And her mouth was moving but Bella couldn't hear what she said, only her father's voice, rough and desperate.

"Don't come any closer, Alice, or I drop her."

The crowd below gathered in clumps. Bella knew there were five stories down to the sidewalk. Five sets of stairs to their apartment when the elevator was broken, which was often. The rain was a drizzle. She heard the sound of a siren. It sounded far away. Would the firemen come like in the book Drake kept by his bed? Would they have a tall enough ladder? And then suddenly they were yanked back, toppling together, Bella landing on top of him in a backwards embrace. Her mother came then, gathering her up in her arms, crying into Bella's hair. She squeezed her eyes shut. Would he come and push them both over? "Run, Mommy, run." Was this a whisper or a silent scream? She heard heavy footsteps on the roof coming towards them. Peeping over her mother's shoulder, she saw two men in blue uniforms. Policemen. They had guns pointed toward the floor. She shifted her gaze. Drake was on their father, straddling him, pummeling him with the heel of his hand. One of the cops yanked him up and still Drake struggled, his arms and legs flailing. "Let me go. I'm not done," he shouted.

She woke, heart pounding, covered in sweat. The clock said 4:21 a.m. Next to her, Ben reached out and pulled her to his chest. "Was it the dream?"

"Yes," she whispered, closing her eyes and burying her face into his chest. "You were there this time. In the crowd."

"I am here," he said into her hair. "I'm here."

CHAPTER FIVE

THE NEXT MORNING, she awakened to her cell phone ringing from the sitting room. She rolled over. Ben was sound asleep, snoring. Stumbling, bleary eyed, she headed for the sound, rummaging in her purse until she found her phone. It was Genevieve. What time was it? Almost ten o'clock. Had she overslept for work, she thought, panicky for a moment? It was Friday morning. No, she didn't need to be on set until eleven o'clock. She would get showered and dressed quickly.

"You all right?" asked Bella.

"No. Something terrible." Genevieve's normally smooth and centered voice was broken and shaky.

"What's the matter?"

"Tiffany was found dead this morning in her hotel room. Strangled."

Bella collapsed onto the couch. "Murdered?"

"That's what they're saying. The county police are all over the hotel. Somehow the press already knows too. They've arrived in droves, like the locusts they are. I don't know how they know so fast."

"Holy shit." Her mind was turning. Ben. Was Ben the last person to see her alive? Except, of course, for the murderer. Next, she thought of Sabrina. Poor sweet Sabrina. "Did Sabrina find her?"

"Yes. When she went to check on her. This morning at like seven. Oh, Bella, it's so awful. Richard said Sabrina howled like a dying animal when they pronounced her dead."

Ben had arrived home a little after midnight. It entered then, the slippery smoke of suspicion. He'd been gone for an hour with nothing to explain his absence but a tale of a drunken, sick girl in a hotel room. Thoughts of deception danced and tossed about her mind like voices in a dark room during the moments before dawn. *How well do you know him?* they said. *Are his laughing eyes only deception wrapped in a pretty package? Might his heart be black, his temper a flame easily sparked into violence, his strong hands capable of murder and lovemaking on the same night?*

No, no, no, she cried out silently to the voices lurking in the dusty, dim corners. He's a man to be trusted. A good man. A kind man. *Trust your instincts,* her mother always told her.

"Bella, are you there?"

"Yes. I'm here. Trying to get my mind around this."

"I know. It's such a terrible thing."

"Gennie, Ben took her home last night. By himself. He didn't get home until midnight. He said she was vomiting and he didn't want to leave her alone."

"Home?"

"Here home. Drake's. I was waiting for him. To talk about things."

"Oh."

"Do you understand what I'm saying?" She got up from the couch and tiptoed over to the bedroom. Ben was still asleep, snoring softly.

There was silence on the other end of the phone for a moment, then, Gennie's voice clear and sure. "Honey, there's no way Ben had anything to do with this."

"But it looks bad. Doesn't it?"

Again, there was a moment of hesitation from the other end of the phone. "Yes. It does."

Suddenly, she remembered Sabrina's confession from the night before. Did Tiffany's death have something to do with debt? Was she into something bad? And the men following her in the bar parking lot? Who were they? Had they gotten to her in her room?

"Gennie, Sabrina told me last night Tiffany's broke. What if those men Ben saw in the parking lot had something to do with this?"

"Like she owed them money or something?"

Her phone beeped. It was another call, this time from Drake. "Gennie, I have to go."

Drake's voice sounded alarmed. "Where are you?"

"In the guesthouse. With Ben."

"Oh." A split-second pause, and then, "The police are coming up the driveway. It's about Tiffany Archer. They want to question Ben."

"Crap." Just then she heard the sound of a car approaching. She went to the window. It was indeed a police car coming up Drake's long drive. "I have to wake up Ben."

* * *

Bella sat on the side of the bed and shook Ben's shoulder. "You have to wake up."

He opened his eyes and then broke into a wide smile. "Good morning, beautiful."

"The cops are here."

He sat up, his face turning from sleepy to shock in an instant; there was a flicker of something else too. Something she couldn't decipher. "What? Why? Is everyone okay?"

"Tiffany Archer's been murdered."

The color drained completely from his face. "Murdered?"

"Sabrina found her this morning."

"Oh, God. They're sure it's murder? Did she choke?"

"No, strangled. According to the police."

"Strangled?" He put his face in his hands, speaking through his fingers. "I stayed with her to make sure she didn't choke on her own vomit and then she's strangled? How can this be?"

"Ben, did people see you go into the lodge last night? I mean, with her?"

He looked at her with a blank expression. "What do you mean?" Then, clearly realizing what she meant, his eyes grew big. "You mean I'm the last person who saw her alive?"

"I mean, you were alone with her in her room and in the morning she's dead."

He didn't say anything. His pale face turned green. "Yeah, she couldn't find her room key. I had to get another one. There were several attendants on duty, giving me the whole once over for being with a drunk actress in the middle of the night. I had this ridiculous urge to defend myself, like, 'Hey my girl's waiting for me at home, not this pitiful thing.' Anyway, they were still on duty when they saw me leave an hour later."

She took his hand. "Just tell them the truth. Every detail you can remember."

"I will. Of course."

Bella dressed in the jeans and sweater she'd discarded the night before. At the window, she saw two detectives dressed in suits get out of a police car. "I'll go inside the house and tell them you're here."

But Ben had already gotten out of bed and was pulling on a pair of jeans. "I'll go with you." Shirtless, he took both her hands in his. "Bella, you know I would never hurt anyone, right?"

"Of course. Don't be ridiculous."

His eyes searched her face. "You think I'm in trouble here?"

"No. They'll interview you and see there's no way you did this. No motive, for one thing."

"Right. Sure." He paused, pulling a blue T-shirt over his head. "But you have to admit, it looks bad. You know, me being in her room alone."

"I should never have let you go alone."

He pulled her into an embrace. "This isn't your fault. Anyway, the truth is I had nothing to do with it. Surely that'll be obvious to them."

She nodded, kissing him and holding him close for a moment. "It'll be fine." But inside she wasn't so sure. He was right. This did not look good.

* * *

The detectives were from Echo Grove, a larger town to the north of River Valley, according to the markings on their car. They were making their way across the driveway to the guesthouse when Ben and Bella came out the door. The weather was damp and gray, the clouds close. A cold wind had come up during the night. Bella shivered and pulled her raincoat tighter.

"Benjamin Fleck?" asked the shorter of the two detectives. He was middle-aged and plump. The other was younger with hair the color of carrots.

"That's right," answered Ben.

"Bella Webber?"

Her voice shook when she answered. "Yes."

"We need you both to come down to the station. Answer a few questions for us about Tiffany Archer."

"Both of us?" asked Bella.

"Yes. We're interviewing everyone who spent the last several hours with her. From what we gather, that includes everyone who sat with her at the bar last night."

Everyone? That meant Stefan and Genevieve. This was going to be in all the papers. Neither of them needed this kind of publicity. Graham would be having an absolute fit about his movie right now. She almost felt sorry for him, knowing how this kind of thing, so out of control of his own power, would make him insane. But that was a fleeting thought. Mostly she was worried about Ben. The good news was that they would all have the same story. Stefan and Gennie would tell the truth as they remembered it.

Behind them, Annie and Drake came out of the house, putting on coats. Her brother had his cell phone in his hand, his face eerily calm whereas Annie was visibly shaking.

"I called my attorney in Seattle," said Drake to both of them. "He recommended two defense attorneys."

"If you need them," said Annie, mouth trembling, her eyes darting to the detectives. "You're just asking questions, right? No one's being accused of anything?"

"That's right, Mrs. Webber. Just gathering information about the victim's last hours."

"Do we follow you, then?" asked Ben.

"No. We'd like you both to get in the car."

Now Bella started to shake. Riding in the backseat of a cop car was not how she wanted to spend the morning. It was supposed to be spent making up Gennie's face, not down at the station answering questions.

"I'll call Peter Ball, too," said Drake to Ben. Peter Ball was a detective with the Seattle Force, assigned three and a half years ago to Drake's wife and daughter's murder case. The two men had become close during the horrific months that followed their deaths, both because of Peter's careful and detailed work on the case and his genuine humanity and sensitivity. No one could unravel something and put it back together like Peter Ball. Bella shivered. If Drake was calling attorneys and Peter, it meant he was worried. And that made her even more afraid.

Chapter Six

THE COP WITH CARROT HAIR interviewed Bella at the police station in Echo Grove. The room was windowless and held only a simple table and two chairs. He sat across from her, his gaze both intense and unflinching, taking notes on a yellow tablet. They'd been together an hour already. She was hungry and the lack-of-caffeine headache was starting, faint still, like the air right before a thunderstorm. So far he'd asked her to tell him as accurately as possible everything she could remember about last night and she'd answered as honestly as she could.

"What is the nature of your relationship with Ben Fleck?"

She returned his gaze, unflinching. "We're sleeping together."

"Is this a purely physical relationship?"

"How is that relevant to anything?"

He shrugged, his hazel eyes cold. "I ask the questions here."

She flushed, hot suddenly. How was her relationship with Ben a factor in anything? Regardless, despite her inclination to sass him, she knew for her sake and Ben's she had to play nice. "We're newly together. My brother's known him forever, though."

"And you were with him in the early part of this morning?"

"Correct. We're both staying at my brother's house. I left him at the bar around eleven. He returned to the house shortly after midnight."

"Are you sure about this?"

Bella felt dampness at the base of her neck where her curls brushed the collar of her blouse. She put her fingers there, fluffing her curls, trying to remain calm. "Yes." *Just tell the truth.* "I'd fallen asleep and looked at the clock when he came in."

"And did you ask him what took him so long to return?"
"Yes."
"And?" Carrot Cop raised his eyebrows and spoke to her in a voice dripping with disdain.
"Tiffany was throwing up and he didn't want to leave her to die in her own vomit."
"You really think a man like Ben Fleck held her hair while she puked for an hour?"
"Yes. He saw Tiffany was in trouble and shouldn't drive so he stopped to help. That's the kind of man he is. I'm quite certain he did hold her hair." She put her fingers against her lips, watching him. There was a trace of meanness in his demeanor he didn't bother to disguise with professionalism. He was a small man and unattractive, with eyes that bulged and one of those mouths where his gums showed over large teeth every time he grimaced. And that awful orange hair? He'd probably been tormented as a child and decided to be a cop so he could become the bully rather than the bullied.

He looked down at his notes for a moment before meeting her gaze, tapping his pen on the table. "How well do you know him, if, in your words, you're newly together?"

"I just do." She hesitated. How did one explain to a man like this one about a man like Ben Fleck? She crossed her arms over her chest and raised her eyebrows. "Surely you can imagine he'd be in a rush to make it back to me. It took a kind man to stay and take care of a girl he barely knew."

"Miss Webber, Miss Archer was raped before she was strangled."

The pain in her head surged then. She stared at Carrot Cop, her thoughts too jumbled to respond.

"Miss Webber?"

"If that's the case, it means someone else was in her room after Ben."

"How can you be so sure about that?"

"A DNA test will prove it wasn't Ben. That's simple enough." She crossed her legs under the table, feeling the soreness from being with a man after a long time without sex. There was no way Ben had raped Tiffany. She felt hopeful suddenly. A DNA test would absolve him. Surely Carrot Cop knew this? "Can I get a Diet Coke? My head feels like it's going to explode."

"In a minute. I have a few more questions. Was Mr. Fleck acting strangely when he arrived home?"

"No. He was tired, that's all."

"And did you have sex?"

"Again, how is this relevant to Tiffany?"

"Again, I ask the questions. You answer them." He spoke to her as if she were a dull-witted child.

She stifled her first response, which was to say, *yeah, dirty, hot sex the likes of which you will never have*, but instead she said only, "Yes."

Carrot Cop got up from the table and headed toward the door. "Hold on. I'll get you that soda."

Halleluiah. Caffeine. Bella went to the window, looking down at the street below. Echo Grove was another sleepy town, thirty minutes north of River Valley but part of the same county. It was nestled in a valley as well, big in comparison to River Valley's population of 1,420, with a population of just over 15,000. Neither of the two towns was prepared for the momentous size of this story, she thought. The number of people from the press that would invade these quiet communities would be unfathomable. She could only imagine what ridiculous theories the tabloids would invent. Bella thought of the film. Would Graham and Richard continue production?

It was unlikely Richard or Graham would want to stop filming. Tiffany had only filmed one scene in the time they'd spent on the movie thus far. With only two days' worth of work, she could easily be replaced. This was Hollywood. Famous one minute, dead the next. No one would care but the fans. As Hitchcock used to say, the actors and actresses were just talent, interchangeable on any given day in Hollywood.

Carrot Cop walked back in and set a can of Diet Coke on the table. "I think we're done here but we still have some questions for your boyfriend. You can wait in the lobby."

CHAPTER SEVEN

BELLA SAT ON A BENCH in the hallway of the station while they kept Ben for several more hours. Around three o'clock in the afternoon he was released from questioning. His usually clean-shaven face was scruffy and his eyes blood-shot. "They wouldn't give me anything to eat. I feel weak," he said, falling into her arms.

"I got something for you." She guided him onto the bench and then rummaged inside her bag for the cheese and turkey sandwich she'd bought for him from the vending machine. "Was it awful?"

"Yeah, pretty much." He bit into the sandwich, chewing quickly before taking another bite. "They kept going over the same stuff again and again, like they were trying to trip me up."

He finished the sandwich in five bites. "Thanks for this. How are we getting home?"

"Drake and Annie are on their way."

He turned to her, taking her hand. "How long did they question you?"

"A couple of hours. Several intense hours."

"Bella, I'm scared. They think I did this."

"It's all right." She lowered her voice. "Listen, did they tell you she was raped?"

"What? No." He looked startled and then a look of comprehension crossed his face. "They were trying to get me to admit to that. They asked me a dozen times if I'd slept with her. I told them there was no way that girl was capable of having sex the way she was when I left her. She was totally out of it. Not to mention it's not exactly sexy to get puked on." His eyes darted to her face. "You know I didn't do this, right?"

"Of course I do." She put her hand on his knee. "But this is good news. Because they'll be able to do a DNA test and prove it isn't your sperm."

Something like relief crossed his face. "You're right. And that'll clear me." He paused. "I guess. There are still ways they could pin it on me though. These small town cops scare me and I have the distinct feeling they're crooked."

"I agree. I didn't want to say it out loud but I'm afraid you're right." She rose from the bench and started pacing. "You said Tiffany was talking crazy in the car. Do you remember what she said?"

He looked at her. "Yeah. I told the cops this too. She was talking about some married guy she was sleeping with. I got the impression she was talking about the director."

Bella felt shock, right in the middle of her chest. "That's impossible. Richard's a family guy. He and his wife have like a million kids, all adopted. He's not the type to sleep with one of his actresses. Especially not one like Tiffany."

"She said it was someone powerful who had a lot of influence over her career and that she didn't even like him but that she felt like she had to keep sleeping with him. Then she started crying and carrying on and I was scrambling to find some tissue in my glove box and it was pouring down rain and all I could think of was getting to you." His voice broke on this last part. "Bella, this is a nightmare." He put his hands on his knees, gazing at the floor. "If they arrest me for this I could lose my job. I'll never recover even if it's proven I didn't do it."

She kneeled beside him, the stone floor cold through her jeans. "It's not going to get to that." An image came to her of Tiffany that day on the swing. They'd talked about Graham. *Someone powerful who had a lot of influence over her career? It had to be Graham. Had he raped her? Was he capable of this?*

Ben raised his head, peering into her eyes. "You won't run away, will you?"

"I promised you last night I wouldn't and I won't. This will be over before you know it." She perched between his legs and kissed him on the mouth, gently, before wrapping her arms around his neck. They were in this embrace when they heard footsteps coming down the hall. It was Genevieve and Stefan.

Stefan had his arm around Gennie, their gazes on the floor, talking quietly. Bella stood, calling out to them.

"Oh, guys, we're so glad to see you," said Gennie. "We've been worried sick. They called us in around noon and before that I was frantically texting you, Bella."

"I'm sorry. I left my cell phone in the guesthouse. They brought us here in the cop car and I forgot to grab it," said Bella. "We've been here ever since."

Ben was on his feet now as well. Stefan reached out to shake his hand. "Quite a thing," said Stefan.

Bella watched him closely for signs of suspicion. Stefan and Gennie barely knew Ben. Would they think he did this? But she read nothing but sympathy on Stefan's face.

Genevieve put her arm around Bella's waist. "We want you guys to know we told them the absolute truth about everything that happened at the bar last night. In detail. Like actors do."

"Thanks," said Ben, "I appreciate it." But his eyes were dull.

Stefan patted Ben's shoulder. "Hey, this is going to be fine. They'll figure out who did this soon enough and you can put this behind you."

"No good deed goes unpunished," said Ben in a way that Bella knew was supposed to be funny but came out hollow.

Just then, Drake and Annie came down the hall, walking fast, looking like two worried parents after a playground accident. "Oh, thank God, you're out of there," said Annie, reaching for Bella and pulling her into a hug. "What did they do to you guys?" She turned to Drake. "This is absolutely ridiculous. How could they keep them in there all day?"

Drake embraced Ben. Next to her brother, he looked smaller than he had the day before, despite the fact that he and Drake were around the same height and build. "Don't worry, I'll hire the best attorney we can find if this goes any further."

"I'm freaked, man. Really freaked," said Ben. "These cops seem dirty."

"I know. They're eager to arrest someone and look like heroes, regardless of evidence." Drake's eyes were steely and determined. Bella felt less afraid in his company. Her big brother would make sure nothing happened to Ben. "I called Peter Ball this afternoon. He's going to take a week off and come down."

Ben's shoulders relaxed. "No way? Peter's doing that for me?"

"Yeah," answered Drake. "He wants to help. Anyone who knows you knows there's no way you did this."

"And Bella, the craziest thing? He already knew about the murder," said Annie.

"From the news?" asked Genevieve.

"No, because Graham Rouse had already called Cleo Tanner's agent about replacing Tiffany," said Annie.

"Holy crap, that was fast," said Bella. "Even for Hollywood." Peter's wife, Cleo, was a former actress and had attended USC with Graham Rouse. Cleo had auditioned for the part in *Stone River* at Graham's urging but hadn't gotten the part because Richard had given it to Tiffany.

"Rouse. Rhymes with louse," said Annie, almost under her breath.

Bella looked over at Genevieve. "Couldn't Graham have let poor Sabrina bury her sister first? Talk about lack of sensitivity."

"You know how it is, Bella," said Stefan. "They're only worried about the budget."

"The show must go on and all that," added Gennie with tears in her eyes. "I can't stop thinking about Sabrina. Tiffany was her whole life. They have no other family that I know of. I called her three times already but she's not picking up the phone. I wanted to offer to pay for the funeral, you know, considering what you told me about their finances."

"Sabrina told me last night they're broke," said Bella to the others. "The drugs and careless living, you know…" she trailed off. Nothing more needed to be said than that. They all understood.

She glanced up at Ben. His eyes were lidded and cold. It was hearing talk of Graham, she realized with a start. Already Graham was so much a part of her past that she forgot it would bother him. She slipped her hand into his and rested her head on his arm.

It occurred to her then that Annie should be at the restaurant already. "Why aren't you at work?"

"Billy's got it covered." Annie put her arm on Ben. "The gang at the restaurant's ready to stand behind you. Tommy and Lee said they would help however they can." Annie motioned toward the exit. "Come on. Let's go home. Peter and Cleo are supposed to arrive in an hour or so. They flew down from Seattle and Drake sent a car to the airport. I'll make dinner and we can talk about what to do next. Stefan and Genevieve, won't you join us?"

"That would be lovely," said Gennie. "Or, it would be for me, if it's okay with you, Stefan?"

"Whatever *you* want," said Stefan, softly. *Adoring*, thought Bella. That was the only way to describe how the man was looking at Gennie.

Chapter Eight

ONCE HOME AT DRAKE'S, Ben and Bella, both grimy, went to their separate quarters to get cleaned up, leaving Gennie and Stefan in the kitchen with Annie and Drake.

After Bella was showered and dressed in clean jeans and a sweater, she heard a knock on the door. She figured it was Ben but it was Annie, bringing a plate of cheese and bread. "Thought you might need a snack before dinner."

"You know me too well."

Annie, smiling, set the plate on the table between the soft chairs by the gas fireplace. "What happened with you and Ben last night?" She sat, munching on a cracker.

Bella sat across from her, grabbing a piece of cheese—it was white and soft, Havarti, locally made, probably—and a chunk of bread. "We agreed to try. Hard. You know, to figure out what this is between us." She paused, putting her piece of bread and cheese back on the platter. "Annie, I know how it looks, but he didn't do this. I know him in a way that belies how long we've actually known one another."

"Honey, I know. He's been living with us for three months. We know him too." She tucked her legs under her. "I just want to say one thing."

Bella laughed. "Oh, here it comes. What?"

"He's vulnerable in a way a man never wants to be. You have to stick by him for real. Like dig deep and figure out how to support him through this. It could get ugly."

Bella looked at Annie for a long moment, trying to think of how to describe this feeling of inevitability, of destiny that was Ben. "I get it."

"Do you?"

"Yeah, no flighty stuff, or selfish stuff. No being self-centered and immature and reckless. You know, no being me."

This time Annie laughed. "That's not who you really are, but yeah, that."

"I'll show you you're not wrong about me, Annie. I made him a promise."

"Good girl. Now eat something."

Bella smiled mischievously. "I bet you never thought you'd have to say that to me."

After Annie left, Bella dried her hair and put on a little makeup before heading to the kitchen. Annie and Drake were chatting with Gennie and Stefan like they'd known one another for years. Annie's pretty face was flushed and glowing as she stood at the stove making some kind of reduction sauce the color of burgundy wine. Stefan and Gennie sat at the kitchen counter nibbling on rosemary bread dipped in olive oil and sipping white wine.

Drake, opening a bottle of red wine, made eye contact with Bella. "You okay?"

"Yeah." She glanced toward the other end of the house. "Hey, where's Alder?"

"He's with Ellen tonight," said Annie. Ellen was Lee's grandmother and Alder's caretaker when Annie was at work. "We thought it best if we could talk about all this without him here. I'm grateful he was at school when the police came. He'll be scared to think Ben's in trouble. They've grown tight the last couple of months."

"Sweetheart, speaking of tight with Ben, did you call Mike?" asked Drake.

Annie, spoon in air, nodded yes. "He said to tell Ben to lawyer up."

"Peter Ball will help us figure out who really did this," said Drake.

There was the sound of a car coming up the driveway. "I bet that's Peter and Cleo now," said Annie.

* * *

Bella's impression of Peter Ball and Cleo Tanner remained intact. They were like an advertisement for athletic clothing with their honey-hued hair and glowing skin and muscular physiques. Cleo's refined, even features and a long patrician neck made Bella think of old Hollywood, like the actresses Richard's mother had so admired, Grace Kelly or Tippi Hedren, delicate and dewy. All of which would be a beautiful contrast on-screen to the sultry and sensual Gennie with her dark hair and olive complexion.

After drinks and introductions were made, they all feasted on a dinner of pork loin with port sauce over mashed potatoes, one of Ben's favorites, of which he ate little. Afterward, Annie took Gennie, Stefan, and Cleo out to the front room for a nightcap while Peter, Drake, Ben, and Bella met in the kitchen around the table near the window. It was dark out, drops of rain sliding down the glass, wind rustling the trees. A storm coming in, thought Bella. How appropriate.

Peter sat at one end of the table, Ben the other, with Bella perched on the windowsill. Drake paced between the stove and the table, listening.

"Who were the men following Tiffany in the parking lot? This seems to me to be the first question," said Bella.

"I agree," said Drake, stopping and leaning against the pantry door.

"Tell us what they looked like, Ben," said Bella. "Actually, tell us everything."

Peter chuckled. "Bella, I'm supposed to be the cop here."

"Oh, sorry. Of course," said Bella, flushing.

Peter ran his hand through his blond, wavy hair. He was nice-looking but the way his eyes seemed to focus and drill into you was somewhat disconcerting and made Bella feel like she wanted to confess to every past sin. "That's fine. I left my partner Brent at home so you'll have to help me out. And, she's right," said Peter to Ben, taking out a small notepad from the pocket of his suit jacket. "Tell us about the two men."

Ben looked up at the ceiling, the way people did when they were trying to recall something accurately. "Lefty's is at the first stoplight, Peter, coming into town, and I was waiting for it to turn green and happened to glance over at Lefty's. There were two men in suits standing under the awning outside the front entrance, looking like they were waiting for someone. I found it odd, given Lefty's usual clientele."

"You found what odd?" asked Peter.

"The suits. But then I figured they were associated with the film."

Peter nodded, jotting something down in his notebook. "What happened next?"

"Just then Tiffany came out the front door, wobbly in these ridiculous high-heels, given the mud in the parking lot, and a tight dress that looked hard to walk in. I recognized her, obviously, from the movies."

"What color dress?"

"Purple."

"Go on."

"She kind of stumbled down the steps and into the parking lot and the men followed her. I don't know why, but my radar went up. Without thinking, I veered into the parking lot and found a spot next to Tiffany's car, just as she was trying to unlock it. I rolled down my window and looked both men square in the face. I said, 'You two need something?' I don't know what got into me, honestly, but like I said, something about them seemed dangerous. Anyway, they didn't answer me, just turned away and went back inside the tavern. I was prepared to wait, just to make sure she got into her car okay until I realized she was hammered."

"Was there any indication that Tiffany recognized these men?"

"No way. She walked right past them. If she'd been afraid I'm sure she would've turned around and gone inside."

Peter twirled his pen on the table, almost absently, watching Ben. "Go on."

"She kept pushing the button on her key, pumping her arm up and down like it was broken. But it must have been the lock button instead of the unlock button."

"How'd you get Tiffany to go with you?"

"I just got out of my car and approached her slow so she didn't get spooked. I asked her if she was all right and she said yes but that her car wouldn't unlock. She was slurring her words and her eyes were all unfocused. I held out my hand and asked if she wanted me to try. She gave me the keys and I slipped them in my pocket. I don't know why I did that, actually. It was a weird thing to do but again I was just trying to keep her from driving. I asked her if I could give her a lift and she turned her face toward me and then upwards towards the sky. The rain was coming down even harder and it was almost poetic the way she held her face up like that and let the rain wash over her face. Then she said something that scared the hell out of me." He closed his eyes, as if trying to remember it exactly. "She said, 'I was going to get in my car and drive out of town as fast as I could until I found the river and then I was going to drive into it with the windows open and let the river fill it and me until we both just drifted away.'" Ben stopped talking and looked over at Bella. "It was the saddest thing I've ever heard anyone say."

Goosebumps ran up and down Bella's arms. She shivered, thinking of poor Tiffany. The world had eaten her alive from the inside out until there was nothing left but a shell of her sad, sunken soul.

"Then she said something about how she couldn't drive and if she was stopped they'd throw her into jail this time instead of just rehab," continued Ben, turning toward Peter once again. "I knew then I had to get her around people, maybe get some food in her and so I took her by the arm and helped her into my car and drove to Riversong."

Ben went on to tell Peter about taking Tiffany to the lodge and how she'd gotten sick almost immediately. "I stayed until it seemed safe to leave her and put her into bed, still fully clothed, by the way."

"Was Tiffany coherent at this point?"

"Yeah, she'd sobered up by this time, a little anyway. She thanked me and then curled into the fetal position and appeared to pass out cold. I left my card on the bedside table and told her to call me if she needed anything."

"And what time did you leave?" asked Peter.

"I believe it was around 11:55. I remember looking at my watch as I closed the door, hoping Bella wasn't going to be mad it had taken so long."

"Did you see anyone else in the hallway or elevator on your way out?"

Ben sat up straighter in the chair. "No one asked me that today. So I didn't think of it until just now. There was a man who got out of the elevator as I was walking in. And you know what? The elevator was coming down, which means he had come from a floor above."

"Can you describe him?" asked Peter.

"About my age, I would say. Maybe a little older. Salt and pepper hair. Medium build. Totally unremarkable. Dressed in sweats and a

T-shirt. He was typing into his phone so his head was down, making it hard for me to really see his face."

Salt and pepper hair and typing on his phone? It had to be Graham.

Ben slumped in his chair, resting the side of his face in his hand. Bella looked over at Peter, who was staring out the window, perhaps thinking through everything Ben had told him. "Peter, can we let Ben go to bed now? This has been a long day for him."

"What? Yes, of course. I'll let you know tomorrow if I have any further questions," said Peter.

* * *

Bella and Ben walked hand in hand across the driveway to the guest quarters without speaking. Once upstairs in the bedroom, Ben sank onto the bed and took off his shoes, leaning over as if it hurt to do so. Then he collapsed onto the bed and put an arm over his eyes. "I keep expecting to wake up from this nightmare but it keeps going."

She sat on the side of the bed, stroking his forearm until he took it from his face and looked at her. "It's going to be all right," she said. "Peter Ball's the best there is. Regardless if the local cops try and pin this on you, he'll get to the truth."

He rolled to his side; she leaned her back against the headboard and gathered his head onto her lap. "Do you think Drake or Annie think I could've done this?" he asked, sounding like a frightened child.

She stroked his hair. "No way. They know you."

He looked up at her. "I don't know what to do about work."

"Just keep on doing what you normally do. No one's accused you of anything yet."

"If I get arrested, I'll lose my job. That scares me almost more than anything. I never realized until now how it's been everything, all I have, my complete identity."

Ben closed his eyes. She felt him relax as she continued to stroke his hair and face. After a few minutes his breathing became steady. She shifted him onto a pillow and placed the extra blanket on the end of the bed over him. She stood, watching him sleep. How was it they were so happy for a brief few hours and now this?

Life, that's what, she thought. Hard most of the time with small moments of bliss. She shook her head, as if to dispel the gloomy thoughts. A drink. She needed a drink. She left Ben sleeping and headed to the main house.

* * *

A few minutes later, Bella stood with Peter Ball on the deck of Drake's house, sipping vodka on the rocks. He held a beer bottle in his hands, peeling at the label. The rain had ceased and the clouds parted to reveal a partial moon and scattered stars. It was cold, and their breath made clouds in the night air. Bella shivered despite her heavy jacket. She'd lived in California too long.

"After dinner on a night like this, I miss smoking," said Bella, shaking her glass so the ice clattered.

"You smoked?" asked Peter.

"Yeah. For like two minutes before I got too vain, worried about wrinkles and stopped. But every once in a while I want one."

They were quiet for a moment. Bella sipped her drink. Peter tipped back his beer. There was the rushing sound of a truck on the highway in the valley below. Something about the sound always made Bella feel lonesome. Perhaps it was the thought of the truck driver, alone, making his way to wherever with his company's goods in the back. Was he sleepy? Lonesome for his family? Did he listen to music or talk radio?

She glanced back up at the stars. They were the same for the truck driver as they were for her and thousands of others who might be gazing upon them at this very moment.

"Bella, you sure Ben didn't do this?"

Her thoughts turned from the stars to Ben. "I am. Aren't you?"

"I'm not a betting man. I'm more of a fact guy. Comes with my job. But if I had to bet on anyone's innocence, it's Ben Fleck's."

"How are you so sure?"

"Gut, mostly. I'm a good judge of character. Can sniff out the truth usually. Plus it doesn't add up. No motive. Unless he raped her and didn't want her to talk."

A jolt went through her. The tips of her fingers tingled. "No way."

"Ben will have to go in tomorrow and give a DNA sample."

"Well, that'll prove his innocence, right there."

He turned to her, his eyes glinting in the moonlight. "You sure about that?"

"Yes." They stood for a moment, watching the stars. "Peter, will you let me ride shotgun with you on this?"

"What do you mean? Like help me investigate?"

"Right." She felt stupid suddenly. This was a real detective. He wouldn't want her tagging along.

"You think you have time?"

"I can squeeze it in. I won't say anything or get in your way. And I know my way around town. That would be a help to you."

"Why, Bella?"

"Why what?"

"Why do you want to do this?'

"Because I love him. It's as simple as that." As she said it, she knew it was true. She'd loved Benjamin Fleck from the first moment she'd spotted him in her brother's living room.

"Okay, then. We'll start tomorrow. At Lefty's. Always start with the bartender."

The door opened behind them and Cleo came out to the deck. "Hi, Bella," she said softly, seeming almost shy. "What are you two doing out here?" she asked, sliding both arms around Peter's waist from behind and resting her cheek against his back. "It's freezing."

"It is," said Peter. "Hey, I'm going to go inside and have some scotch with Drake." He paused, nudging his wife slightly. "Go ahead, ask Bella the stuff you wanted to ask her."

Cleo pulled her jacket tighter. "Yeah, okay."

After Peter left, Bella turned to Cleo. "You nervous about tomorrow?"

"I'm a wreck. It's been so long. And being in the same room with Stefan and Genevieve tonight I realized how screwed I am—they're pros and I haven't really acted in ten years. Not to mention taking the place of poor Tiffany Archer. I want to turn around and go home."

"You'll be fine. I'll make you look perfect."

Cleo laughed. "Yeah, there's that too. My God, Genevieve's gorgeous. The camera doesn't lie, does it?"

Bella looked at her for a moment. "You know what I've noticed in the years I've been doing this job?"

"What's that?"

"Women never think they're beautiful. And trust me I've worked on the most beautiful women in the world by anyone's standard and none of them think they're half as lovely as they really are. And what's even sadder is the rest of the world is comparing themselves to the women in my makeup chair. If they don't think they're beautiful there's absolutely no hope for the rest of us." She paused, cocking her head to the side, taking in Cleo Tanner. "You're as lovely as Gennie, just different."

"Hollywood." Cleo looked up at the sky, shaking her head. "I can't even get my mind around that. Yesterday I'm teaching Montessori and looking forward to going home to Peter at the end of the day. Next thing I know I get a call from my agent that I need to get down here as fast as I can. And there's this script waiting for me, like I'm a real actress or something and I have lines to learn and, well, I'm terrified."

Bella squeezed her hand. "Don't worry. I'll be there to talk to between takes. That's what good makeup artists do. We're like bartenders that way."

Cleo laughed. "Good to know."

"Who's your agent?"

"Camille Bradbury. Graham hooked me up with her."

Bella shivered. Camille Bradbury was a shark in a well-preserved, fifty-year-old, human form—a tiny body that lived on vodka and cigarettes. Behind the Botox that made her features unreadable and sleek, precisely-cut, bottle-blond hair was the soul of a great white shark that could rip a person apart and leave them bleeding on the urine-scented streets of Hollywood in the time it took to order a skinny latte from the nearest Starbuck's barista/actress.

Cleo stomped her feet and pulled her jacket tighter. "They always say you're truly living if you're doing something that scares you. I guess I'm about as alive as you can get."

Yes, me too, thought Bella.

After Cleo went inside, Bella wandered to the edge of the deck. She sat on the steps looking up at the sky. The countless peppered stars glittered and sparkled and felt close. Might she gather them in her hands? Perhaps put them in a Mason jar to draw upon later for strength like children did with fireflies back east? On that summer night with Ben, standing near the rose garden, they'd held hands and gazed upward at the Milky Way. He'd pointed to the Big Dipper, the Little Dipper, and Orion's Belt. And she'd known then she'd never seen the sky. Not in Seattle where the clouds rarely moved aside and one only suspected the stars were there, hidden, waiting for a shift in the wind. Not in Los Angeles where the lights of the city and the pollution scarred an obscured sky. But here, they were close and tangible and splendid. She'd gasped from the beauty of it and moved closer to Ben, the scent of sun-drenched rose petals sweet, and leaned into him to welcome his kiss that changed her heart.

And now, under this October sky holding these flecks and slivers of light, she sighed. A sense of peace that began in her changed heart soothed the hidden dark places where fear and worry dwelled, as if the stars had been conjured just for her by a nameless force. All will be well. Surely this was true, she thought, reaching up toward the sky with her fingertips. It gave one the idea of limitless possibilities, if the universe held such things as this.

* * *

Inside the house, Drake and Annie were putting away the last of the dinner dishes. "I was thinking I should let Cleo and Peter have the guest quarters in the house. I'll move out to the guesthouse with Ben," said Bella.

"Isn't that a little soon?" Drake looked at her, his face concerned, although he was trying to hide it, which Bella found amusing.

Bella shrugged, ready for a fight. "You need the space. And Peter's doing us a favor by agreeing to look into this unofficially while Cleo's working on Stone River."

To her surprise, Drake agreed. "You're right. We're lucky to have him investigating this when he has no jurisdiction here, especially given the obvious ineptitude of the local police. I'll let Peter and Cleo know to bring in their things."

Bella packed her clothes and toiletry items quickly, feeling suddenly so exhausted she could barely think straight. In the guesthouse, she left her suitcase packed, setting it quietly by the bureau so as not to wake Ben. She brushed her teeth and washed her face and then, stripping down to nothing, slipped into bed. Ben shifted, murmuring something in his sleep. She moved close to him, pressing her cold backside against his front and wrapping his arm around her waist.

"Bella, you feel so good in my bed," he whispered in her ear.

The spark of desire shot through her. But not tonight. Tonight Ben needed to sleep.

"Where have you been?" he asked.

"Looking at the stars."

"Ah. The stars and the scent of roses were there when I kissed you for the first time. Do you remember?"

"Every detail." She moved so she faced him, kissing his neck, taking in his scent. "Peter's agreed to let me tag along this week to see if we can figure out who did this."

"Why would you do that?"

"Because."

"Because why?"

"Because I believe in you. And I'm scared. And when I'm scared I try and take control."

She felt him smile against her head. "Bella, you're a menace. You know that?"

"I've heard this before. Mostly from my brother."

"A force of nature."

A force of nature. Her fire had been called worse. "Go to sleep," she said. "You need to be strong tomorrow."

"But it's hard to keep my hands off you." His hand traveled up the back of her leg and over her hip.

And then, like the inevitability of the stars' return on any given night, they let themselves be lost in one another until their energy was exhausted and they fell into the dreamless sleep of lovers.

Chapter Nine

EARLY THE NEXT MORNING, Bella was jolted awake by a text from Richard Greenwood's assistant. "Cast and crew meeting on set at 8:00 a.m. Saturday morning. Mandatory."

She sat up, yawning. It was only six thirty. Ben was still asleep, breathing steadily. How nice it would be to stay in bed all day, especially since it was a Saturday. *But duty calls,* she thought. Her mother had often said that before she left them for the day. *Duty calls.* On those mornings, more frequent than the others when their mother stayed and made them pancakes, Drake had taken care of her, gotten her breakfast and made sure she was dressed, hair combed, and teeth cleaned and on the bus for school. She'd been a skinny child and it was always raining. The frequent wind would make its way up her pants legs so by the time she walked up the steps of the school bus her teeth chattered. But her mother had given her a red raincoat with a faux fur lining and red boots for Christmas the year she was in fourth grade. How proud she was of that coat and boots. And warm.

She'd gotten her little niece Chloe a pair of pink boots and a matching raincoat for Christmas. They were still stuffed in Bella's closet, on the floor behind shoes she never wore. Chloe had died before Bella was able to give them to her. And then it came, the sadness, like it was fresh, pulling her into grief like an unexpected riptide. She wrapped her arms around her knees and buried her face in them, letting the tears come. *Lean into the grief,* her therapist Valerie advised. *Let it take you. Don't fight it because it will find its way back to you anyway.*

Ben stirred next to her, sitting up and reaching for her. "Bella, what is it?"

She told him then of Chloe and her mother, how sometimes the loss felt like a new wound instead of scar tissue.

"Well, all this with Tiffany's bringing it up. Of course it makes all the loss just rush back into you." He put out his arms. "May I hold you? Would that help at all?"

"It would." But the tears wouldn't stop. She sobbed into his bare chest until he was damp. Finally, the tears ran out and she rose up on her elbow to look into his eyes. "Thank you for letting me cry."

"My mother always says it takes a real man to let a woman cry without trying to fix it."

"Your mother's very wise." She leaned down and kissed him. In the kiss she gave all the love she felt for him with her big and yearning heart, her tender underbelly. And he returned it in a long and searing kiss she wanted to never end. "Ben, I love you," she said into his mouth. "I can't help myself."

"Bella," he breathed into her as he pulled her under him, looking into her eyes. "You make me feel like the person I want to be, like I was meant to be, like I want to be. Is this what love is, then?"

"I think so." She bit her bottom lip, because it quivered and the lump was in the back of her throat again, only this time it ached with longing and love and gratefulness for this man destined to love her.

She hated to leave the bed but knew how important it was to be on time. She showered and dressed in jeans, a long wool sweater, and riding boots. Ben was in one of the easy chairs typing on his laptop. "Everything all right at work?" she asked.

He looked up at her. "Yeah. Just a few fires to put out, as usual."

"Do you like your work?"

He closed his laptop and set it on the ottoman. "Most of the time. It's pretty stressful. The expectations for someone at my level are intense and I'm under terrible scrutiny to stay within budget. Plus, the personnel issues are endless. Did you know there are a lot of crazy people out there?"

She laughed. "Um, yeah, I do work in the film industry, so I'm familiar."

"And moving around every two years to open yet another call center gets old. Sometimes I think about cashing in all my stock and opening a fly fishing store here in River Valley."

"Are you serious?" She sat on the arm of his chair, peering at him.

He returned her gaze. "Would you still love me if I said I was?"

"Of course I would. I might love you more, actually. Well, no, that's not possible." She hesitated, running her fingers along the collar of his T-shirt. "I have an idea for something too." She told him of her discussion with Mike about changing the mill into a factory for her cosmetic line.

"Bella, that's really exciting. You know I could help. If you wanted."

"Being with an MBA is so hot."

He pulled her onto his lap. "You really think you could live here?"

"In a second."

"I could run my little store while you turn into a cosmetic tycoon." He looked into her eyes. "Everything that's happened the last couple of days—us—and then this awful mess with the police—it's made me think a lot about what I want, how I want to spend the rest of my life. I've been so happy here, especially now, knowing you want to be part of my life. The stress that comes with all this ambition doesn't feel worth it. I've done it, you know, the whole corner office thing, and I think it might be time for a change."

"I understand. Do you think Drake would invest?"

"Maybe. The numbers are small compared to what you're trying to do so I could fund it myself. Rent's cheap here and I could carry other outdoor equipment besides just fly-fishing gear. Plus, the town needs guides for the tourists and I could run that out of the shop too."

She shook her head, amazed at him. "You've really thought this through."

"I had to think about something so I wouldn't think about you. Which didn't work, by the way."

She kissed him lightly on the mouth. "I have to get to set. Don't spend all day worrying. Peter Ball's going to figure out what really happened. I promise."

"Bella, if we get through this, I want to take you somewhere. Like Hawaii maybe?"

"When, not if, we get through this. And Hawaii sounds awesome. I'll wear my pink bikini." She got up to go but he pulled on her hand and brought her back onto his lap.

"You're going to marry me, Bella Webber, if it's the last thing I ever do."

She stared at him. "What did you say?"

"I said I want you to marry me. But this isn't me asking you. I'm going to ask you properly, in a way worthy of you. But you should know my intentions."

"Benjamin Fleck, you know how to make a girl swoon. And getting me to marry you won't be the last thing you ever do. It'll just be the beginning. I promise that too."

Chapter Ten

IT WAS POUNDING RAIN as she drove to the set; her wipers on high couldn't keep the front or back windows clear. She was one of the first to arrive, but soon the rest of the cast and crew came in, holding coffee cups, looking tired and worried and scared. A few of the women were crying. *Poor Tiffany*, thought Bella. *If you only knew how much some of us cared.*

She searched the room for Graham but he was not there. *Typical*, thought Bella. Richard ambled to the front of the room. Bella had never seen him look as poorly as he did this morning. His clothes looked like he'd slept in them and his bushy hair stood up like it hadn't been combed in days. He took off his glasses and cleaned them before he began to speak in an unsteady voice.

"Gang, I don't know how to begin to speak about this in a way that will comfort any of us. I certainly can't think of one way to explain how or why a talented young person should have to go out of the world in the way that she did. I will not pretend she wasn't a troubled person but she was doing her best, as we all do, day in and day out, to be better than she was the day before. It's my understanding she had a relapse the night she was killed. Would she have been forgiven by me and welcomed back into the fold? Yes. I believe in many chances for those with good hearts, knowing from my own experience that sobriety is not easy. Those of us with that particular addiction struggle for it each and every day." He looked around the silent room that seemed as if no one dared breathe. "I've been sober for twenty-five years. I was just a little younger than Tiffany when I took the first step into an AA meeting. Tiffany Archer was a good girl, a talented girl who struggled as I did, as I do. We're never fully safe—each day is like the first day. Regardless of her disease, she will be missed, most especially by those of us who looked forward to seeing her triumph like Phoenix Rising in the next several months. I believe in my heart she would have. But she won't have that chance now and I won't pretend like my heart isn't broken. However, we must continue forward, not only for the sake of all the jobs represented in this room but also because the only way to fight against evil is to live. This is all we can do. Make art. Kiss in the rain. Hold our children close. Love hard and without restraint. So we will." He paused, his eyes skirting to Stefan and Gennie, who were holding hands, both in tears. "I've already shared this with Stefan and Genevieve, but you should all know we've hired a new actress. I know it sounds beyond callous; I can hardly think of how to go on today, let alone offer Tiffany's role, her comeback role, to someone else. But it must be done."

His voice broke. He took off his glasses once again, wiping under his eyes with the sleeve of his shirt. "When I cast the film there was an unknown actress who auditioned for me. She goes way back with Graham—theatre school at USC—and I would've given her the role if it hadn't been for Tiffany. We've offered it to her now and she's accepted." He put his glasses back on, shaking his head. "But I cannot film for the next several days. I cannot bear it. Instead I'll find an AA meeting, in honor of Tiffany and to ensure my own demons do not yank me over to the dark side. Tonight my wife's arriving with our five children so that I may hug them and hold them close and take them to dinner and tuck them in for bed at night. So please, all of you—take the day off. Do something you love. Live. In honor of Tiffany's memory. And to say, we will not succumb to the evil that wants more than anything to bring us to our knees. Not today. Not tomorrow. Not ever."

In the parking lot, Gennie grabbed Bella and they hugged one another in a tight embrace. "How's Ben?" The rain came down upon them but neither seemed to notice.

"Scared."

"Oh, Bella, me too. And heartbroken. I think it sunk in this morning. This is real. Tiffany's gone."

Stefan came up behind them, his eyes sad and red. It appeared as if none of them had slept last night. He embraced her as well. "What's your plan, Bellalicious?"

"Peter Ball's picking me up. We're going to poke around, see what we can figure out."

Stefan nodded and glanced at Gennie. "Come on, sweetie, I'll take you back to the lodge."

Gennie nodded and took his outstretched hand. "Call us later, okay?"

Call us? Since when were they an "us"? And since when did they hold hands? Kiss in the rain, she wished for them. *Just kiss in the rain.*

* * *

Moments later, Peter picked her up and they headed toward town. "Like I said last night, always start with the bartenders," he said to her. "They know everything."

"And makeup artists," said Bella.

They parked in the muddy lot outside Lefty's Tavern and went inside. It was cold and empty but for a couple of drunks at the end of the bar and smelled like a damp ashtray. The walls were made of stone; there were no windows. How long had this place been here, she wondered?

Peter spoke under his breath. "Places like this always depress the hell out of me."

"Yeah, me too."

They sat on two barstools in the middle of the counter and waited for the bartender to acknowledge them. He was white-haired and overweight, with a red, bulbous nose. Sampled the goods too often, thought Bella. Was he Lefty?

"What'll it be?" asked the bartender. His eyes were half-closed. Suspicious of them?

"Nothing for now," said Peter. He pulled out his badge. "I'm a cop, looking for some information."

"This about the actress?" He leaned against the counter with both hands, shaking his head. "Terrible thing. But the cops have already been here. I told them everything I remembered."

"I'm on the case as well," said Peter. "They want us to be as thorough as possible."

"That don't make no sense. Why would there be more than one cop assigned to a case? That ain't how it is on television. She a cop too?" He indicated Bella with a jut of his chin.

Bella scooted to the edge of her barstool and looked him in the eyes. "No. Just a friend of Tiffany's. I'm a makeup artist on the movie set. She and I were close. I'm devastated and can't rest until we find her killer." How easy it was to lie, she thought. It just rolled off her tongue. She thought of Ben, home and scared, and let her eyes fill with tears. This must be how Genevieve did it, she thought. Just think of what you're really sad about and let the tears come.

The bartender visibly softened. "Well, I'm real sorry to hear that. Hard to lose a friend."

"Are you Lefty?" asked Bella, keeping her voice vulnerable.

"Oh no, that was my old man. He's been dead twenty years already. Gave me this heap of stones that's like a dead weight around my neck." He put his hands, red and chapped with short square fingers, on the surface of the bar as if he wanted to shake hands but then thought better of it, hiding them under the counter in the next instant. "I'm just plain Spike. Spike Lawson."

"I'm Bella Webber and this is Peter Ball."

"Wait a minute. You Annie Bell, I mean, Annie Webber's sister-in-law?" asked Spike.

"Yes. Drake's my brother."

"Oh, well, anyone family with Annie is all right in my book."

This surprised Bella. She would have thought Spike would consider Annie competition. "You know her?"

"Sure. She and Lee Tucker been real great to me and great for this town. Brings people in here to spend money and that's good for all of us. Plus, Annie sends me down dinner every now and again. Knows my wife died last year and that I sleep down here in my office most nights. Gotten to where I hate to go home."

"I know how that is," said Bella. "Hard to live alone."

"Sure is," said Spike. "It was a heart attack that took her. Just like that, she was gone." He said this as if she'd asked.

"I'm sorry." Bella hesitated, her heart twisting. "I've lost so many people."

He nodded, knowingly. "Most folks have. Guess it's the way of the world." Spike looked over at Peter, the wariness gone from his face now. "So what do you need to know?"

"I just have a few questions for you," said Peter, taking out his notepad. Bella noticed his gun then, just perched at his side like a cell phone or something. He was a cop. A real cop. The enormity of what happened in the last forty-eight hours hit her then. Tiffany was dead. Raped and murdered. She felt the pastries she'd eaten earlier rising to her throat. Peter glanced at her. "You okay?"

She took in several large breaths. *Keep it together*, she ordered herself, *or Peter will make you stay at home.*

"Yeah, I'm good."

"Spike, what do you remember about Tiffany that night?" asked Peter.

"Well, she came in around ten, give or take. She'd already had a few if I was to guess. Real chatty with me, like we were old friends or something. Ordered straight shots of tequila. Two of them. Drank them one after the other then went to the jukebox and put in at least ten dollars worth of music. And then came back to the bar and asked for two more shots."

"Was it crowded for a Thursday night?"

"No, it was slow. Everybody was down at Riversong listening to Tommy's band. It was just some of my regulars and the girl. And two suits, sitting over in the corner, nursing beers." He pointed at the far corner of the bar, near the restrooms.

"Were they here when she arrived?" asked Peter.

"No, they come in right after her."

"You recognize them?"

"No, never saw them before."

"Did they leave before her?"

"Yeah. Sort of. They went outside, I figured to smoke, but instead they just stood under the awning, like they were waiting for someone to pick them up. After the girl left, they came in and put some money on the table for the beers and left."

"Did you hear anything the two men talked about?" asked Bella. "You know, to give you a clue about who they are?"

"Not really. They were quiet, didn't seem to speak much as far as I could tell, even to each other."

"What did Tiffany talk to you about?" asked Bella.

"Shoot, only her life story. The girl was as plastered as they come. She told me she was an actress because I didn't recognize her. I'm not partial to movies—I like hunting and fishing shows mostly—but anyway, she seemed real surprised by that and said she was glad to be in a bar where no one seemed to know who she was. I asked her why she wasn't out with her movie friends and she said none of them really liked her—that they all felt sorry for her because she'd had some trouble."

"Did she tell you what kind of trouble?" asked Peter.

"Said something about drug rehab and..." He searched the ceiling as if for answers. "What did she call it? A declining fan base. That was it. Said this movie was kind of her last chance but that the acting stuff didn't come easy no more like it did when she was a kid. Said she wanted to quit the whole business but knew she couldn't because of her sister."

"Her sister?" asked Peter.

"Yeah, apparently her twin sister is her manager or something like that. Said her sister'd be lost without all the money she makes in the movies. Then, she said something about how she had a best friend for a while but they'd gotten in a fight because the friend accused her of taking something that didn't belong to her."

"Do you know who she was talking about?" asked Peter.

"Well, I asked her, 'cause by now I was real curious and I'm hanging on every word—it's like watching a show, you know, and my life's pretty boring. So I asked and she said, 'You ever read in the papers about Jocelyn Zinn?' And I said, 'That the one accused of running a brothel?' And she nodded in the affirmative. I started feeling embarrassed given the fact I would never have gone to a place like that because of my wife Myrtle, but I know they exist and everything."

"What did she say next?" asked Bella, horrified and curious at the same time.

"She said Madam Zinn was her roommate at rehab and they became best friends, until she accused Tiffany of taking her customer book and blackmailing some of the men who are in it."

Both Peter and Bella stared at him. This was motive. Blackmail? She could only imagine the list of names in that customer book.

"I told her a nice girl like her should stay away from anything like that and find a nice man to marry. And she said she had a boyfriend but he was married. And I told her to run away from that as fast as she could. Nothing good could come from seeing a married man, I told her. Then I told her a story about one of my customers getting bludgeoned to death by a jealous husband one night a few years back. But she was the type of girl who doesn't listen. You know the type?" He said this to Peter, as if it were only something another man would understand.

Peter nodded, serious, and then wrote something in his pad before looking up, his placid expression suddenly animated. "How loud was she talking? Could the suits hear her, you think?"

Spike looked at the counter, thinking. "She talked loud for sure. However, the jukebox was playing so I'm not sure if they could hear her or not."

"Do you remember if they seemed agitated at all when she was talking about the blackmail stuff?"

"Can't say I noticed."

"Could you describe the men to me?"

"Clean cut. Military-looking haircuts. Like secret service types for the president or something."

"Did you tell the other cops all this same information?"

Spike looked blank for a moment. "No, matter of fact, they never asked much about Tiffany. Those two buffoons didn't know which end was up. They just wanted to know if I'd seen the man who picked her up in the parking lot."

"Did you?"

He nodded, picking up a towel from under the counter and rolling it into a ball. "I didn't want her to drive in her state, especially because I'm liable now for over-serving. But when I tried to get her to stay and let me call someone to pick her up, like her sister, I suggested, she got furious and threw her empty shot glasses at me. Knocked down three bottles of booze." He pointed to the shelf behind him. "Yep, went totally crazy like a mama bear surprised in the forest, I swear to Jesus. Next, she came up over the bar and pushed me so hard I fell back, knocking a bunch of glasses to the floor. After she practically demolished my bar, she charged out the front door, making this clacking sound in those shoes of hers. It took me a minute to recover—I ain't young, you know—anyway, after I got up, I ran out the backdoor to try and stop her at the pass but by then there was the young man who works for Hylink—I recognized him from his photo in the paper when they announced the call center coming here—offering her a ride. Once I saw he had it under control, I came on inside. Can't trust folks these days not to help themselves to a couple of drinks while I'm gone."

"Okay, just one more thing," said Peter. "Can you describe to me exactly what you saw in the parking lot?"

Spike proceeded to describe what he saw. It matched Ben's story almost perfectly.

After Spike finished, Peter handed him his card. "Call me if you think of anything else."

"You're with the Seattle cops?" said Spike. "What're you doing down here?"

"Making sure an innocent man doesn't get blamed because of faulty police work," said Peter.

"You sure you two don't want a beer?" asked Spike.

"Not today, Spike," said Bella, putting her hand on top of his rough one. "But I'll come back. I promise."

"Say hi to Annie for me."

"Will do."

* * *

In Peter's car, they sat for a moment, taking in what they'd just learned. After a moment, Peter took out his phone. "Jocelyn Zinn, right? Yeah, here it is." He shook the phone in the air, almost triumphantly. "Rumored Madam is what the press calls her."

"There's no rumor about it in Hollywood. I'm sure that little black book of hers was filled with half the actors and two-thirds of the elected officials in Los Angeles. But seriously, I can't imagine Tiffany was doing this. For one thing, where is the money? Sabrina said they were broke."

"The industrious Miss Zinn's been arrested a bunch for refusing to give up her client list. Could make her angry enough to kill if she thought, even erroneously, that Tiffany took it and was blackmailing some of these guys."

"Which means we have yet another suspect," said Bella. "What do we do next?"

"Let's go back to Drake's and tell Ben what we learned. Should give him some peace of mind."

On the way, Bella's phone rang.

"Bella, it's Sabrina."

"Oh, Sabrina, I've been worried about you. Did you get my message?"

"No. My phone's so full I haven't been able to sift through anything. I've just been sitting in my hotel room staring at my hands. I can't believe she's gone. And the police are saying she was raped. Her room was torn apart too, like someone was looking for something." Her voice broke. There was the sound of tears on the other end of the phone. "I can't stop thinking about her final moments."

"Oh, Sabrina, don't think about that. You'll make yourself crazy."

"I'm glad our parents aren't alive to see any of this."

She glanced at Peter and mouthed, "Sister."

He nodded, understanding.

"Bella, the cops told me they brought Ben in for questioning."

The wipers were on intermittent. Rain fell steadily, causing the window to blur until the wipers wiped them clean. She fiddled with the car vents, moving the lever up and down. "Yes."

"I told them how nice he'd been to pick her up outside the bar and that he didn't seem the type, what little I knew of him, to be violent. But they didn't seem to believe that. Bella, they seem like complete idiots. Or worse, not on the up and up."

"I know. Ben's scared and so am I. We had a friend come down from Seattle. He's a detective, Sabrina, with the Seattle Police Department. He's helping me poke around a bit."

She heard Sabrina sigh. "You have no idea how much better I feel to hear you say this. I want whoever did this brought to justice. Do you think your friend can help us do that?"

"They say he's the best." She glanced over at Peter. He reminded her of the Australian actor Simon Baker, only younger. Had anyone ever told him that?

"Will you come see me? I feel so friendless here and the press and paparazzi are swarming the hotel. I'm like a trapped animal in here. Maybe I could tell your cop friend something that would be helpful?"

"Of course, we'll come."

"Now?"

She made eye contact with Peter who nodded in the affirmative. "We'll be there in five minutes."

Bella filled him in on what she knew about Tiffany's financial situation, according to what Sabrina had told her the night before. At the lodge, they parked in visitor parking. Sabrina was right. Every big and small news station, magazine, and newspaper seemed to be represented. As they walked past the vans and cameras and reporters wearing heavy coats and sipping coffees, several of the reporters gave them the once over, but clearly decided they were no one important and turned away.

The lobby was quiet; the two front desk people nodded in their direction as they walked past the desk to the elevators. There was no one in the elevator or the hallway. All the movie folks were inside their rooms, thought Bella, probably in shock over the news and also hiding out from the press.

Sabrina answered the door wearing one of the lodge robes. Her hair was dirty and she wore no makeup, making her crimson scar seem more vivid than usual. Bella's hands itched, wishing she could dim it with foundation and powder. But Sabrina had never let her do her makeup, refusing to attend any public events with her sister. "I don't want to deal with the stares," she had said once.

The two women embraced; Bella held her tightly for a moment before releasing her. There was an open bottle of wine on the table. Bella looked at her with surprise. "I've never seen you drink."

"I don't really. Well, I never wanted to in case it made it harder for Tiffany. But today I just felt like it. Would either of you like some?" She put her hand to her mouth. "Oh, I'm sorry. I'm Sabrina Archer." She held out her hand to Peter.

"No thanks on the wine," said Peter, shaking her hand.

"Me either," said Bella. She needed one. But she'd wait until she was back at Drake's. She thought of Ben then, at home with Drake and Annie, probably scared out of his mind. How could this be happening? What had Tiffany Archer done to her life? This was the inevitable question. What was it that had made her self-destructive? Early fame as Stefan had suggested? Or something deeper, some seed of madness that lay in wait, dormant until the cruelties of the world made it bloom and take root? Why else would someone as talented and privileged as Tiffany Archer destroy her life? Not that she deserved to be murdered and raped, of course.

The three of them sat in the easy chairs in the sitting room. Sabrina, seeming to have forgotten her wine, folded and unfolded her hands, alternately staring at the gas fireplace and the ceiling. "I've arranged for her body to be sent back to Los Angeles after the coroner's done with her. She wanted to be cremated. We talked about it once."

"Will you have a memorial for her?" asked Bella. "I could help you, if you need it."

"No, I don't think so. We have no family." Sabrina pulled on her unwashed hair. "She did good work, you know, when she was clean."

"Sabrina, she was talented and respected by many in the industry. No one can take that away from her. Or you," added Bella.

"But all anyone will remember is her drug use and that she was murdered. This is the legacy she'll leave. Not her body of work." Sabrina picked at a bandage around her thumb.

"What happened to your thumb?" asked Bella.

"I cut it yesterday. In the afternoon. Opening a box for Tiffany. New shoes she had sent up from her favorite boutique in Beverly Hills." She fiddled further with the bandage. "Seems like a million years ago now." Sabrina turned her gaze to Peter. "I'd give anything to know the truth. Otherwise I'm afraid I'll lose my mind. I need to know what happened. Do you find this to be true for all victims' loved ones?" She asked it almost clinically, as if she were conducting a survey for scientific study.

"I do."

"No matter how horrific the end?" asked Sabrina.

"Right," said Peter.

And then, there it was. The memory of Drake sitting with Peter in his Seattle home after Esther and Chloe were murdered. Drake had asked for every detail. "Tell me exactly." After Peter told him every detail, he'd asked for it again. This had surprised Bella. Might it be too painful for him to know? But she understood later he wanted to measure the suffering in their final moments. They hadn't known what was happening, Peter Ball had told him over and over. It was too quick. This had given them both a small amount of peace.

"Can I ask you a few questions?" asked Peter.

"Of course," said Sabrina. "Anything. Not that I'll be much help."

"Tiffany told Ben Fleck you two had a fight. Bella tells me you said that wasn't the case. But do you have any idea what might have triggered her binge drinking?"

Sabrina's eyes went cold; she waved her hands around dismissively. "Anything could trigger her binges. She didn't take her sobriety seriously. Thought it was something the rest of us were manufacturing, this idea she actually had a problem. She saw it as partying." She made quotes in the air. "'I'm young,' she always said to me. 'I have every right to be out having fun whenever I want.' Which might have been the case if she could have kept it from spiraling out of control. But she couldn't. She was an addict."

Peter hesitated; he tugged on his ear. Bella could see his mind working behind his green eyes, debating about whether or not to tell Sabrina what they'd learned from Spike. "Did Tiffany tell you much about her last stint in rehab?"

"No, not really. Why?"

"Did she tell you who her neighbor was?"

Sabrina smiled, reaching for her glass of wine but not drinking from it, merely holding it in her hands and studying its contents. "Yes. Jocelyn Zinn. Of course, Tiffany would befriend her. She had radar for other self-destructive people. Attracted and attached to them time and time again. The two of them were best friends for a month or so, spending every minute together shopping or lunching. But then they had a falling out, which is the inevitable path for all Tiffany's friendships."

"Do you know what they fell out about?" asked Peter.

"Tiffany told me Jocelyn accused her of something she didn't do." She took a small sip of wine. "Although, knowing Tiffany, there's always more than her side of the story. It's always everyone else's fault, never her. She's the victim." Sabrina's lips trembled. "I sound terrible, speaking ill of my dead sister. It's just she was so difficult. The fact that she's gone doesn't change that."

"We understand," said Bella. "You took good care of her."

"I sacrificed my own career ambitions for her but she never understood that I might have any other interests but her. In the end, it didn't matter, I suppose."

Peter shifted in his seat. "Do you know anything about Miss Zinn's client list?"

Sabrina stared at him, turning pale. Her hands trembled so violently the wine in her glass swayed to and fro like the waves of a lake on a stormy night. "What did you say?"

Bella reached for Sabrina's glass, taking it and setting it on the table next to Sabrina's chair. "She mentioned to the bartender the night she was killed that Ms. Zinn believed she not only took the book but was also blackmailing clients. You think it's possible?"

"I can't imagine Tiffany showing that much initiative. Blackmail?" said Sabrina, shaking her head furiously. "She couldn't even log into her own Facebook fan page or get money out of her bank account. There's no way she was blackmailing people. Plus, if that was the case, where's the money?"

"But it's motive for her murder," said Peter. "Big time motive if it's true."

"And it would explain why her room was torn apart," said Bella. "Someone was looking for that book."

Sabrina went to the window and opened the curtains a few inches. "Did you see all those idiots down there with their cameras? Just waiting for something to put on their ridiculous shows. And all for what? To feed this fascination for scandal?" She shut the curtain, hard, and wheeled around to look at them. "If this is true, that she was blackmailing a man or men, how will we ever know for sure?"

Peter rose to his feet and went to meet her in the middle of the room. "I'm not sure exactly. But we'll start with scouring bank and phone records, that sort of thing."

"Right." Sabrina poured more wine into her glass. She held it in both hands. "We'll know it's true if you can find the money."

"We'll get to the bottom of this and it just may lead us to her killer."

"How can you possibly do this work?" asked Sabrina.

Peter smiled. "My wife asked me that one time. And I don't know the answer except to say it's what I'm made to do. It's the way I'm wired."

Sabrina tugged at the tie around her waist. "I used to think that about something too, but it wasn't to be. Instead I ended up my sister's keeper."

Bella wanted to ask her what this something was. What had Sabrina wanted to be when she was little? She'd always seemed so oriented toward making her sister's career a success that it had never occurred to Bella she might have had other aspirations.

Sabrina sank back into the empty chair. "Now what am I supposed to do?" She took a large swallow of wine.

Peter leaned forward, covering Sabrina's small, white hand with his. "Give it some time. Let's get you some closure first. Then you can decide what to do next."

She nodded. Her eyes filled with tears. "I'm lost without having her to worry about."

Bella scooted into the bathroom and came back with tissues. "Have you gotten any rest?"

"No. I can't sleep."

"Could you get a doctor to prescribe you something?" asked Peter.

Sabrina shook her head. "No drugs. I'm my sister's twin." Her eyes were flat now, without expression.

Bella suddenly had the impression of a young person in class who day after day cannot understand the lesson. They've accepted their fate, their doomed march toward a hopeless future. *I cannot understand; I cannot figure a way out.* She glanced at Peter. He was gazing at Sabrina with an expression of kindness despite his professional demeanor. He was probably trying to think of something to say but there was no offer of comfort within their grasp for this lost twin.

Bella stood. "We'll go. Try and get some rest. I'll call you later."

"Yes, thank you." Her eyes were still glazed.

"Order some food, maybe?" suggested Bella.

"Sure. I'll do that." This was said without any guise at pretense. There would be no food ordered. No sleep would come. The room was dim except for the glow of the gas fireplace. Bella switched on a lamp near the window. Outside, the autumn afternoon was growing dark already. The rainstorm the night before had stripped off the last of the colorful leaves and the trees were leafless and skinny against a close, gray sky. Gray. Everything seemed gray, ugly. Bella felt a sudden homesickness for Los Angeles and her tidy, cozy apartment in Venice near the ocean. Her neighbors were artists and musicians with tattoos and purple hair. At night the bars and restaurants opened their doors and people spilled out onto the sidewalks with drinks, music blaring from unseen speakers. It was like a carnival all the time, she often thought. Today, if she were home, she would walk to the beach in her flip-flops and her wetsuit and her boogie board. The sidewalks would smell of spilled beer from the night before. The stretch of beach would smell of salt water and seaweed and marine life. She wondered for a moment, which life was real? This one with Ben and Drake and this police detective she barely knew or the one she'd left behind? Just as quickly as those thoughts came, she remembered Ben's face that morning. It was a mixture of fear and gratitude. "You don't have to do this," he'd said, referring to her stint as a police detective.

But she did. This was not the time to be the selfish young woman who lived for the surf or a night out with her friends. This was the time to do something for someone she loved without worry for her own needs.

With that thought, she indicated to Peter they should go. With a sympathetic pat on the shoulder for Sabrina, he nodded. In the hallway that smelled of new carpet, they walked toward the elevator. "It's for the family," he said, as if she'd asked him the question. "That's why I do this work. For the families."

Bella punched the button for the elevator, feeling the familiar sadness. Loss. The sadness never left, never faded like the moments of joy did. The finality of death made sure of that. "I know. I was the family once."

The elevator doors opened. They stepped inside. Peter ran his index finger over the braille next to each floor button, gazing at the floor. She felt the weight of his thinking as the elevator dropped five floors until it reached the lobby. There, waiting to get on the elevator was Fred Hughes, River Valley's deputy.

"Fred?" Bella said, reaching out her hand. "How are you?"

"Hey, Bella." He shook her hand vigorously. "Terrible thing, this. You must've known her, what with working on the movie."

"I did. Knew her for years actually. We were just up talking with her twin sister."

"That's a shame now. Poor girl."

Bella indicated to Peter with a lilt of her head in his direction. "Fred, this is my friend Peter Ball. He's a detective with the Seattle Police Department."

"Wow. Cool." Fred's pale blue eyes were wide as he held out his hand for Peter to shake. "You made detective, huh? That's a big deal." He sighed. "Won't ever happen for me, you know, working here in this little town. Matter of fact, Bella, the cops from Echo Grove just swept right in and took this whole thing over."

"I know. They took me in for questioning. I had that awful little red-haired troll grilling me for hours."

"Shoot, yeah, he's a real piece of work." Fred shuffled his feet. "Hey, Annie called me about Ben Fleck. Said they worked him over pretty good."

Bella lowered her voice, looking around the lobby. Fortunately for them, the staff at the lodge was successful in keeping the press outside in the cold, where they belonged. "They're targeting him for it, Fred, and we're all scared."

Fred looked up at Peter. "You poking around for Ben's sake?"

Fred. Not as dumb as he looks, thought Bella.

"I am. He's a friend of mine. And my wife's down here filming so I tagged along." Peter, sounding conspiratorial, leaned closer to Fred. "You want to help me?"

"Could I? Well, shoot, yeah, I would."

"You have access to her room?" asked Peter, sounding a little too casual. Fred didn't seem to notice.

"Yep." He nodded toward the front desk. "These guys know me. I'll get a key right now."

"You're more than a tad bit evil," Bella whispered to Peter. "I like it."

"Takes one to know one," he whispered back.

* * *

Room 501 was blocked off with crime scene tape that Fred gingerly moved so they could cross over before using the key to unlock the door. Bella suddenly felt strange entering the room, and a shiver went up her spine, given what had happened here. The light was dim, making it hard to see much except the bed and chairs similar to the ones in Sabrina's room. Fred turned on several lamps. Bella stifled a gasp.

The room was ransacked. Every bureau drawer was open, clothes and shoes strewn about, magazines tossed on the floor. There were several empty bottles of airplane-size tequila bottles on the bedside table. Dirty towels were in a pile on the floor in the bathroom, with evidence of someone getting sick in the splashes around the toilet. A crumpled up washcloth was on the sink, dry now but obviously wet at one time. The one Ben used to wipe Tiffany's face after she was sick—just as he'd indicated.

Had they been looking for Ms. Zinn's black book?

Peter was on the floor with a small flashlight that must have been attached to his key chain, looking under the bed. "Don't see anything under here." He scooted onto his stomach, reaching under the bed with his right arm. "Ah, I feel something," he said, scooting a few inches farther, his face plastered against the side of the bed. "Somebody hand me a tissue."

Fred did so, placing it in Peter's outstretched hand. Peter made a stretching noise, grunting softly. "Got it." He straightened, coming to his feet and holding something shiny. "A lighter. Stuck between the bed's leg and the wall. They must've missed it the first time."

The room began to tilt. Bella took in deep breaths but still black spots appeared.

"Bella, what's the matter?" she heard Fred say, sounding like he was inside a tunnel.

But she couldn't answer, her vision darkening. The nausea came, swift. She stumbled. Fred caught her and brought her to an empty chair.

"Put your head between your legs," said Peter.

She did so, taking in deep, calming breaths, until the feeling of faintness dissipated enough for her to speak.

"What's wrong?" asked Peter, his brows wrinkled in concern. "Too much for you to be in Tiffany's room?"

"It's not that," she answered, bringing her hand to her mouth, the nausea in waves now. "That's Graham Rouse's lighter. I'd know it anywhere. It was his father's. He takes it everywhere with him. Loves to light people's cigarettes with it. Especially actresses, apparently."

"Graham Rouse? The producer?"

"Yes." She looked up at him. "And my ex-boyfriend. My *married* ex-boyfriend."

"The married man she told Spike about is Graham Rouse?" said Peter, in a way that was more a statement than a question.

Fred's gaze bounced between them, like he was watching a tennis match. "Another suspect, then?"

"I suspected it but I wasn't sure," said Bella. "But this proves he was here. I think he's the man Ben saw get off the elevator that night."

Peter shrugged. "We don't know when he dropped it. Could've been any night and it certainly doesn't mean he raped and murdered her."

All Bella could think was, she was raped. She was raped. Could Graham Rouse be capable of rape? And murder? He was a liar, sure. But he'd only been aggressive with her once and that was after he'd had a lot to drink the night she told him she was done. He'd shaken her, thrust her against the wall before he charged out of her apartment, slamming the door so hard her neighbor, Tim, a Venice Beach body builder, had come over to check on her.

As if he'd read her mind, Peter asked her the question. "Bella, was he ever violent with you?"

She glanced at Fred, feeling self-conscious to talk about it in front of him. What did he think of her? The feeling of shame washed over her, as it did when she had to talk about her relationship with Graham Rouse. But it was for Ben. To save Ben. She had to tell the truth. *Graham? What have you done?* she thought. "Once. When I broke it off the last time. But nothing close to rape. He just shook me. Almost like a child throwing a temper tantrum." She thought back to what Spike had told them earlier. "You know, Peter, she didn't tell Spike she was afraid of her married lover. Did she?"

"No, she didn't," he replied. "But murders are more often than not committed by someone the victim is intimate with. I think it certainly puts Graham Rouse on the suspect list."

She felt nauseous again. "How do we get him to talk to us without letting it be known we were in here snooping around?"

"That's where you come in," said Peter.

"I don't know."

"Think about Ben."

"Graham's not going to tell me anything."

"You might be surprised."

Chapter Eleven

WHEN THEY RETURNED HOME, she found Ben in the guesthouse watching television from the bed. She knew by the way his eyes were glazed over that he was merely making an effort to stay distracted.

She sat next to him as he shut the television off with the remote. "How'd it go?" he asked, with that same wary fear in his eyes he'd had for twenty-four hours now.

She filled him in on everything they'd learned, saving the part about Graham Rouse for last.

"Son of a bitch," he said, sitting up.

"I'm going over to the hotel to talk to him. Peter suggested I try and get something out of him myself before we go to the police with anything."

He made a stop gesture with his hands. "Absolutely not. There's not a chance in hell I'm letting you alone with that guy." He paused, looking at her like she was insane. "For so many reasons, not the least of which is that he might be a rapist and murderer."

"I'm doing this." She rose from the bed, heading toward the bathroom.

He followed her. "You are not."

"I am."

"Dammit, Bella, let Peter handle this. He's a pro."

"Peter suggested I go. No one can get Graham Rouse to talk like I can. I know him so well. He'll open up to me if I ask the right questions."

"You just might be the most stubborn, infuriating woman I've ever met." He yanked a towel from the rack and twisted it in his hands. "I cannot let you put yourself in danger for my sake. I got myself into this. I should get myself out of it."

"You got yourself into this because you're a great guy who was trying to help a woman in trouble. I'm not abandoning you now. Peter's going to figure this out. You should've seen him in action today. The guy's awesome."

"That's my point. He's a professional and you're getting in over your head."

She turned on the shower, stripping off her clothes. "Are you going to fight with me or get in here with me?"

But he didn't smile like she thought he would. "I'm serious, Bella. This is not okay, no matter how hot you are, and trust me, there's nothing I'd rather do than get in there with you but even I have my limits. I'm pissed at you. Seriously." With that, he turned and left the bathroom, shutting the door firmly behind him.

When she was done with her shower, he was gone, his jacket missing from the coatrack and the bedside table empty of his keys.

Fine, she thought. *Be angry. I'm still figuring out who murdered Tiffany if it's the last thing I do.*

* * *

She met Graham Rouse for dinner in his room. He ordered room service: a vegetable stir-fry with tofu for him and a steak for her. *Yes, that's right*, she said silently, when he showed surprise at her request. *I eat steak now. And you can suck it.* For years it was the almond milk and tofu and wheatgrass shakes and waiting for him to call. Why? Why had she done it for so long? The familiar feeling of regret came to her, like something bitter in the back of her mouth she couldn't rid herself of.

After he hung up the phone, he turned to her, indicating the open bottle of red wine on the minibar. "I got you the good stuff."

"Thanks," she said. "I'll pour."

"Figured you missed good wine now you're no longer with me."

"I'm perfectly capable of buying good wine with or without you," she said, pouring two glasses for them. *Keep it nice*, she told herself. But how she would like to deck him. Or karate kick him. Not that she knew karate. Just kick him, then, right in the chest.

"Bella, did you hear me?"

"What? No. Sorry."

"Why did you call?"

She handed him a glass of wine. "I wanted to talk to you about Tiffany."

Was it her imagination or had he turned pale under his tan?

He shook his head, took a sip of wine, and then sat on one of the chairs, crossing his legs, revealing a bare ankle next to his loafer. The pretentious ass never wore socks. Did he not realize where he was or that the temperature was in the 40s? "Terrible. Just terrible. Richard's shook. Never seen him so shook."

"You didn't waste any time replacing her."

He took another sip of wine, watching her over the rim of his glass. "You know how that goes, Bellie, budget and stuff. Can't stop production over another dead actress. Sad as it is."

"Another? Really? That's how you're going to talk about her."

He shrugged, playing with the cuff of his pants with his manicured fingers. "Come on, Bella. Don't sound so righteous. These crazy bitches always do themselves in one way or another."

"Jesus, Graham. Have a little respect for the dead."

"Sorry to bother your sensitive side, babe, but that girl did everything she could to fuck up her life. And she hurt a lot of people along the way."

"Hurt? Or do you mean cost a lot of money?"

"Isn't that the same thing in Hollywood?" He took another sip of wine. "This is good. Not sure a hundred dollars good but hey, only the best for you." He gazed at her with a half-smile on his face. "You miss me? That why you called? You don't have to make up some excuse to see me, you know. I'm always here for you."

"Graham, cut the shit. I know you were sleeping with Tiffany."

He flinched. "Excuse me?"

"She told me." There it was, again—the lies just slipping off her tongue. *This is for Ben*, she told herself. *All for Ben*.

"Did she now?" He downed the rest of his wine and went to the bar, filling his glass.

"Yes, she did." She took a sip of wine, enjoying playing with him. "I could use a smoke."

He looked at her like she had two heads. "You don't smoke anymore."

"I've decided to take it up again." She reached in her purse for the pack of cigarettes she'd bought on her way. "Want one?"

"You know I don't smoke."

"Tiffany did."

"Yeah. So what?"

"I forgot to pick up any matches. Do you have your lighter?"

He did turn white under his tan then. "Can't find it."

"Really? When was the last time you used it?" She said it innocently, with her head cocked to the side. She took a cigarette from the pack, sniffing it. "Still smells good to me even after all these years."

"Bella, what the fuck?"

"The fuck is Fred Hughes, a friend of mine who happens to be the local deputy here, found your lighter under Tiffany's bed. Wouldn't surprise me if the cops come calling tomorrow and haul your cheating ass into the station in Echo Grove, where they will ask you every question under the sun, including swiping your lying mouth with one of those little DNA thingies to find out if it's your sperm they found in Tiffany. And I just came over here to hear your side of the story, you know, maybe vouch for you if you're suddenly accused of rape."

He sank into the chair. "Crap. Bella, I was sleeping with her, but I swear I didn't rape her. I had sex with her earlier that night, before she went out, which by the way, I tried to talk her out of. She'd already had a bunch to drink."

"So you just let her go? Let her drive like that?"

"Listen, I couldn't control her. No one could. Not even her sister."

"Well, someone should've looked out for her that night that actually gave a crap about her and that way Ben Fleck, a perfect stranger, wouldn't have had to pick her up in his car and get involved in this mess that has nothing to do with him. Unlike you, who had vested interest in her both as an actress on your damn film but that…" She choked on her own words, on her anger. "You were sleeping with her, for fuck's sake—sleeping with her when you knew how fragile she was, how much she needed this film to restart her career. If nothing else, couldn't you have thought about Richard staking his reputation and his film on her?" She stopped, glaring at him.

"You have a mouth like a sailor," he said, shaking his head as if disgusted.

She chose to ignore that insult. "Did you rape her?"

"Of course not. Why would I do that? She gave it up freely. You know how it is with me."

"God, you're the biggest prick in Hollywood. And that's really saying something."

He put his hand over his heart. "That hurts."

"Good."

"Bella, don't be like this. You know I still love you. Tiffany was my way of trying to get over you." He tilted his head, with an indulgent expression that at one time had turned her heavy with desire. It no longer did anything but fill her with rage.

"The fact that you think I still care is almost sad."

His face flushed; he sat up straighter in his chair. "Listen, I may be a prick but I'm not a rapist or murderer." He set his glass on the table. "Seriously, you think I'm in trouble here?"

She softened slightly. "I think you'd better come clean before they figure out it's your sperm. You won't look nearly as guilty."

"Yeah, I suppose you're right." He picked up his glass of wine, swirling it around the glass as if they were at a wine-tasting event instead of talking about a dead girl. "If this gets out, my marriage is over."

She stared at him. "Did you really just say that to me?"

"Oh, come on, Bella."

"Come on?"

"You know my situation." He went to the bar and poured the rest of the bottle into his glass. "You want me to open another bottle?"

"No, I should go."

"But what about dinner?"

"I'm suddenly not hungry."

"That doesn't sound like you."

She looked at him for a long moment. "Did you ever really contemplate leaving Susannah? Or was it always just lies to keep me where you wanted?"

He blew air out of his nose like he was exasperated, like they'd talked about this too many times. "Bella, I love you, have since the moment I met you but I cannot get divorced."

"Why?" She wanted to hear him say the truth. "You've never really told me your reasons. Instead it was just empty promises that you would."

"Because I'd have to give her half of everything. You know the divorce laws in California."

There it was. The truth. Finally. It was about the money.

"Did you make empty promises to Tiffany?"

He wrinkled his brows, as if what she said was difficult to understand. "Of course not. It was just a casual thing."

"According to what she told others, she was afraid of you."

He made a scoffing sound. "In what way?"

"Afraid she'd lose her job if she didn't sleep with you."

"That's ridiculous. You know I'm not like that. I thought we were just having fun."

"You know, Graham, your idea of fun and a vulnerable woman's idea might be two entirely different things. Have you ever thought of that?"

"Babe, you and I were totally different. This Tiffany thing was just a way to pass the time. I was willing to give you everything. You know that."

"Except a marriage certificate. You really think that was fair to me?" She paused, watching the shadows on the wall made from the gas fireplace. "I didn't get it for so long that I deserved more than the crumbs you gave me at the end of every day. I regret every moment I waited for your call. I have to live with that the rest of my life. And, sadly, I can see that means nothing to you." She stood, gathering her bag from the table. "I have to go."

"Please stay." He went to her, putting his hands on her upper arms. "I really need you to stay."

"I really can't, Graham." She backed away, toward the door. "Call the police. Tell them the truth." At the door, she turned to look at him. "I'm going to marry Ben Fleck when this whole mess is done."

"I'll believe it when I see it."

She was already out the door when she heard him call out, "Thanks for nothing."

"No, thank *you*," she muttered under her breath, buttoning her coat in preparation for the dark and cold October night. *I need to get home to my family*, she thought, *and Ben.*

Chapter Twelve

WHEN BELLA RETURNED to the house, Annie was putting dinner on the table. Alder was staying another night with Ellen, Drake told her. Cleo, Peter, and Ben were already seated and talking quietly when Bella joined them. Annie, looking considerably better than the day before, served them all squash soup while Drake passed around freshly baked bread and butter. As they ate, Bella filled them in on everything she'd learned from Graham.

"There are so many suspects in this case I hardly know where to start," said Peter. "Do you think Graham's capable of this, Bella?"

She shook her head, vigorously. "He's a coward and a worm but, no, I cannot believe he's capable of murder. And there's no motive. It's better for him if the actress on his film remains alive."

"I think we should fly to Los Angeles tomorrow," said Peter. "See if we can talk to Ms. Zinn."

Bella glanced at Ben, who had barely said two words to any of them since she'd arrived back from seeing Graham. He moved his spoon around his bowl of soup and didn't look up.

"How could we get her to speak to us?" Bella asked Peter.

Cleo smiled, placing her hand on Peter's arm. "You're going to pretend to be a customer, aren't you?"

He grinned back at his wife. "Maybe. Unless we can think of something else. Pretending to be a customer is fraught with, um, danger."

Cleo, her face animated, poked at his chest. "You mean, like you'd have to figure out how to order a prostitute without actually ordering a prostitute."

He rolled his eyes. "Yikes. Yes."

Bella laughed. "Peter, you could tell her you just want to talk."

"Perfect," added Cleo, patting the table playfully. "I know, tell her it's because your heinous wife doesn't understand you."

Peter, deadpan, nodded his head. "Maybe I can talk about my childhood, work through my father issues."

Cleo, her smile turning slightly melancholy, dropped her head onto Peter's shoulder. "Honey, that's not so funny."

He looked over at Bella and then Annie. "I really do have father issues, is what she means."

"Don't we all," said Bella. "Right, Drake?"

But he seemed not to hear the question. He was frowning and playing with his knife. *Thinking hard*, thought Bella. He'd been this way all his life. *Got the brains in the family*, Bella always said, only half-joking. "What's that, Bella?"

"Oh, nothing," she answered. "What're you thinking about in that big fat head of yours? You've got an idea, don't you?"

He pointed his knife at her, still with the serious wrinkle in his brow. "Maybe. What about one of your Hollywood friends? Surely someone knows her."

"I could ask Stefan. He's not the type, though. At least I don't think he is," said Bella. "But he might know someone who is."

Ben, looking at her for the first time that evening, pushed his plate aside. "What exactly do you hope to accomplish by talking to her?"

Peter answered, catching Bella's eyes for a moment, as if to say, *I've got this*. "Couple reasons. One, to see what she knows about Tiffany and the blackmail situation. And to rule her either in or out as a possible suspect."

"I'll call Stefan from the kitchen," said Bella, reaching for her phone and pretending not to notice Ben's glare in her direction

* * *

Stefan answered on the first ring. "Hey Bella. You okay?"

Always the first to think of someone else, she thought. "Yeah, I'm fine. I have a weird question for you." She relayed everything they'd learned that afternoon, asking at the end if he had any ties to Ms. Zinn.

"Don't take this the wrong way but, yeah, I do. Have ties, that is." He chuckled. "It's not what you think."

"Hey, no judgment here. A person has needs."

"No, really, it's not what you think. I have an actor buddy from theatre school filming the television movie about her life—you know, from the autobiography she wrote a couple of years ago. Apparently she sold the studio the rights to her book with the caveat that she had some say in the script. She's on set almost every day, driving the director crazy and giving notes to the actress playing her. He's always texting me stuff about it—hilarious."

"You think she'd talk to us?"

"I could call my friend, see what he thinks."

"Badass!"

"Badass?"

"That means good." She chuckled. "You Canadians are so sweet."

"Whatever, Bellalicious. I'm totally badass. I know hookers and stuff."

She laughed out loud. "Yeah, total street cred, Stefan."

After they hung up, she went back to the living room. Annie and Drake were snuggled together on the couch, talking quietly. "Where is everyone?"

"Peter and Cleo went out for a drink. Wanted some time alone, I think."

Annie looked up as she approached the couch. "Ben said he'd wait for you in the guesthouse." She faltered, as if trying to think what to say next. "He's a mess."

"Yeah, I know," said Bella. "We got in a fight this afternoon, to make matters worse. He didn't want me to be alone with Graham."

Just then her phone rang. It was Stefan. "You're in," he said. "My buddy—Chris Weaver is his name—said he'd introduce you guys to her if you come to the set. And the director is a guy I've worked with before. I'll call and tell him to let you guys in. He's a good guy—I'll tell him the truth about why you're there so he can help you out if needed."

"That's great," said Bella. "Thank you."

"Told you I'm badass."

"Totally badass."

* * *

Bella took off her shoes and tiptoed up the stairs in case Ben was asleep. He'd looked dreadful at dinner and he had to work in the morning. Perhaps he'd fallen asleep already? But he was awake, sitting up in bed with an unopened book on his lap.

"Where have you been?"

"Talking to Stefan. He figured out a way for us to interview Jocelyn Zinn."

"I don't know what you're doing here." He tossed his book onto the bedside table.

"What do you mean?"

"Running around acting like Miss Marple." His voice was almost scornful and definitely accusatory.

She couldn't think of what to say. A painful lump formed at the back of her throat. "Why're you mad at me?"

"You were in Graham's room for a long time. What was I supposed to think you were doing over there?"

"I, literally, cannot believe you just said that. Do you know how humiliating it was to have to talk to the lying prick? I did it for you. And this is what I get? Accusations? Jealousy? How long until you trust me? Or will you ever trust me?"

She wanted to cry but held it in, watching his face turn from stony to angry.

"If you're so innocent, why didn't you answer your phone?"

"I didn't know you called." She glanced at her bag on the easy chair. "I had the ringer off when I was with him." She went to the bag and pulled out her phone. There were five missed calls. "Are you these all from you?"

"Probably," he mumbled. "I called you four times." He ran both hands through his hair. "Bella, please tell me you didn't sleep with him."

"The man was sleeping with Tiffany. He's a freaking murder suspect. And you actually think I was over there having sex with him?"

"I'm a murder suspect."

It hung there in the room then, suspended between them.

Then, he spoke. "You have no reason to believe I didn't do this."

"Yes, I do."

"You don't know me that well, Bella. Yet you're running around town trying to figure out who did this like an Agatha Christie heroine."

"What's your point?"

"That maybe you have some doubt about me and you're trying a little too hard to figure this out."

She stared at him. This was ridiculous. Of course he didn't do it. She was running around, as he put it, in order to prove his innocence to the world, not to herself.

He went on. "You've been on a dead run on this thing since it happened. And there's no reason for it. Peter's a real detective. He doesn't need you on the case. You're acting like a woman with something to prove. What are you trying to prove? That I'm not a murderer? How do you not know that already? You know that about Louse, apparently. What was it you said at dinner—there's no way he's capable of murder—how is it you don't know the same thing about me?"

"But I do."

"And Louse is so trustworthy." His voice dripped with sarcasm. "It's not like he's a liar or a cheater or anything. Yeah, he has way better odds of not being a murderer than me."

"Regardless of his questionable character, a cheater and a murderer are not even close to the same thing."

"They bring up the question of moral integrity, Bella. Have you lived in Hollywood for so long now you've lost sight of that?"

"Jeez, you sound like my brother."

He continued without pause, his speech rapid, almost manic. Had he heard anything she said? "How can I blame you, really? You had a relationship with Louse for three years. You've known me for three months."

She squared her shoulders and tossed her head, hot and angry and hurt now. "You can say whatever you want, Benjamin Fleck. Or think whatever you want. Doesn't change the fact that I love you. Or that I believe in you." The tears were scratching at the insides of her lids, threatening to explode forth like those of a hurt little girl. *Dammit. Do not cry in front of him.* How she hated crying. She took in deep breaths. *Just pack your things. You can cry in the house.* She turned away and began tossing her clothes, neatly folded in the bureau by the ever-efficient but elusive housekeeper, into her suitcase.

After she collected her toiletries from the bathroom, she headed toward the bedroom door. Ben stood at the window now. He turned as she came out of the bathroom. "So this is it, huh? Just leave when things get tough, when the hard questions get asked? Glad to know this now because I have a feeling I'm getting arrested tomorrow. Good to know I still can't count on you."

She held her toiletry bag close to her chest. "When I first met you I thought I was the crazy, self-destructive one. I guess I had that figured wrong. When you wake up out of this delusional madness you've created in order to protect yourself from hurt, you'll see how ridiculous it is to push me away." She turned and grabbed her suitcase. At the bottom of the stairs, she stumbled and had to grab the handrail to keep from falling. Her mind was spinning; she felt as if she might vomit. She opened the door and burst out into the breezy night air that smelled faintly of wood-burning smoke. It was dark except for the porch light, which Annie insisted remain on, regardless that they never had any visitors not announced at the gate.

Instead of going inside, she went around to the deck, careful not to slip on the wet stone that made a path to the back of the house. The kitchen light was on, shedding light onto the deck. The night was cold but she barely felt it, her anger and confusion a cloak against the late autumn night. Where was she going to sleep tonight? The couch? She set her suitcase near the kitchen door and sat on the steps. *Just sit for a moment. Have a good cry*, she thought. And then make some notes of everything they learned today. Perhaps something would come to her that she and Peter hadn't thought of. No matter that Ben was angry with her—she would not rest until they figured out who really did this. For Tiffany and Sabrina—and for stubborn, bull-headed Ben.

Ben. Ben. Why do you have to be like this? They could be wrapped up in one another's arms right now.

Was it too much to ask, she wondered, to be held in the night by someone you loved? To feel the warmth of someone else when you awakened in the dark night, the demons that come in the hours before dawn tugging at you, wanting to pull you into the abyss where despair and doubt and fear all waited to say, we got you this time, your friends' hope and love and persistence are no match for us? Just to be held in the night by a man who loved her? This, apparently, was too much to ask for.

But the tears that had threatened to come earlier were dry now. She felt numb. And exhausted. What right did Ben have to act so crazy? She believed in him, was trying to help him, and she was repaid with this? Why did she always choose the wrong men? Just give up on this, on him, she thought. Just accept the fact that she'd picked another one too damaged to have anything resembling a healthy relationship.

Suddenly she felt the cold. She pulled her sweater tighter around her and blew out a long breath that was a puff of white reflected in the light from the kitchen. She turned her gaze upward towards the sky. A cloud shifted, revealing a skinny moon. Then she heard a noise coming from the yard, beyond Drake's rose garden with its dormant bushes waiting for the spring sun that would remind them of their future blooms. It was just a rustling in the leaves and fallen branches. Perhaps footsteps? Was it a person? No, no one could get into the property. Drake kept it locked up with the electric fence, ever diligent against outside danger, given what had happened to his wife and daughter. One's scars remained intact, despite our ability to move forward.

Then, a doe appeared in the grass, a half-dozen feet from where Bella sat. She gazed at Bella with soft brown eyes. They looked like Alder's eyes, she thought, not for the first time. *Your kiddo has the same gentle eyes as deer*, she'd said to Annie last summer.

The doe remained, perfectly still except for the flicker of her ears. What did she hear? Did she have babies, near but out of sight? She thought of her mother then, for no reason and without warning. Her mother. *Mommy*. Bella had slept with her every night after their father left for the last time. Until she was ten years old she'd fallen asleep with her backside next to the heat of her mother's slender form as she read, usually a paperback novel from the library. She'd read at least a book a week, never television, only novels, all different kinds. As long as it has a good story, she'd told Bella again and again, encouraging her to read more, like her brother did. Her mother, Bella understood now, had so few moments of relaxation or peace and must have lived in the pages of those books. The only travels she'd ever had, the only love story she'd ever known, the only victory and redemption. And in the morning, Alice Webber had risen again and again, her feet still aching from the day before, and gotten dressed and fed them breakfast, washed dishes, packed lunches, and hurried them out the door to the bus all before going to her job as a clerk at the local drugstore. On the weekends she worked the breakfast shift at the local chain diner. Free meals for the two of them as an added bonus, which Bella had found delightful (she'd stuffed herself on all-you-could-eat pancakes every Saturday and Sunday morning for years) but that Drake found humiliating. *How generous they give Mom a barely edible $2.99 breakfast as part of her pay as if that's something that actually helps us. Maybe they should try paying their staff better than minimum wage and we could buy our own damn breakfast.* Drake was fourteen when he said this, and Bella, eight at the time, was awestruck by not only his understanding of minimum wage, which apparently *was not enough to live on or mom wouldn't need two jobs in the first place*, but that he'd said a curse word. She'd put her finger over her mouth and made a shushing sound, so their mother wouldn't hear. Nothing mattered more to Bella than making sure neither of them ever did or said anything to hurt her. Their mother hated curse words, or any harsh words at all, for that matter. *You can attract more bees with honey than with vinegar*, she always told Bella.

It does help us, Drake, Bella had said to her brother. *Two meals she doesn't have to cook for us or pay for.*

Someday, little sister, I'm going to be worth so much we can buy fifty crappy diners if we want to.

Fifty breakfasts?

No, fifty damn stores.

But why would we want fifty stores?

We won't. I'm just saying we could if we wanted to. Trust me, Bellybear, someday I'm going to give you and Mom anything and everything you ever wanted.

And he could have. Unfortunately, their mother hadn't lived to see this come to be. Bella shivered, tears coming now. Sixteen was too young to have to say goodbye to her mother. *Mommy.*

Died of the flu because they didn't have insurance.

No fucking insurance, Drake had shouted the night after her funeral. *That's what did this.*

And she'd shriveled up then, in her angry brother's presence, in the humiliation it felt to be poor, in the indelible sadness that felt like a cavern in the middle of her chest. The ache had begun in that moment and remained tonight, even as she watched the deer watching her.

That's right, she had shouted back to Drake that night. *No fucking insurance.* The first curse word she'd ever said. This was the beginning of her potty mouth. Because if her mother wasn't around to care anymore, why should she? And it felt good to say the bad words. And to take tequila shots at parties. And to kiss boys her mother wouldn't have approved of.

Out of desperation after Esther and Chloe were killed she'd made the first appointment with Valerie Short. She hadn't slept more than a couple of hours a night for a month and she hoped the shrink could give her something to help her sleep. That was all, really, because she didn't actually believe in therapy—what could a shrink do to help you? Talk over all the old hurts? Fine. But it wouldn't mean they'd go away. Her mother was still dead. Her sister-in-law and her precious little niece were still buried side-by-side in a cemetery in Seattle.

But she went. And to her surprise, she found the therapy sessions helpful, more so than she could have ever imagined. Every week for two months she went to see Valerie and sat in the chair that looked out on the blue water. She sat in the chair next to the miniature Zen garden with the tiny rake and polished rocks and talked about her grief. Nothing was solved but she had an hour in which to cry and shout and sometimes just stare out the window into the waves that crashed onto the shore again and again and again. And she wondered, why. Why all the suffering? Why all the pain? Why was life nothing but a series of losses? She'd asked Valerie these questions, none of which the poor woman dressed in long silky skirts and soft cotton blouses and wrap dresses could explain. At the end of two months, Bella accepted a gig for a movie shoot in New Mexico and she'd stopped going. She met Graham a month later, on that movie and, well, then it was the waiting game. For three years. Until finally, she'd had enough and escaped to Oregon, to this little town no had ever heard of and she'd fallen in love with it and her brother all over again and his new family and the river. The river that teaches you your name. *Bella Webber. Bella Webber* it had called to her when she floated on its surface or sunned on a rock with only her hand dipped there in the cool green of the water. Bella Webber, your mother's daughter. And in the ripples there were whispers. *You are not a girl who gives her life away to a married man. You are a girl that deserves to be loved properly. A badass chick. Alder's Auntie Bella and he should admire you and hold you up to the women of his future. You are not someone who leads a compromised life.*

And when she returned to Los Angeles she called the Eileen Fisher-draped Valerie and made another appointment.

At their first session Valerie crossed her arms and smiled but had no expression in her bland and all-seeing eyes. "It's been almost three years since I've seen you."

"Yeah."

"Are you ready to dig deep?"

"Dig deep?

"That's right," said Valerie. "It's time."

Now, the deer startled and ran out of the yard and into the forest. Bella stood, glancing into the kitchen. Annie was there, making coffee. Perhaps the deer had seen the light shift. Bella knocked softly on the kitchen door. Annie, her back toward the door, jumped, but seeing it was Bella, waved and opened the door.

One look at her face and Annie opened her arms. "What happened?"

Bella told her everything.

"You're absolutely right he's trying to push you away before you can push him away. The key is not allowing him to do that," said Annie.

"How?"

"By remaining steadfast in your devotion."

"What does that mean?"

"It means figuring out who murdered Tiffany Archer. Until his name is cleared the poor man isn't going to be able to give in to his feelings for you. It's all he can think of right now. Not to mention that guy has major trust issues. Who can blame him? His fiancée runs off with his cousin? I mean, Bella, it's awful to think of."

"And I'm not trustworthy in his eyes because of Graham."

"You will be. Just give it time. Keep doing what you're doing. Do you want some cake?"

Bella shook her head. Even cake wouldn't do tonight.

"Come on then, I'm putting you to bed. You can sleep in Alder's room tonight," said Annie. "I'll give you one of Drake's sleeping pills."

In Alder's room she put on her pajamas, which smelled like Ben. She brushed her teeth and climbed into the twin bed. Staring at the shadows on the wall, she fought against the hollow feeling in the pit of her stomach. This was just an argument between them, not the death of their relationship, she told herself. Perhaps he would wake tomorrow and feel more rational? She had to hope for this. After a few moments Annie came in with a pill and a glass of water.

"Where's your phone?" asked Annie.

"In my purse." She'd left her purse in the kitchen. Ben wouldn't call. He was too stubborn and insane.

"Okay, good. Because Drake says people can do weird things on this drug and not remember doing it, like calling someone they really shouldn't call."

Bella swallowed the pill. "Will you sit with me?"

"Of course." Annie perched on the side of the bed and stroked Bella's hair.

"Is this what it's like to have an older sister?"

Annie smiled. "I suppose. I wouldn't know." She tugged at the blanket, making it tighter about Bella's shoulders. "I'm proud of you. I know it's not easy to love someone when they're not acting very lovable but that's when you know it's real. Ben will come to his senses, probably in the morning, and feel like an idiot. Until then, I'm impressed by how you're handling this whole thing."

"You always make me feel like a better person than I really am."

"Nonsense. You're better for real."

"Did I ever tell you that you remind me of my mother?"

Annie smiled. A gentle smile. Just like her mother's. "That's just the drug talking"

And then it went blessedly black.

Chapter Thirteen

BELLA WOKE THE NEXT MORNING feeling refreshed. She showered and dressed in slacks and a light sweater and followed the smell of blackberry syrup and pancakes into the kitchen. Annie was flipping pancakes. They were dark. This was a shame. It meant they were whole grain laced with wheat germ and other healthy ingredients. But Drake stirred dark purple syrup, the source of the delightful smell of blackberries, at the stove. Peter and Cleo were at the counter. Peter was eating pancakes between sips of coffee. But Cleo, looking a little green, was reading her script.

"Morning, Bella," said Annie. "You want some hotcakes?"

"Yeah, I guess."

"Sleep okay?" Drake asked, his light blue eyes actually soft and sympathetic.

"Rock-like. That stuff's powerful."

"It is. You shouldn't take it much, though. Totally addictive."

"Yeah, big brother, I know," she said, glancing at Annie and rolling her eyes.

"I saw that." Drake poured the syrup into a pitcher. Normally she'd be dumping as much as she could get away with over a giant stack of pancakes but this morning her stomach turned at the thought of eating. Was her appetite permanently suppressed? *Damn you, Benjamin Fleck*, she thought. *You've messed with my stomach.*

As if she conjured him, Ben was suddenly there in the kitchen doorway with wet hair and dressed casually in a jeans and a t-shirt that matched his eyes. Sunday, she thought. He was off work. Why did he have to look so good in jeans? Everyone greeted him, except

Bella. She avoided looking at him, her heart pounding in her chest. Don't give him the satisfaction, she thought, of letting him know how much he'd hurt her. She poured some coffee, added a dab of half-and-half, and headed towards the door.

"Bella, no breakfast?" called Annie.

"I'm not hungry." She didn't turn around.

"Just coffee for me too," she heard Ben say.

* * *

She was in the living room, pretending to read a magazine, reclined on one of the tan couches, when Cleo came through, still carrying her script. "Bella, I'm off to work with the coach Richard suggested. Wish me luck."

"You'll do great. She's the best coach around from what I hear."

Cleo came to the couch, kneeling on the floor and resting her forearms on the cushion next to Bella. "Don't worry about this thing with Ben. He'll come around. He's just been hurt and is trying to push you away. I did that with Peter but he'll figure it out. And Peter will figure out who did this."

"Promise?"

"He's relentless." Cleo patted her knee. "I'm so glad you'll be there tomorrow to make me look decent."

"This will not be hard."

A few minutes after Cleo left, she heard the front door open and shut and Alder shout out his standard greeting. "I'm home, peeps."

Alder. He would cheer her up. "In here," she called out to him, tossing the magazine aside.

"Auntie Bel, whatcha doing?"

"Nothing."

He perched on the coffee table, scrutinizing her face. "You sad?"

Behind him, Ellen White was coming in, carrying a pie. "Bella, I brought you a pie."

She sat up. Pie? "What kind?"

"Apple."

She clapped her hands. "Pie's good." The room filled with the scent of cinnamon and cooked apples and butter. "Is that a butter crust?"

"Is there any other kind?"
"What's for breakfast?" asked Alder.
"Whole grain pancakes."
"What? Whole grain? Seriously, Bella, you've got to do something about Mom's health kick. She's ruining perfectly good pancakes by putting that awful stuff in them."
"I know," said Bella. "But there's nothing I can do. Plus, Peter's here. You know what that means."
Ellen chuckled. "You two just come on over to my house if you get hungry. I'll make you some real pancakes."
"Maybe tomorrow?" He grinned. "No school."
"No school on Monday?" Bella asked.
"Parent/teacher conferences," said Alder. "I get to stay with Momo and Goldie." Momo was Alder's pet name for Ellen, and Goldie was her dog. Alder was crazy for both of them.
"Should we be worried?" asked Bella.
"About my conference?" asked Alder, looking perplexed.
"Right. Just thinking of my own experiences," said Bella, smiling. "I wasn't the best student."
Ellen jumped in. "Of course not. Alder's an excellent student." She sniffed, somewhat judgmentally, and added, "He hardly studies because it's all too easy for him." She wagged her finger at him. "However, young man, it's not a good idea to develop lazy habits just 'cause things are easy. Someday you'll be challenged and then you won't have the proper study habits in place."
"But Momo, what am I supposed to study if I already have my homework done?"
"Smart boy like you should be asking for extra credit. Matter of fact, I'm going to suggest that to your mother this morning." She handed Alder the pie. "You take this into the kitchen. I need to talk to little miss here for a minute."
Bella sat up, crossing her legs, readying herself for one of Ellen White's life lessons. No idea what it would be about this time but Ellen White was always at the ready with advice, whether one asked for it or not.
She lowered her voice to just above a whisper. "Annie told me on the phone that Ben's acting like a real nincompoop. Men can be

profoundly idiotic, unfortunately. But Ben's a good one. Needs a little grace I suspect, given this ridiculous police business."

Bella remained quiet.

Ellen went on, speaking louder now. "I was awake last night—Vern snores like a bear some nights—and I started thinking about this whole darn thing and something occurred to me."

Behind them, both Drake and Ben were coming out of the kitchen. "What occurred to you?" asked Ben.

Ellen motioned for them to come sit by pointing to one of the couches. "Good, get on in here. Both of you." If there was any doubt in anyone's mind that Ellen White was a former high school English teacher, there certainly shouldn't be. She eyed Ben as he sat on the opposite couch from Bella. "Where's Peter Ball? I need him to hear this too."

"I'm here," said Peter, carrying a coffee cup into the room. He sat in one of the easy chairs.

"You need a chalkboard?" Ben asked Ellen, grinning. Bella looked at him in surprise. Was he teasing Ellen? When had she last seen him smile? Three days ago. Ben glanced her way. They locked eyes for a moment before she looked away. The doorbell chimed. Who could that be?

"I'll get it," said Bella.

Annie had beat Bella to the door. It was Linus. He was wearing one of his blue silk suits and a red tie. "Good morning, ladies."

"Linus, what're you doing here?" Annie had a towel in her hand and was still wearing her apron, which was smeared with pancake batter and blackberry syrup.

Linus slipped off his coat and placed it carefully on the bench near the door before turning to Annie with his hands on his hips. "Oh, sweetie, why are you wearing an apron at home? You should be running around here in that negligée I got you for your wedding. Do you girls never listen?"

"Linus, your expectations for my sexiness are way too high. I have a house full of people, and, in case you don't remember, a ten-year-old boy living here."

"That's absolutely no excuse." Linus turned to greet Bella, giving her air kisses on each cheek. "You look gorgeous." He pursed his lips and cocked his head to the side. "Falling in love agrees with you."

Bella shook her head, trying not to let the tears flood her eyes. Linus being kind to her might send her over the crying precipice. And she was done crying over Benjamin Fleck. At least for the next hour. *Damn you,* she cursed him again silently. "He's already dumped me," she said in a whisper.

"That isn't true," said Annie, matching Bella's whisper. "He's just acting crazy because of this whole thing with the police."

Linus glanced toward the front room. "Is he here now?"

Annie nodded. "And Ellen."

"She says she has something she wanted to discuss about the police," said Bella.

"I have an idea I want to run by the gang too," said Linus. "But we have to wait. Lee and Tommy are on their way over as well. And Mike and Sharon. Everyone's concerned about Ben and we want to get on the same page on this thing. Make sure we're all in this together to figure out the real killer."

Bella smiled, squeezing Annie's hand. "Your gang of misfits always comes through when it counts."

"You know it," she said as they went into the living room.

Annie made more coffee while Drake found a white board. Bella took Peter into Drake's office. "The whole gang's on their way over. They all want to help." She said it almost apologetically but there was no need.

"Good. The more people we have on this thing the better."

She left Peter to set up the whiteboard on an easel and went to fetch another cup of coffee. Lee and Tommy must have arrived because Alder was in the kitchen holding their toddler, Ellie-Rose, on his lap and feeding her small bites of pancake. "She needs tiny bites so she doesn't choke," he said. Her heart twisted, remembering doing the same with her little niece. *Don't think of it now,* she told herself. *Just focus in the moment.*

Ellie-Rose, a smaller version of her pretty redheaded mother, grinned at Bella. "'Pakes." She raised her arms in the air. "Yay."

"Pakes are yay." Bella poured more coffee into her cup and added cream that Annie had placed out for the guests.

"They banished us to the kitchen. I'm too young to hear all the grizzly details, which totally sucks because I'm a great detective," said Alder.

"I'll fill you in later," she promised, with her hand on his sweet head. "Just without the R-rated parts."

"But Bella, those are all the badass parts."

"I know. But you're too young for badass parts yet. Give it a couple more years."

She was almost to the door when he called out to her. "Bella?"

"Yep?"

"Ben's not going to jail, is he?"

"Absolutely not. He didn't do anything."

"Yeah, but sometimes innocent people go to jail. Look at what happened in *To Kill a Mockingbird*."

"No way this gang will let that happen."

"More 'pakes," said Ellie-Rose, tugging on Adler's arm.

He fed the baby another piece and kissed her forehead. "Bella, I know Ben's acting like a jerk but that's just what men do when they're afraid."

She chuckled. "I know, honey." She paused. "But thanks for saying that."

"Badass," said Ellie-Rose, crystal clear. Bella couldn't help but laugh. She couldn't say *pancake* but *badass* came out as though spoken by a classically trained actress.

"Oh no," said Alder, grimacing. "I'm in so much trouble."

Bella continued to laugh. "You better teach her a new word before her parents come back in here. Seriously."

Alder made a clicking noise with his tongue and shook his head sadly. "Why are people so worried over conventions?"

"You better start worrying about them or your mother's going to have you banished to your room until Thanksgiving."

"Oh, Bella, I'm not made for this world."

"Badass," said Ellie-Rose, grinning.

* * *

In the living room, Mike and Sharon had arrived and were sitting together on one of the couches next to Tommy, Lee, and Ellen. Ben was talking quietly with Drake and Linus near the fireplace. Annie was pouring coffee for everyone and had somehow produced pastries. There was a never-ending supply of food in this house, thought Bella. Such a shame she felt like road kill. She hated to waste good pastries.

Ben and Linus took seats as Annie settled next to Drake on the loveseat closest to the stone fireplace. Bella stood in the corner of the room, feeling awkward. Why couldn't her place be by Ben? Why did he have to act like such a fool and ruin everything between them? Finally, she opted for the chair nearest Peter.

Ben cleared his throat and looked around the room. "Listen, I just wanted to say thanks for rallying behind me. You all have no reason to believe I'm innocent but I'm grateful you do. I hope this all blows over but, I don't know, I have a bad feeling. The way those cops interrogated me the other day I feel like they want to pin this on me just to meet the demands of the public. Anyway, thank you."

"We take care of our own here," said Mike. "Always have, always will."

"That's right," said Tommy.

"And all this because you did the right thing for that poor girl. Just shameful," said Ellen.

Peter, using the whiteboard, charted out what they knew thus far. "Ben arrived with a drunk Tiffany at eleven and left at midnight. The clerk at the front desk substantiated this. We also were able to see him arrive and leave from the security cameras."

Ellen, looking up from her pad, raised her hand. "Were there any other people in or out of the lobby on the security cameras?"

"No," said Peter. "Which tells me one thing."

"That it was done by someone staying in the lodge?" asked Lee, sitting forward on the couch, her intelligent eyes snapping.

"Exactly," said Peter. He twirled the pen between his fingers like a baton and gazed at the white board. "The problem with this case is there are too many suspects." He went on to tell them about Graham Rouse admitting to an affair with Tiffany and the two men in suits who had followed Tiffany that night, along with the blackmail scheme.

"So this Jocelyn Zinn—she could have hired someone to do it, right, Peter?" asked Tommy. "Those two men could be working for her?"

Peter nodded. "Yes. Only problem is we can't seem to find them. It's like they disappeared into thin air. But we know they exist because the bartender at Lefty's corroborated what Ben told us."

Mike's brow was furrowed, like he was thinking hard. "I've followed this Zinn thing in the news and that woman's not somebody to mess with. Her client list, it's assumed by the press anyway, has everyone from men in the mob to elected public officials, all with deep motivation to keep their names out of the paper."

"Any of them could've hired someone to kill Tiffany if they thought she was blackmailing them," said Tommy. "Don't you think, Peter?"

"Absolutely. If she was blackmailing them, which I'm not totally convinced of. From what her sister says and what we know of her personality it seems unlikely," said Peter.

Ellen raised her hand again.

"Ellen, you don't have to raise your hand," teased Tommy. "This isn't your classroom."

Ellen slapped him on the knee. "Good thing for you it isn't. I'd have you in detention so fast it'd make your head swim."

"Detention?" Tommy's eyes went wide. "I've never been in detention or anything close to it in my life."

"Goodie-two-shoes," said Bella. "That's totally obvious."

Drake, from where he and Annie sat on a loveseat near the fireplace, laughed. "Let's tell them how many times you've been in detention, Bella."

She blushed and shot him a dirty look. "Keep quiet, smart boy. Shouldn't you be in the front row with the other nerds?"

"Front row's where all the best students sit," said Drake. "Right, Lee?"

Lee, with a prim smile, pushed a strand of her strawberry-blond hair behind her ear. "It's where I always was, yes."

Linus pointed at Tommy with his half-eaten croissant. "Tommy wasn't in detention, he was wherever the ladies were, probably reciting poetry to them and telling them where to meet him after school."

Tommy laughed. "Well, I did have a way with the ladies."

"Still do," said Annie.

"I only have eyes for my wife now. Right, honey?" Tommy looked over at Lee. She was writing something in her notebook. "Um, hello, Lee, they're talking about my charming ways."

She glanced up with a blank expression. "What's that?"

Tommy, with his characteristic grin, shook his head and rolled his eyes. "Never mind. The honeymoon's over."

"Of course it is, sweetheart. Don't be silly." Lee went back to her notebook.

"Oh, that hurt," said Tommy. "I'm not writing any more love songs about you."

"I doubt that," said Lee, smacking his knee. "Now focus on what we're doing here."

"You can't distract the best student in class by flirting with her," said Drake.

Annie kissed Drake on the cheek and put her finger through one of the curls by his ear. "You sure about that?"

"No, I'm not, now you put it that way." He leaned over and kissed her on the mouth.

"Oh my God, get a room, you two," said Linus. "You breeders are so inappropriate."

Ellen waved her pen in the air. "Laser-like focus, people. We have a murder to solve here. If any of you were in my class you'd all get a D minus for effort." She turned her gaze to Peter. "I have something I want to propose, Peter, as a possible angle to this case."

Peter's eyes were amused but he kept his face straight. "Do tell."

"I think the cops on this case are crooked."

"I agree but what makes you think so?" he asked, all amusement gone from his eyes.

Ellen tapped her pencil on the palm of her hand. "Because I had that red-headed cop in class years ago and he was nothing short of a liar. His brother was a big athlete and good student—went off to Yale or Harvard, can't remember which now—and now he's a big shot in the Los Angeles attorney's office. Gale and Rawley Hough."

"Gale's the local cop, right?" asked Peter.

"Right. Gale was always trying to prove he was as smart as Rawley but he wasn't even close. And then there was the problem of his name. Gale? A name that's also a girl's name plus red hair, the kid was doomed. Anyway, let's just say this Gale has an agenda. He wants to solve this case and look like a big shot. But he's lazy. Plagiarized a paper in my American Literature class when he was a junior. Cried like a baby when I confronted him, begged me to give him another chance, which I did and probably shouldn't have because he needed to learn his lesson. Anyhow, this shows his character. Once a cheater and a liar, always a cheater and a liar. And, no offence, Peter, but there's a fine line between those who choose the criminal life and those who choose the life in law enforcement."

"Unfortunately, that's true," said Peter. "Ellen, do their parents still live here in town?"

She shook her head no. "There was no father that I can remember and their mother's dead. Died ten years ago in a house fire."

Lee raised her hand, seemingly without realizing she was doing it. Just like her grandmother, thought Bella, smiling behind her hand.

"What're you thinking, Lee?" asked Peter.

"I remember both of the brothers from school. I'd forgotten about them, honestly, like I have so much of my childhood until Momo just brought them up. Gale was in my grade and not the brightest kid, for sure, and was constantly picked on. I remember thinking to myself, just fly under the radar like I did, despite my red hair."

Tommy interrupted. "Your hair is beautiful. Poor Gale's is the color of carrots."

She smiled at Tommy before continuing. "I didn't know Gale that well but he always seemed shifty to me. But the older one, Rawley, who was the smart one—there were rumors about him, you know, stuff I overheard from the lunch room and all, since I didn't really have any friends."

"Like what kind of things?" asked Tommy. His voice was soft, almost coaxing: He was in the habit of getting his shy wife to speak, thought Bella.

"That he was somewhat of a sexual deviant."

"What do you mean exactly?" asked Tommy.

Lee's alabaster skin was flushed. "Like he forced himself on several girls. I mean, I don't really know exactly." She looked down at the notebook in her lap. "And now I don't even know why I'm bringing this up. It has no relevance to his brother or the case. It just popped into my mind, that's all. I didn't know he was a big time attorney." She looked over at Mike. "Do you remember them? Were they friends with your son?"

"No, and I can't say I remember the brothers much except when the older one got into Yale." He glanced at Ellen. "I believe it was Yale, not Harvard. Made the front page of our newspaper that spring.

They weren't friends with Zac that I know of but I was busy those days running the sawmill so didn't keep up on things like I do now."

"Well, anyway, it's not relevant," said Lee. "I'm sorry I brought it up."

"No, it's good, Lee," said Peter. "Any information that helps us understand that there might have been some strange stuff going on in their house could explain a crooked cop. I'll look into him, ask around a little and see if I can get a better read on him." He glanced down at his notebook. "I think that's it, folks. Next step is for me and Bella to take a little trip south tomorrow and meet Miss Zinn in person."

* * *

Later, Bella chewed on one of the cold pancakes and stared out the kitchen window. The clouds had lifted and sun glittered on the wet grass in the backyard. Alder was right, she thought. People went to jail for crimes they didn't commit all the time. She'd seen it on Oprah. Something moved near the rose garden. It was the doe. The creature pranced closer, with the grace of a ballerina, and stopped at the edge of the deck. Perfectly still, she seemed to be listening for something, her ears twitching, before bounding into the thicket of trees on the edge of the yard.

Bella turned from the window. There was Ben, standing at the stove, watching her.

"Hey," he said.

"Hi." Suddenly she didn't know what to do with her hands. The actors she worked with often told her stories of their early training and they all agreed the hardest thing to figure out was what to do with your hands. She stuffed hers into her pants pockets, looking at the floor, unable to think of anything to say. The hurt was in her throat. Even if she could speak, she shouldn't. She couldn't trust herself. The ridiculous tears might come again.

"Bella, I'm sorry."

What had he said? She raised her head, meeting his eyes. His green eyes. So beautiful. They appeared soft, not laughing like they sometimes were, but without the accusatory and jealous glare they'd had last night.

"You heard me." He paused. "I'm an idiot."

She smiled, but her lips trembled. "Yeah. Kinda."

He approached her, almost cautiously, she thought, as if not to spook her, like the deer in the yard. "I'm a jealous fool."

She sighed and shook her head slightly. "You have no reason to be."

"Take a walk with me?"

"It's freezing out there." She glanced out the window. A large rain cloud had moved over the sun.

"Come over to my place, then?" He indicated the front room with a shake of his head. "Drake and Annie are in there and I want to talk alone."

The way he was looking at her it seemed he had more on his mind than talking. She held out her hand. "Fine, but you have a lot of apologizing to do."

He ignored her hand and instead pulled her into his chest and spoke into her hair, holding her tight. "I know I do. I'm an idiot."

"You really are."

* * *

They walked up the stairs to his bedroom without speaking. Once inside the room, he sank onto the bed and brought her onto his lap. She buried her face in his neck. How good he smelled. She felt his heart beating against her breasts. He kissed her, gently. "I'm a complete crazy person, I realize this," he whispered against her mouth. "But when it comes to you I'm not rational."

"I know the feeling," she said, her eyes filling with tears, thinking of how desperate and helpless she'd felt the night before. "You have the ability to hurt me like no one ever has, which makes no sense considering how long we've been together."

"Bella, can you give me another chance?"

"Yes, but you can't do this jealous thing about Graham. He's nothing to me. He never should've been. Last night when I was with him all I could think was why and how." She paused, kissing his neck and the sides of his face and then his mouth. "And getting back to my family. And you. Mostly you. I can't deal with you doing that to me again. You just have to trust me. I know it might not seem like it but I am a girl who just wants a nice man to love me, to hold me when I'm sad, to be by my side through all the shit life flings at us."

"You have such a potty mouth." He kissed her, exploring her mouth with his tongue until she ached for more.

"You're going to pay for making me cry." She kicked off her shoes and panties and straddled him, pushing her small hands into his muscular chest until he fell back on the bed. "I'm going to make you suffer a little."

"Don't hurt me," he said, his voice hoarse.

She flicked her tongue along his neck until she found his mouth again. Then, still straddling him, she unbuttoned his shirt. He tried to help but she batted his hands away. "No, we'll do it slow so you have to wait for it."

He let his head fall back onto the bed, grinning. "Fine, but payback's a bitch."

"I'm counting on it."

The last button was undone. She pulled him up slightly so he could shrug out of his shirt. Then she knelt on the floor, tugging his jeans and boxer shorts off. She stood, looking at him, taking in every inch of him, before running her hands up his thighs. They twitched under her touch. She straddled him again, guiding him inside her. He sat up, suddenly, pulling her closer to him, looking her in the eye, before kissing her. "Nice and easy," he whispered.

But her goal to make him suffer was gone. She felt herself losing control, as she always did with this crazy man. She whispered his name and wrapped her legs tighter around him. He had his hands on her hips, was almost all the way inside her, just a small movement in and out. And then she felt it coming and it took over as she moaned. The shudders came one after the other. Without moving from inside her, he moved so she was on her back and he thrust deep into her several times before he gasped and exploded inside her.

Afterward he held her against his chest, stroking her hair. "I know it's no excuse," he said. "But when you've been left at the proverbial altar it's hard to trust again. I question every woman's motives I've dated since then. I find I'm suspicious about everything and I'm just always waiting for the other shoe to drop. The betrayal, Bella, was like nothing I'd ever experienced before. I trusted her with everything I had. I would never have thought in a million years she would betray me." He stopped, tightening his grip around her waist. "Anyway, never mind. We've talked about this enough."

She pulled away and turned on her side so she could see his face. "Why is it so hard for you to talk to me about this?"

He smiled; his face crinkled in the way so dear to her now. "I'm a guy. We don't like to talk about this kind of thing."

"But then you do stupid things that make us cry."

His face went soft. He stroked the side of her face and ran his finger along her lip. "I'm sorry for that."

"You're going to have to talk to me, Ben, or this isn't going to work. It can't just be all hot sex with us."

"It can't?"

"No." *Let yourself be vulnerable,* she thought. *Like Annie.* "Not if you're really serious about me."

He played with one of her curls. His eyes were the color of the fir trees swaying outside the window. "I am. You know that."

"I was thinking about my mom yesterday." She let the old sadness come inside her, feeling it, like Valerie had encouraged her to do, looking into his sympathetic eyes. "When she died, I changed. I loved her so much and I was a lost little girl for years afterward. I've made decisions from that hurt place for too long. No matter how we try, we can't escape the pain. It gets into everything. Like something sticky that creeps into every crack and crevice."

"It's been two years since Sheri called off the wedding. It hurt every day for all that time until I met you. My brother told me the only way to get over someone is to fall for someone new."

"Do you think that's true?"

"I do. With one caveat. The baggage that comes with betrayal doesn't leave. It's the same as what you say about your mother's death. It messes with you. It's made me so distrustful and I was never like that. I would've sworn on a stack of bibles I didn't have a jealous bone in my body, but, well, we know that isn't the case, now don't we?" He smiled but it didn't reach his eyes. "I hate that I hurt you yesterday. I'm sorry."

She kissed him. "I know you are. I forgive you. How did you find out about Sheri?"

"It was a week before the wedding and I came home in the middle of the day because I forgot something I needed for a meeting that afternoon."

Bella shut her eyes, knowing what was coming next.

"And yeah, there they were. In bed together. In our bed we'd shared for three years."

"I'm so sorry," she whispered.

"You know what's weird about it? They were just in bed talking, albeit without their clothes on, but there was an intimacy between them that hurt worse than if I'd seen them in the actual act. The way they were looking at one another—she'd– she'd never looked at me that way."

The shadow of the pain in his eyes made its way into her body as if osmosis of emotion was physically possible. "I want to look at you that way."

"You are. Right now. You are." He pulled her under him, kissing her. And then talking was over once again.

* * *

They woke to pounding on the door of the guesthouse. Bella sat straight up, filling with sudden and swift unease and dread. Ben rolled to his back and put his arm over his eyes. "Bella, I have a bad feeling about this."

Heart pounding, she wrapped a blanket around her shoulders and went to the window. More clouds had come in while they were inside and it was raining hard. Below, in the driveway parked next to Ben's red Porsche, was a cop car. Her knees felt weak. She turned, reaching for the back of one of the easy chairs.

"It's the cops, isn't it?" he asked.

She couldn't speak and merely nodded.

He got out of bed, reaching for his clothes strewn about the floor, hastily discarded just an hour ago when the possibility of what was happening now was only a worry. "Sweetie, get dressed," he said to her. He was oddly calm, she thought. Resigned to his fate.

She nodded and found her panties and bra, shaking so hard she could barely fasten the clasp. Once they were both dressed, he reached for her. "Listen to me. It's going to be all right. Drake has an attorney lined up for me. Peter will figure out who did this for real and we'll be back here in no time, together again. Knowing you love me gives me strength to go through anything." The pounding on the door started again.

Fighting tears, her voice shaking, she pressed against him. "Drake will post bail, whatever the cost. I'll be waiting until then."

"When this is over I'll take you someplace tropical and buy you drinks on the beach. Hold onto that. Okay?"

"Okay."

"Nothing they do to me can touch this place inside me that loves you. Nothing will break me, knowing you're here waiting."

"I am. For however long it takes."

He kissed her trembling mouth as the pounding continued. Finally, they parted. "You stay here," he said. "I don't want you to see this."

"Absolutely not," she said. "I want to look that son of a bitch Carrot Cop in the eye so he knows I know he's a liar."

"I love you, Bella Webber." With that, they walked down the stairs hand in hand.

* * *

Wearing heavy rain gear, Carrot Cop and his partner were waiting right outside the door. Just like on television, Carrot Cop read Ben his rights and handcuffed him as the rain fell steadily from a dark sky. Annie and Alder were huddled together under the front porch awning.

Bella had on only her light sweater; in their angst, she'd forgotten her jacket and so had Ben. She shivered, crossing her arms. Her hair was wet now, like she'd come from the shower. Ben's head was down. Water dripped from his nose. He tried to wipe at his face but his hands were cuffed behind his back so the movement was more like a careless shrug of his shoulder. Annie waved for Bella to come to the porch but she shook her head. If Ben was getting wet, so would she.

Roughly, the cops pushed Ben towards the car. "I'm sorry Alder had to see this," Ben called to Annie.

Annie said nothing, just put her hand over her heart.

"Stay badass, Ben," shouted Alder. "My dad will take care of this."

Bella began to cry then. *My dad.* And he was right. Drake would take care of this. He always had and he always would. *Take care of things—that's what I do,* he used to joke. But that was before his wife and daughter were murdered and all the cockiness was snatched from him. But he was Alder's dad now. Surely that was something good in this messed up world.

Peter and Drake rushed into the yard. "Carl Schmidt's on his way down," Drake said. *The attorney. Drake would take care of this,* she said silently to Ben. *Whatever it cost, he would take care of it.*

As the car drove away, Ben put his forehead against the window. Bella blew him a kiss. And then the car disappeared around the corner. She put her hands to her wet face. How was this happening?

Alder and Annie were beside her now, leading her toward the house.

"Bastards," said Alder.

"Bastards," said Annie. "Fucking bastards."

"Mom!"

But Annie didn't apologize. Her face was flaming red. "Ellen's right. These cops have to be crooked. What evidence do they have to arrest him?"

"Drake, I'm scared," said Bella, stumbling in the stone walkway. Rivulets of muddy water trickled between the stones.

Drake, his eyes steely, put his arm around Bella. "Don't worry. This shark I hired for him is the best defense attorney in Seattle. And Ben's innocent, which is more than Schmidt can say about most of his clients."

They were all dripping wet and Annie steered them into the mudroom. Everyone disposed of shoes and jackets before making their way into the front room. Bella's clothes were soaked through; her hair was dripping and she was shaking, perhaps with cold, perhaps fear.

"Hot shower?" suggested Annie gently.

"Yeah, I guess."

"Come to our room."

She nodded but turned to Peter. "Let's get to Los Angeles and talk to this Miss Zinn. There's no time to waste."

"I'll get you tickets for the first flight out in the morning," said Drake.

CHAPTER FOURTEEN

PETER AND BELLA LEFT early Monday morning for the airport. Their flight arrived just before noon. Bella turned on her cell phone as they were waiting to disembark. There was a message from Mike.

"Bella, hey, just wanted to let you and Peter know I called my son to ask him about the Hough brothers. Zac remembered them and said Lee's recollection was right. Apparently this Rawley thought himself quite the ladies man and was aggressive with girls. Zac said several of the girls in their grade told him that Rawley had basically forced himself on them. They didn't call it rape but it sure sounds like that now. Regarding Gale, Zac said what Lee said—he was picked on and bullied at school. Apparently his own brother would have nothing to do with him and didn't protect him either. I have no idea if any of this is relevant but wanted to pass it on anyway. Hope you guys are doing okay down there today. Call us when you return."

They walked through the airport, Bella filling Peter in on the voicemail Mike had left her. "Do you think any of it is relevant?" she asked.

"In this work, you just never know. The more information we have the better."

After they rented a car, they drove to the film set on one of the studio lots. Bella knew the guard at the gate. After exchanging pleasantries, he allowed them through without even asking her what film she was associated with.

"Wow, Bella, you're kind of a big shot in this town."

"Hardly."

"I'm going to call Brent and tell him I've replaced him with a younger and better-looking partner."

They parked and walked over to the film's set. It took only a few moments for Bella to spot a cameraman she knew who pointed them towards Chris Weaver's trailer.

She knocked on the door and Chris answered almost immediately, shaking her hand and then Peter's. "Come on in, guys. Bella, great to meet you. You're one of Stefan's favorite people ever."

Chris was plump, bearded, short, and looked vaguely familiar. She'd probably seen him in a dozen movies without ever knowing his name. This was the difference between being a movie star and a character actor. Stefan, because of his looks, was a movie star. Chris Weaver was an actor.

"Good gig this time," he said, smiling. "Have my own trailer. I play the frumpy district attorney." He pulled on his beard. "This thing's driving me crazy but the real guy has one. Itchy as hell." Pointing at the small table and chairs, he asked if they wanted to sit. "Stefan told me you want to talk to Jocelyn but didn't say what about." He held up his hands in a gesture of submission. "Not that I need to know. Or want to know, most likely. She's on set today—just saw her at the craft table. Do you guys have a way to get her to talk to you?" His brown eyes were curious. All actors were curious about everything, all the time.

"I thought I'd just flash my badge," said Peter.

"Wow, man, that's cool. I played a cop once," said Chris. "The fat sidekick."

"Oh, sure, I saw that movie," said Peter. "Saw it with my real partner, Brent. He was bitter—says the sidekicks are always portrayed as overweight."

"Totally," said Chris, grinning. "But I'm here to represent the ugly fat guys."

"You're adorable," said Bella. "And a great actor."

"A great actor no one's ever heard of," said Chris. "And I like it that way. Stefan and I go way back and I hate the way he's hounded wherever he goes."

Peter nodded in agreement. "I couldn't stand it." He glanced at his hands, shaking his head. "My wife's an actress and I'm not sure I'm ready for it if she becomes well known."

Bella explained that Cleo was taking Tiffany's role. "Cleo went to school with Graham Rouse."

"The producer?"

"Right," said Bella, flushing.

"Stefan says he's a douche," said Chris.

"Yeah, that about sums it up," said Bella with a glance at Peter.

"Dude, super sad about Tiffany," said Chris. "I worked with her years ago. She had the chops back in the day." He opened the minifridge and reached inside, pulling out several bottles of water. "You guys thirsty?"

They both took one and sat at the small table.

Chris joined them, wiping condensation from his bottle of water with his shirtsleeve. "Not that Tiffany would've even remembered me or anything. It was one of my first movies—I had only had three scenes or something—but they were all with her and she was huge then. There were hundreds of screaming fans outside the studio every night waiting for her." He shook his head, obviously remembering. "And her sister—wow, I had the biggest crush on her."

"You did?" asked Bella. "Sabrina?"

"Totally gone for her. She seemed so smart and was impressive, you know, especially to me, being new to Hollywood back then, how she worked the industry and the press and everything. But she wouldn't give me the time of day."

"Did you ask her out?" asked Bella, intrigued by this insight into Sabrina. She must remember to tell her. Maybe there was still a chance for them?

"Once." His eyes clouded over at the memory. "She said something like, 'Don't you mean my sister?' And I was like, 'No, I mean you,' and I swear she looked through me like I was a ghost, and then she pointed at her scar. 'What? You'll pretend like it's Tiffany if I'm angled the right way?'"

"No way," said Bella. "That's harsh."

"Completely. Sent a shiver down my spine. I'll never forget it. Something so broken about her I didn't see until that moment. You know how that is sometimes?" Chris stood, gesturing toward the door. "Anyway, let's go see if we can find Jocelyn. Talk about a piece of work. I'm surprised I'm not madly in love with her, actually. She's as crazy and mean as they come. Totally my type."

They found Jocelyn sitting with one of the associate producers near a table lined with sandwiches and fruit with an open flask in her hand. So much for rehab, thought Bella.

Peter introduced himself, showing his badge.

"This about Tiffany?" asked Jocelyn.

"Yeah. I just have a few questions," said Peter.

"Why's a Seattle cop investigating a murder in Oregon?" she asked, standing, pushing long brown hair out of her eyes. She was tall and slender, almost pretty if it weren't for pockmarked skin and a crooked smile. And an overly exuberant nose job, thought Bella. Who the hell was her plastic surgeon? The man or woman should be court-martialed.

Peter shrugged. "We have our reasons."

"Why should I talk to you?"

"Do you have anything to hide?" asked Peter.

"No."

"Then why not?"

Jocelyn shrugged. The numerous bangles around her wrists made a clattering noise. "Fine."

"You want to use my trailer?" asked Chris. "You know, for privacy."

"That'd be great, doll," said Jocelyn. She took a swig from her flask, smacked her lips, and wiped her mouth with the back of her hand. "Come on then." She pointed at Bella. "This your partner?"

"Yep," said Peter.

"You're kinda pretty for a cop," said Jocelyn to Bella. "I know a way you could make a lot more money."

Bella laughed. "That's okay, I'll keep my day job for now."

* * *

Back in Chris's trailer, they sat at the table. Peter took out his notepad without taking his eyes from Jocelyn Zinn, who returned his gaze without so much as a flinch.

"What's up?" she asked, taking another swig from her flask.

"When was the last time you heard from Tiffany Archer?" asked Peter.

She crossed her arms over her small chest. "It was at my house. A month ago. The day my client book went missing." She was matter of fact, and quiet, almost eerily so, thought Bella.

Peter proceeded to fire questions at her, one after another, matching her calm tone. "You think she took this client list?"

"No doubt in my mind." Jocelyn's eyes flickered, like a cat watching a fish bowl.

"Why?"

"Because a week later, four of my best clients, extremely high-profile, called me to tell me they were being blackmailed. Didn't know by whom. But I know."

"Why Tiffany?"

"Tiffany's bad news. And she was broke. Doesn't take a cop to figure that out." Well, maybe not, thought Bella. If Carrot Cop was any indication.

"Did this make you angry?" asked Peter.

"What do you think?" Jocelyn's eyes flipped to Bella. "Could you look in the fridge and see if he has any beer?" She pointed at the miniature refrigerator near Bella's feet.

Bella, without getting up from her chair, opened the refrigerator door. Six beers were lined up neatly on the top shelf. "Corona or Sierra Nevada?"

"Is there any lime?"

"No lime," said Bella, stifling a smile. This Jocelyn Zinn was nothing short of outrageous in the best possible way. That is, unless she was a cold-blooded killer in addition to being a boozed up madam. She needed a reality show. Why hadn't any of the idiots running this town figured that out yet?

"Sierra Nevada then," said Jocelyn.

Using the opener on the top of the fridge, Bella popped off the cap and handed Jocelyn the beer. What would come next? She had a feeling it would be shocking. Something about Madam Zinn guaranteed it. Regardless, it was better than anything television provided, she thought, settling into her chair to enjoy the show.

Peter shifted slightly in his seat, his eyes flat. He didn't like Jocelyn Zinn. Bella could tell by the way his handsome features had turned stony. He was no fish in a bowl. No, more like a panther meeting a mangy alley cat. Neither would back down, despite the ferocity of the other.

"Angry enough to kill her?" asked Peter, as if the conversation about the beer hadn't interrupted his questioning.

Jocelyn raised an eyebrow and tilted her head to the side. "Yeah, probably."

"Probably?"

"I didn't, but I would've liked to. I would never take the risk of murder—I have no intention of going to jail if I can help it. It's impossible to commit the perfect murder. Isn't that right, Mr. Ball?"

"In my line of work we like to think so."

"Wasn't sad to hear she was dead. Got rid of a bunch of my problems. But I didn't kill her."

"Did you send men up to Oregon to get your client list back?"

Jocelyn's grip around the beer bottle tightened but her face remained passive. "Is that a crime?"

"Could be."

"I wanted what was rightfully mine. She could've hurt a lot of people with the information in that book. So yeah, I sent my guys up there to get it. A pair of private detectives I use frequently...for various things."

"And did they?"

She played with the silver locket that hung just above her breasts. "They did not."

"Did they kill her looking for it?"

Jocelyn took a long swig of her beer before looking Peter directly in the face. "No, they did not. They would not have, as those were not my instructions. And they're private dicks, not hired killers. It's my understanding hired killers are much more expensive."

"Why should I believe, given how much you had at stake, that you didn't hire those thugs to murder Tiffany Archer?"

She crossed her arms over her chest, like a sassy teenager in the principal's office. "You can believe it or not. Regardless of your unfounded suspicions, it's the truth. None of this is complicated. I'm a businesswoman hell-bent on protecting my clients. I'm not a whore like the girls who work for me. I'm not a murderer. Nothing's worth taking some silly bitch's life, no matter how perfectly worthless she was." She tossed her hair over her shoulder and then moved her beer in a circle around the table. "They followed her the night she was killed but got nowhere. Some guy picked her up outside of the bar where they planned to confront her and convince her to give them the book."

"Miss Zinn—"

Jocelyn interrupted him. "*Ms.* Zinn."

"*Ms.* Zinn, do you think either of these so-called private investigators you hired are capable of rape and murder if pushed far enough, despite your lack of orders to do so?"

"Tiffany was raped?" Jocelyn's stoic mask cracked for an instant before being reassembled. Was it Botox or a cold heart that made her features so unreadable?

"Yes. Perhaps they broke in and decided to rape her and then murdered her to hide the rape?"

"No. I don't."

"How are you so sure?"

"Both my boys are gay. They're married to one another, actually. Ceremony just last month. Strangest thing you ever saw—two men who look like they should be Marines fighting in one of those God awful countries, saying I do and kissing on a Santa Monica beach." She crossed her arms over her chest again and must have dug her feet into the floor because her chair tilted back several inches. "Plus, they weren't in her room that night."

"Can you prove that?"

"Depends on if anyone saw them go back to their hotel. After she left with the man at the bar, the tools had the brilliant idea of dealing with her in morning."

"Where were they staying?"

"How should I know?"

"It's important you remember because it could determine their innocence without question."

"How's that?'

"The murderer had to be a guest at the hotel. Surveillance shows no one but the man who picked Tiffany up that night entering the lobby after eleven."

Jocelyn bounced the bottle cap back and forth between her hands like a game of air hockey. "Okay, give me a minute. It'll come to me. Something like Second Chance Inn or something. Told me some stuffy gay boy runs it and he had an unexpected cancellation so they were able to get a room there."

Linus's inn. The detectives couldn't have killed her.

"I want to talk to your henchmen," said Peter. "How do I get in touch with them?"

"My *detectives* have an office on Wilshire."

Peter wrote something in his notebook. Then he took a business card out of his suit jacket and set it on the table. "Call me if you think of anything that might be helpful."

"Stop by my place sometime. I'll have my girls take good care of you."

"No offense, Madam Zinn, but it would be a cold day in hell before I ever set foot in your establishment or laid a hand on any of your girls." He shuddered. Yes, physically shuddered, thought Bella. She must remember to tell Cleo his reaction.

"And why is that exactly?" asked Jocelyn with a slight smile. How could a smile be so thoroughly nasty?

"For one, it's illegal. Two, your business is debasing to women. Three, I have no intention of exposing myself and therefore my wife, who's an angel I'm privileged to have by my side in this cruel and unpredictable world, to whatever diseases your girls, as you so affectionately refer to them, may or may not have. And four, I'm married. It means something to some people."

Jocelyn laughed. It was husky and sarcastic. "Go easy now, choir boy. There's such a thing as condoms."

Peter's mouth was a straight line. "I'll keep that in mind. Thank you for talking with us."

"My pleasure." Again, the nasty smile before she left, leaving her empty beer bottle on the table.

"So much for rehab," Bella said to Peter.

"Vile woman."

"You think?" She chuckled and poked him on the arm. "Choir boy. I'm going to call you that from now on."

"I'll have you know I used to be a player. I'm retired now."

"Now that you're married to an angel."

"Exactly right." He opened the door for her, stepping aside so she could pass. "Let's get something to eat on the way. I'm starving."

"I know a great taco truck." They stepped out into the bright sunshine of late afternoon. The palm trees swayed in a warm breeze. She squinted, looking at the sky. It was actually bright blue today without the usual haziness that came with smog.

"God no. Do you want to be poisoned? How about vegetarian Thai or sushi?"

"Poisoned?" She searched the bottom of her bag for her sunglasses.

"Those places are not clean. And the amount of grease in that food can clog your arteries in one sitting."

"It's impossible you were once a player."

He laughed. "Being health conscious and a player are not mutually exclusive." He put on his sunglasses. "Now watch your step. The sidewalk's uneven."

* * *

Bella took Peter to a sushi place in Beverly Hills, not far from the private detectives' office. The weather was a pleasant 72, as it so often was, although not usually in October. Peter was quiet during lunch, nibbling on a plate of sashimi he dipped in low sodium soy sauce. Bella could only imagine what his sharp and precise mind was doing with everything they'd learned thus far.

She picked at her spicy tuna roll, thinking of Ben, of his face as he was hauled into the police car yesterday. Peter's cell phone rang. "It's your brother," he said to her. "Hang on."

His face turned from serious to grave as he listened to Drake. After a minute or so, he hung up, running a hand through his hair and staring at the table.

"What is it?"

He looked up at her. "They set the bail at a million dollars. And the District Attorney held a press conference. They're going for the death penalty."

A roar started between her ears. What she'd eaten of her lunch felt as if it might come up. "I can't believe this is happening."

Peter dipped a napkin into her water glass. "Put this on your face and take deep breaths."

"What're we going to do?"

"We're going to find the killer." He smiled and squeezed her hand. "Well, first we're going to interview those two assholes and find out what they know."

* * *

They found the private detectives' office in an alley off Wilshire Boulevard. The two men were as Ben described, clean-cut and in their early thirties with an air of having served in the armed forces. Bella would never have guessed they were gay. These weren't the kind of gay boys she was used to. The taller one by several inches was Matt Reed. He was fair skinned and blond, trim and muscular, but with a bland expression that seemed never to change. His partner, in life apparently as well as business, was Jose Torres. Obviously Latino, given his dark eyes and skin, his expression was as apathetic and unreadable as his partner's, except for eyes that seemed to display an inquisitive nature.

"You know why we're here?" asked Peter as they took seats in a small conference room adjacent to the main office.

Matt nodded but didn't say anything.

"It's our understanding you were in southern Oregon, with the intent to recover Ms. Zinn's book? Is that right?"

"Yep," said Matt.

Jose pointed at Bella. His head was almost square, emphasized by the way he wore his hair short and spiky. "Who's she?"

"My partner," said Peter.

Matt shifted his eyes to Bella. She wanted to cringe under his scrutiny but held steadfast. No way was this guy going to intimidate her. "Bullshit. Where's her badge?"

"I'm a friend of Ben Fleck's," said Bella. "He's the man that picked Tiffany up outside the bar. Remember him? You know when you were following her into the parking lot? He was arrested for Tiffany's murder this morning."

Matt, without moving a muscle, asked, "Did he do it?"

"He did not," said Bella, as firmly as she could.

"How do you know?" asked Jose.

"I just know."

"Look, guys, we're looking for any kind of lead. There could be a connection between the blackmail scheme and her murder. Do you have any clue who the men were that were being blackmailed?" asked Peter.

Matt shook his head. "Ms. Zinn only told us that there were four of them. She didn't give us their names. She's careful to protect the anonymity of her clients."

"According to Ms. Zinn, you guys went back to the Second Chance Inn after you were unsuccessful in making contact with Tiffany that night," said Peter. "Is this correct?"

"Yes," said Matt. "We intended to talk with her in the morning and gently persuade her to give us what belongs to Ms. Zinn."

"This clears you of any suspicion," said Peter. "The murder was committed by someone staying at the lodge."

Neither man showed any sign of relief or even acknowledgment. Matt sat forward slightly, his eyes livelier than the moment before. "The book wasn't in her room, at least not that afternoon when we searched it."

"Wait a minute, you were in her room earlier that day?" said Bella. "How did you get in? She didn't say anything had been disturbed."

Matt interlaced his fingers on the desktop. "We're professionals, Miss Webber. How we got into the room isn't the point. We were there. There will be no fingerprints to prove it but we were there just the same. We searched the room thoroughly. The book was not there."

"That means whoever searched the room later didn't find it either," said Peter, almost under his breath. He looked at Bella. "We have to get the names of the four men being blackmailed."

And where was the book?

They stood. Peter shook first Matt's hand and then Jose's. "Thank you, gentlemen, for your help. Please call me if you think of anything else."

Jose walked with them to the door. "You know, Mr. Ball, there's a way to get Ms. Zinn to give you the names of the men being blackmailed."

"What's that?" asked Peter.

"Tell her you'll get her book back if she tells you who they are."

* * *

Chris met them outside his trailer. "She's in there. I got her to come by promising to play backgammon with her."

"She plays backgammon?" asked Bella.

"I know. Weird, huh?" said Chris.

Jocelyn Zinn appeared nonplussed to see them again, her eyes skirting to them and back to her game in a matter of a split second. "You again?"

Peter proposed Jose's idea to her.

She didn't take her eyes from the board. "What makes you think you can find it?"

"My gut tells me at least one of these four men knows something that will help us locate it."

"You're a cop. You really think I'm going to trust a cop with my client list? If you could even find it, which I doubt."

Peter paused for a moment, surveying her, before seeming to come to a conclusion. "I'm going to level with you, Ms. Zinn. I'm not actually assigned to this case. A good friend of ours has been accused of Ms. Archer's murder and I'm trying to clear his name. I have no interest in making trouble for you. They're threatening to try him for the death penalty."

"And I'm not a cop. I'm a makeup artist," said Bella.

Jocelyn Zinn looked up then, her impenetrable eyes softer for the first time. "I thought you looked familiar."

"I can't emphasize enough how little interest we have in causing you or your clients any troubles," said Peter.

"The man accused is my boyfriend. I'm desperate." Bella's voice caught. She swallowed against the lump in her throat before continuing. "I'm trying to help him. He's a good person who was at the wrong place at the wrong time."

Jocelyn looked at Peter. "And you're sure this dude didn't do it?"

"We are," said Peter.

"Well, shit, I know how it feels to be falsely accused of something. Plus, I don't think an innocent man should die, especially over something like this." She put her hand out, with an open palm. "Give me your notebook. I'll write the names down. But you cannot tell them I told you. You'll have to say you uncovered the blackmail plot when she was murdered."

"Fine," said Peter.

There was nothing but the sound of the pen scratching on the paper for a moment. She handed the notebook back to Peter.

His face showed no emotion as he scanned the list. "Are these all current clients?"

She shrugged and tossed her hair. "Depends on what you mean by current. I'm technically not in business any longer."

"No need to play games, Ms. Zinn," said Peter. "I could care less about whether or not you're currently in business. We're here to solve a murder, not pass judgment on your business. Honestly, I don't know why anyone gives a crap about prostitution considering the real crimes being committed."

Jocelyn appeared to consider him. Was it Bella's imagination or did she shift her perspective of Peter just then? She got up from the table and sidled up next to him, tapping the book twice. "These two are no longer clients."

"Why's that?" asked Peter

"The first one was too rough with my girls. The second one found Jesus when he married America's Sweetheart."

"Thanks for this," said Peter, closing his notebook and stuffing it in his jacket pocket. "Come on, Bella. We've got work to do."

"Remember, keep me out of it," they heard Jocelyn say as the trailer door slammed.

Now we're getting somewhere, thought Bella. *Ben, just hang tough. We're going to figure this out.*

Peter was quiet until they got to the car. He opened the passenger door and she slipped inside the warm car. Specks of dust had settled on the black dashboard. It smelled of new car and leather. Silently, Peter handed Bella the list. There were four names, all with phone numbers.

Cash Cutler. He was the lead actor of a popular television show and well-known bad boy about town. No surprise there.

Connor Jenkins. CEO of a major discount grocery store chain.

Austin Blu. Lead singer for the rock band Crazy House. Married to popular movie actress Carlie Cullen, nicknamed America's sweetheart. Classic nice girl marries bad boy.

The last name on the list caused her to gasp.
Rawley Hough. Los Angeles Assistant District Attorney.
"Holy shit," said Bella.
"Yep," said Peter. "And he's the one who was too rough with the girls."
They drove south toward Los Angeles. The late afternoon sun was bright on the asphalt, and the brown hills in the distance seemed stark and barren to Bella after the lush green of the dramatic Oregon mountains. "How do we get them to talk to us?" This seemed impossible.
"Leave that to me. How do we get to your apartment?"

* * *

In Venice, they turned onto Bella's street, parked in her garage, and took the elevator up to the third floor. Once inside, she opened the screen door to the deck. The ocean breeze brought all the familiar smells of home. Or was it home? Perhaps home was up north now with the swaying firs and rushing river.
"Cute place," said Peter almost absently.
Peter went out to the balcony. She shivered when she saw him lean against the ledge. Averting her eyes, she called out to him. "You want something to drink?"
"You have any tea?"
"Like iced?"
"No, like green."
"Seriously, you're like a chick."
"And you're kinda like a guy."
"I know. I'm badass."
She heard him laugh as she put the kettle on. "You'll have to come inside to drink this."
From the balcony, "Why's that?"
"I never go out there. I'm afraid of heights."
He came inside. "Is that why there's no furniture out there?"
"Right." She set a cup of tea on the kitchen table for him.
Peter paced in front of the sliding glass door, pausing every so often to gaze out toward the water. Finally, he perched on the edge

of the table, pulling out the list from his pocket. "Okay, I'm going to make some phone calls. See if we can get these guys to meet with us."

"I'll leave you to it. Think I'll take a walk out to the boardwalk." Reaching into the coat closet by the front door, she slipped off her heels and into a pair of athletic socks from the pile she kept in a basket and then into her tennis shoes. "Call me when you're ready for me to come back."

But he seemed not to hear, already dialing the first number on their list.

* * *

The three-mile beach itself was deserted; lifeguard towers stood alone and barren next to sand the color of Melba toast. The wind, chilly this time of year, whipped the orange flags as if to say, *we're still here*, waiting for the months when the sand would be covered with bathing-suit clad bodies. There were several surfers, wearing full wetsuits, sitting on their boards, waiting for the next wave. But the boardwalk was active as ever. She walked past the sign for the Medical Marijuana Doctor, and the skateboard park, never empty, always with the whooshing sound of boards on concrete. Did these lost boys go to school, she often wondered? Soon she came upon the body builders, ever vigilant and shirtless, arm muscles the size of small watermelons bulging and glistening in the sun. She passed various street performers: a mime; the famous roller blade guy playing his guitar and singing; two acrobats, one doing a handstand on his squatting partner's knees. And then the tattoo shop where the hummingbird had been etched into her hip after she ended it with Graham. She'd wanted a tattoo reflective of freedom and a new start. Gennie sometimes said she was like a hummingbird when she worked and it had seemed like the perfect symbol.

Her thoughts turned to Ben. Would she have the chance to bring him here one day? She imagined him laughing at the antics, at the murals and shops with everything and anything one could imagine. Everything was big here, and bright, and loud. Ben would love it. He would laugh here. She knew it. They might sit at her favorite bar on a Saturday afternoon, wearing only their bathing suits and drinking beer and sneaking kisses between bites of curly fries and chicken wings. Imagining it, she filled with a physical longing she'd never before experienced, thinking of the life they could share, the way everything felt like an adventure with him.

She turned around, walking back toward her apartment. Men and women on rollerblades, runners, and bicyclists weaved around her. The sun was on her back now and she was able to gaze at the ocean without squinting. Her mother had loved the ocean, had loved Venice Beach. When Bella was ten and Drake sixteen, they came here for vacation, the only vacation she could ever remember taking. Her mother's great aunt died and left several thousand dollars to them and instead of putting it in the bank, she'd surprised them both with a trip to California. They'd stayed, by accident really, in a dive motel in Venice that her mother had stumbled into a coupon for. The hotel was no longer there; it was torn down years ago and replaced by a nice hotel. But during the week they'd stayed there it had seemed to them a certain kind of paradise. All three enjoyed themselves, but perhaps her mother most of all. She'd seemed young that week and carefree, surprisingly open to the alternative lifestyles of the residents of Venice. One afternoon, strolling the boardwalk and licking ice cream cones, she'd pointed to a particularly bright mural depicting early California and said, "I dreamt of being an artist when I was a kid. Did I ever tell you that?"

She couldn't remember if she or Drake had asked a follow-up question. Perhaps Drake had? He was older and more aware and curious about the time before she was their mother. But Bella was ten and distracted by her ice cream and the sea air that made her feel alive in a way the damp Seattle air could not. She'd vowed after that trip to come back to live with the colorful people and the sunshine and palm trees, which were not native to California, Drake had pointed out more than once. He was so pedantic when they were kids. Well, he still was. People didn't really change. Bella was still the wide-eyed child she'd been, enamored with the tan sand and blue water and brown and green mountains of the coastline. And Drake was still wise and bossy.

An image came suddenly of that day with the ice cream. She'd had strawberry, her mother peach (she loved anything peach flavored), and Drake chocolate (he always ordered chocolate). They were all laughing and had stopped to sit on one of the benches that lined the grass and overlooked the sandy beach. Why were they laughing? What she would give now to remember. Her mother wore a yellow sundress and cheap flip-flops she'd gotten at the dollar store before they left. Bella could remember this, she thought, but not what they'd laughed so hard over.

She could see now her mother's feet in those flip-flops. Bella had painted her toenails pink like the wild roses that bloomed in August in Seattle. Yes, her mother's toes. Alice tossed the flip-flops aside and wriggled her toes in the grass. "Oh the grass tickles and this ice cream is so good," she said, turning to look at Drake and then Bella. "You know something I've learned?"

"What's that, mama?" asked Bella, biting into the sugar cone, wishing this ice cream could be like in a fairy tale, always refilling as soon as the last lick was done.

"It's the smallest moments in life you remember, like this one, just this perfect one with the ocean and the ice cream, and the grass and sitting with my two favorite people in the world. I'll remember this for the rest of my life." She stood in her bare feet on the grass and flung her arms wide. "Just take it in, my loves. Just take it in."

Alice's second toe was slightly longer than her big toe, just like Bella's. That small thing they shared was something Bella held onto even all these years later. Sometimes in bed, with the windows open and the sea breeze moving the white curtains she'd hung herself, she would gaze at her feet and think, *some part of you is still here. It proves you were here. You gave me these crazy toes.* Drake's daughter had had them too.

Bella's eyes filled and she walked blindly for a moment until she spotted a bench. She sat and wiped her eyes, watching the waves come in one after the other. *The waves are slower here,* her friend from Florida had said to her once. *They come in less frequently,* Bella had replied, *but with more strength.*

How desperate her mother must have felt about money, alone with two children. Why hadn't her mother ever dated? Bella hadn't really thought of it before but she must have been lonely. Perhaps she never met anyone she liked well enough to bring him into her children's lives. As it so often did when she thought of her mother's sacrifices, the hollowness of loss and pain and regret was like something alive, emptying her insides until there was nothing but a cold mist whipping and tugging there.

Her cell phone buzzed in her pants pocket. Peter. He'd reached each of the men on the phone and arranged times and places to meet them.

"I'll be right there," she said into the phone, leaving her memory of peach ice cream and laughing next to the bench. For now. She would visit it another day.

* * *

They were to meet Austin Blu first, at his Malibu home. It was four in the afternoon as they headed out, Bella driving while Peter filled her in on what each of the men had said when he called. The coastal highway was surprisingly uncongested and the sun low on the horizon, making diamonds on the blue water. This was one of Bella's favorite drives. When she was heartsick over Graham, she often drove this stretch of highway on a weekend afternoon, with the radio cranked and the windows open so the salt air could find its way to her. Not that it helped. Nothing had helped. When you love a married man there is no escape from the inevitable loneliness that comes when one chooses to participate in betrayal.

All the men had been surprisingly open to meeting with him, Peter told her as they approached Malibu.

"How did you get them to agree?" Bella asked, genuinely curious. This Peter Ball was good at his job.

Peter smiled. "Well, for lack of a better explanation, I kept it simple without revealing I have no jurisdiction over the case. Told them I was a cop and knew they were being blackmailed. They all agreed, rather quickly, to meet with me."

"What about Rawley Hough?"

"He didn't admit he was being blackmailed, like the others did. He was mostly silent but agreed to meet with us at his home office."

"He's involved, Peter. He has to be."

"I agree. There's no way it's just a coincidence. Carrot Cop has way too much incentive to pin this on Ben as a way to keep his brother out of it."

"Especially if Hough murdered her."

"That's right."

Austin Blu lived in a gated community in one of the highest priced areas in the country: Malibu beach property. When they arrived at the gate, a middle-aged security guard with a substantial beer gut came out of a booth with a clipboard. "Yes, Mr. Blu was expecting them," he said as the gate opened. "Last house at the property. A terracotta with no windows on the driveway side."

They found it easily, parking in the driveway near pots of blooming flowers. The house was rectangular and barren, very modern looking, except for white clematis climbing up the side of the house. Perched on the edge of a cliff, like many of the houses along the shore, with a trail around the house hinting at the Pacific Ocean and sandy beach below.

Bella was surprised when Austin Blu answered the door. She'd expected staff of some kind since the man was listed as one of the richest men in the world. He had the standard long hair of a rocker, although artfully cut so that it lay just so, and blue eyes the color of the ocean outside his magnificent windows. His nose was on the long side but it didn't detract from what could only be described as attractive of the raw sexuality variety. Why would this man need to visit Madam Zinn's girls? He could have any woman in the world. And there was his wife, the princess of romantic comedies. She was the girl-next-door daydream of countless men across the country with her blond cap of curls and big blue eyes. And she had the type of personality so many men seemed to like: perky and sweet and nonthreatening. Bella assumed this was close to her real personality because actresses like Carlie Cullen always played characters similar to their own. Regardless, Carlie Cullen was like gold at the box office.

Austin shook both their hands and motioned for them to come inside. The part of the house that faced the beach was floor to ceiling windows, giving the feeling that one was on the water as opposed to merely looking at it. The décor was angular and modern, accented with bright reds and yellows. Masculine, thought Bella. Did Carlie live here with him? Was their marriage real or just for the press? She'd been in Hollywood long enough to know it happened more often than the American public was aware of.

"Would you like something to drink?" She'd never heard him speak before and was surprised by his New Jersey accent. "There's sparkling water or regular water. No soda or booze. Carlie won't allow it. Always worried about my sobriety. Well, and my caloric intake." He was charming and surprisingly soft-spoken, with an intelligent glint in his eyes. Not what she'd expected, considering the hard rock his band was known for.

"Is your wife here?" asked Peter, after declining the offer for a drink.

"No, she's filming in Hawaii." He indicated the sofa. "Please, come sit."

They did so. He sat opposite them, picking up the electric guitar from an ottoman. "It's not plugged in, don't worry," he said, grinning. "I won't blast you." He glanced toward the windows and then back to them. "How did you know someone was blackmailing me?"

"Had a tip from another man being blackmailed for the same thing," said Peter. "How long had it been going on?"

"A month ago I got a call. The voice was distorted, you know, like they do in the movies. But she knew all the details and asked for $100,000 mailed to a P.O. box here in Los Angeles to keep quiet. I agreed, obviously. I didn't want this out in the world."

"Because of your wife?"

He shook his head, his eyes dull. "No, she knows. I met Carlie three years ago and have been faithful to her all that time. Carlie knows everything about me—the good, bad, and the ugly. And if you've done any research on my past, you know there's a lot of bad and quite a bit of ugly. I used to be a frequent visitor to the ranch when I was still drinking but all that changed when I met Carlie. She's the best thing that ever happened to me and there's no way I'd mess that up at this point. And we just found out she's pregnant. I'm thrilled. Utterly thrilled."

"So why did you care if your name was exposed publicly?" asked Peter.

"Because I don't want Carlie publicly embarrassed. Our life is enough of a media circus as it is. You know, bad boy rocker marries a girl like Carlie—the press loves this shit. I knew if it came out, the whole circus would start again. They'd start running the clips of my mug shot from years ago and the time I punched a paparazzi in the face and I don't want her to have to go through all that again, especially since it's finally died down. Does that make sense?"

"It does." Peter glanced at his notepad. "Did you make any other payments to the blackmailer other than the initial $100,000?"

"Yes. Last Thursday I got another call, asking for another $100,000. I sent it to the same P.O. box as the first time."

"What time of the day did you get the call?"

"It was the morning. The call woke me up. I was grateful Carlie had left the day before so I wouldn't have to explain it."

"So Carlie doesn't know everything about you?" asked Peter, not unkindly or accusatory, more like they were just two men out for a drink.

Austin looked at him blankly for a moment before understanding crossed his intelligent features. "Oh, right. No, I haven't told her about this. I don't want to risk her being upset. She's had two miscarriages. I want to get her through the first trimester. She lost the last one after the press crucified her because of her performance in *Cat on a Hot Tin Roof*." Bella had forgotten that Carlie had played Maggie in one of the big theatre houses in Los Angeles. The press had not been kind. It wasn't Carlie's fault, Bella had thought at the time. Who casts a movie actress known for playing the girl next door in fluffy romantic comedies as the ferocious and sexy Maggie the Cat? Someone concerned with people buying tickets instead of worrying about the integrity of the play or the poor Hollywood starlet completely miscast.

Peter glanced at his notepad again. "And you're sure it was Thursday morning you heard from the blackmailer?"

Austin nodded his head in the affirmative. "I think so."

Peter wrote something in his pad. Austin plucked at the strings on his guitar, staring at the floor before looking over at Peter. "Do you know who it was?"

"We have a suspicion but we're unsure," said Peter.

"Can you tell me?"

"Tiffany Archer."

He blanched and turned pale. "What?"

"We believe her murder could be tied up in this."

He put his guitar down and walked to the window. "So that's why you're here. You think I could have something to do with her murder?"

"That's right."

Austin turned to look at them. "If it was her blackmailing me I wouldn't have murdered her over it. I might've eventually decided it wasn't worth it to keep paying her but it wouldn't have been the end of the world if it had come out. Carlie and I have good publicists. It was mostly Carlie I was worried about, just getting her through this first couple of months without miscarriage. And, I don't say this to sound arrogant, but a couple hundred thousand dollars isn't going to break me."

"Where were you Thursday night and Friday morning?"

"Thursday night I played a charity gig at the Hollywood Bowl. Bunch of bands participated. Cancer research. 18,000 people saw me that night. Saturday I spent the day here, writing songs and surfing. My housekeeper can vouch for me. She was here all day as well."

Peter asked him to call them if he thought of anything else. They both gave him their cards. "You're in the business, then?" he said to Bella.

"I'm afraid so."

* * *

Cash Cutler's home was in Beverly Hills. It was enormous, with sprawling lawns and fountains, although not even close to the largest on the street, which Peter noted with a dry quip about sit-com actors not making as much as rock musicians. This time they were let in through a security buzzer, similar to the one Drake had at his home, and pulled into a circular driveway. The house had large columns, like southern plantations might, and Bella remembered then that Cash was from Alabama or Georgia. His current television show was about a country singer who hit the big time and moved to Beverly Hills. Cash was a good singer and a surprisingly talented actor, completely believable in his current role.

A Hispanic maid answered the door and without a word led them outside to a swimming pool. Cash, fit and tan, dressed in long shorts and T-shirt, was reclining on a chaise lounge reading a magazine. There was a glass of white wine and a martini with two olives on the table next to the chaise. A young blond woman stood next to him, her surgery-enhanced breasts barely covered in a pink tank top. Her cut-off jeans were so short her butt cheeks were peeping out as she leaned over and pointed to something in the magazine that made them both laugh.

Cash looked over at them as they approached. "Hey y'all. Come on out. What're you drinking? I'll have Lulu here fix you up one."

Lulu was the girl, not the maid, apparently, because she straightened up, gave them the once-over, and broke into a huge smile. "Of course I will, darlin'." Her accent was southern, noted Bella. He must have imported this one from home.

They both declined the drink. "Well sure, you two are on the job," said Cash, his voice a slow drawl. "I played a cop once in a movie and my character was always sipping from a flask but I guess y'all don't really do that in real life." He pointed toward a table with a cocktail umbrella. "Come on over here, I'll get Martha to bring us some grub."

"No, we're fine," said Peter. "We just have a few questions for you and then we'll let you enjoy your evening." His eyes slid to Lulu. "Best if we talked to you alone."

"Much obliged. Sure thing. Lulu, baby, go get changed. I want to take you to dinner."

Lulu squealed and jumped up and down. Those breasts were a couple of weapons, thought Bella.

Cash grabbed his martini and the three of them sat at the table. "What can I do you for?" asked Cash.

"Like I said over the phone," began Peter, but Cash interrupted him. "This is about the blackmail thing."

"Right," said Peter. "Can you tell us when it started?"

Cash looked around the yard like he was nervous, his eyes darting to every corner of the yard. "See, the thing is, whoever this blackmailer person is, she said if I went to the police she'd leak the whole damn thing and well, I really don't need that right now."

"We believe the person who was blackmailing you is dead," said Peter. "You're safe to talk to us."

"Dead?"

"When was the last time you heard from her?" asked Peter.

"Thursday."

"What time?"

"Around lunchtime, I think. I was at the studio between takes. They've got this whole sexy storyline going this season and this sweet little thing I'm filming with needed a break. It all looks sexy on television but filming love scenes ain't as much fun as you might think. It's all move your arm there and throw your head back there. This poor girl was freezing and needed something hot to drink, not to mention how horrified she was to be almost buck naked next to me wearing nothing but one of the darn dick socks, excuse me for saying so, Miss." His eyes darted to Bella and back to Peter. "I suggested a swig of tequila or something to loosen her up but she's one of these girls who never eats or drinks, legs as big 'round as a toothpick. I like my girls with a little southern fried meat on their bones. Wait a minute, now, where was I going with this? My mama always says I never know when to shut my mouth and let someone ask a question."

"How many times had you received calls like this?"

"Three times. This was the fourth. Each time she asked for a hundred grand. Which hurt me to hand over, believe you me, but like I said, I'm trying to build a new image—away from the bad boy stuff—and more of a recovering sweet ol' southern boy who wasn't prepared for fame. You know, that kind of thing."

"That kind of thing can be real, you know," said Bella, warm, thinking of poor Tiffany.

"Oh, hell yeah, sure. But that's not really the case for me. I'm reckless. Have been all my life, even before I came out here, so me and my mama can't really blame Hollywood on my troubles but my publicist sure can. You know half the crapola you read in them big magazines ain't really the truth. Publicists run this town, let me tell you. And the thing is, I don't care what people think of me, really. I just want to keep working and my manager and agent think it's better if I play up all this poor ol' me routine."

"Poor old me?" asked Peter, watching him with those piercing eyes that seemed to see everything in at once.

"Oh, you know, the sharks of Hollywood got a hold of me and now I'm fighting hard against my demons, blah, blah, blah. Get my drift, here?"

"Is it important enough for you to murder over?"

"How's that again?"

"Tiffany Archer was blackmailing you."

His eyes were wide, disbelieving. "Tiffany Archer? Wasn't she just a kid? May she rest in peace."

"Twenty-seven," said Peter.

"Shoot, she was blackmailing me? How'd she know about it?"

"She got ahold of Ms. Zinn's little black book, for lack of a better term."

"And now she's dead. Holy cow. Murdered? Am I a suspect?" Strangely he didn't look scared, more intrigued with the idea.

"How important was it that this be kept from the press?"

He shrugged, glancing toward the house. "Shoot, not enough to kill over it. I wasn't sure what to do next, honestly. I've had some money problems, you know. Gambling and, well, as you know, whores, and some parties I've thrown I really shouldn't, so I really couldn't afford to keep paying her, but on the other hand, I really didn't need any more bad press. But, heck, I couldn't kill anyone. I love the Lord, for one. And He's already displeased with me over the gambling and the whores and not giving enough money to the church and all that, but Jesus knows my heart and it ain't the murdering kind."

"Where were you Thursday night and early Friday morning?"

He scratched his chin and took a sip of his martini, glancing toward the house. "I was with a girl. Not Lulu, as it turns out."

"Were you seen in public with her?"

He grimaced. "'Fraid not. We were here at the house." He snapped his fingers. "But the security log will show when I came in and when I left. That'll prove it." Pausing for a moment before taking a swig of his martini, he looked over at Bella. "You look familiar. Have we met before? I've had a couple run-ins with the cops out here. Do I know you from that?"

"Maybe," said Bella evasively. She looked at her hands.

"It'll come to me later. Probably tomorrow when the martini isn't making my head fuzzy." He turned back to Peter. "Anyway, I feel real bad she was murdered but it does solve some of my problems, I ain't gonna lie. But I had nothing to do with it. I hope you believe me."

"We'll check the security log, as you suggested," said Peter, putting his card on the table. "You give us a ring if you think of anything that might be helpful in this case."

"Sure as shootin'."

* * *

Connor Jenkins's home was a few streets over from Cash's and four times as big. Besides the main dwelling there were several guest cottages and multiple pools and a tennis court. "How much money does this guy have?" Peter asked her as he parked the car.

"He owns all those stores plus a basketball team and I don't know what else. I'm pretty sure he's on the Forbes 100 list."

Peter kept shaking his head as they waited for someone to answer the door. Finally, a maid wearing an actual old-fashioned black and white uniform answered the door. "This way, please. Mr. Jenkins asked me to show you into his study."

They followed her down a hallway, catching a glimpse of a sitting room ornately decorated and a dining room with a large chandelier. Connor Jenkins was tall and rotund and balding, dressed in an expensive looking sweat outfit and slippers. The study was dark and masculine, with leather chairs and mahogany walls. A large desk held a computer and several neat stacks of paper. There was a bar in the corner with various hues of liquor in crystal decanters. He smoked a cigar, sitting in a leather chair next to a lit fireplace, but stood when they entered, shaking both their hands. He picked up the humidor from the coffee table, opened it and offered one to Peter. "Cigar? Best in the world."

"Thank you, I don't smoke," said Peter.

"Drink?" he asked, his eyes on Bella.

"No thank you," she said, unable to break eye contact.

"I insist."

"I'm on duty," she lied, feeling warmer.

"There isn't a chance in hell you're a cop." His black eyes glittered. He pointed at Peter with his cigar. "That's a cop. You, my lovely, are something else entirely. But never mind. I don't know what game you're up to, but Peter Ball, Tiffany Archer's murder is no more your case than this little girl over here is a cop."

If Peter was as shocked as she, he didn't show it. His expression never changed. "You know Tiffany Archer was blackmailing you?"

"Figured it out the night before she was killed. Had some folks looking into it for me. All roads turned to her. Next morning I wake up to the news she's dead. Couldn't say I was sad to hear. Solved me having to take care of it myself."

"Did you have her murdered?"

"Course I didn't. Not my style. I was prepared to send my boys up there to Oregon and have her roughed up a bit, threaten her if she didn't agree to back off. She was in way over her head and that would've done the trick."

"How did your people figure out it was her?" asked Bella, curiosity overcoming her fear of this dreadful man.

"I don't tell my secrets, Miss Webber."

"How did you know my name?"

"Again, I have people."

"Why should I believe you didn't have her killed?"

"Mr. Ball, I am one of the richest men in the world. I would not risk prison for something so easily taken care of."

"Why didn't you take care of it sooner then?" asked Bella. Something about this man made her speak when she really should keep her mouth shut.

"She only blackmailed me once. I didn't intend for her to come back for more."

"What was the amount?" asked Peter, taking out his pad.

"A million dollars."

Clearly Tiffany knew he was the richest of the people on her list.

"It was worth it to keep her quiet until I could figure out who she was. I'm a married man."

"So the usual reasons for wanting it kept quiet," said Peter. "Wife. Children. That sort of thing."

He set his cigar in the ashtray on the table. "My wife could care less who I sleep with. She's busy spending my money instead of having orgasms. No, it's the public. I'm well aware of how hated I am and have the daily death threats to show for it. But I'll be damned if I'll give them any further ammunition to hate me more than they already do. This country isn't that far from its puritan roots. I would be hammered in the press for this, made fun of on every late night show. There'd be picketers in front of my stores. All of which is bad for business. This country's full of haters, Mr. Ball. Especially the rednecks that live in these little towns that claim they hate me for closing down all the mom and pop poorly run hardware stores and grocery stores and drug stores but fight like cats over a can of tuna at the half-price bargain bins in my stores like the uneducated, ignorant trash they really are."

"Technically, Mr. Jenkins, uneducated and ignorant are the same thing," said Bella, her armpits prickling and damp. She wanted to hurt this man. Bad. Very, very bad.

"Ms. Webber, did they arraign your boyfriend today? Is that why you're so nasty this evening? Pity he murdered a girl when you'd only just started dating. You really should let me pour you a drink."

How did he know this? She opened her mouth to make a retort, but Peter stopped her with a light touch on her shoulder. "Mr. Jenkins, thank you for your time. We'll be in touch if we have any further questions."

They all stood. Bella's legs were shaking, making it difficult to walk. How dare this arrogant greedy man insult Benjamin Fleck? Someone good and decent. Someone who took care of the people who worked for him. Someone who respected his customers.

At the doorway of the study, Jenkins put his chubby fingers on Bella's forearm. "You give me a shout when you decide to dump that loser boyfriend. I'd love to show you what a real man could do for a girl like you."

"It would be a cold day in hell when I'd let you anywhere near me," she said through gritted teeth.

Peter took her arm, steering her out of the house and almost shoving her into the car. "Not worth it, Bella. Not worth getting your hands dirty. Trust me."

"I want to take him down, Peter. Hard."

"You and half of America."

"Wait until I tell Mike about him. He'll want to chew nails. After all the effort he's put into saving River Valley and an asshole like that is spending all his time trying to figure out how to ruin towns just like it. Makes me sick. How's the little guy supposed to survive in this world, Peter? The little business owner doesn't stand a chance."

Peter chuckled. "You're starting to sound like a River Valley resident. Those friends of Annie's are contagious with this stuff."

"I know. It's just I never thought about all these small towns going under because of Connor Jenkins's giant stores and meth until I spent time in River Valley."

"Yeah, I know. The town I grew up in on the Oregon coast, same deal."
"I hate Connor Jenkins."
"Why do guys like that always win?"
"They won't in the end."
"Why's that?"
"There's one major difference between a guy like Mike and a guy like Connor Jenkins that matters in the end."
"What's that?"
"Mike has a soul."

* * *

Rawley Hough was tall and ruggedly handsome with just a beginning of a receding hairline. His home was modest compared to the ones they'd just visited, but nice just the same, set on a corner lot in Brentwood.

A petite blond woman wearing yoga pants and a spandex top opened the door. A yoga mat and a gym bag were on the floor. "May I help you?" she asked. Her features were bland and blond. *Vanilla pretty*, thought Bella. She looked like so many upper middle class women in Los Angeles—soccer moms, PTA leaders, professional shoppers for dresses to attend their husband's work functions, obsessive daily trips to the gym, a little Botox now and then.

Peter took out his badge. "Your husband's expecting us."

She flinched. "About what?"

"Official police business," said Peter, without taking his eyes from her.

She'd flinched and looked frightened. Or had Bella imagined this?

Rawley was behind them now, carrying a drink in his hand. Probably scotch by the looks of it. *Expensive, no doubt*, thought Bella. "It's all right honey. I know why they're here. Just work stuff. Nothing to worry about."

"I'm Julia Hough," she said, holding her small, tanned hand out first to Peter and then to Bella. She trembled slightly, almost like someone with a degenerative disease. "I'm just on my way out to yoga. I go in the evenings after I get the girls to bed." Why the need to explain this, wondered Bella? Was it to convince them of the normalcy of the household? Just a happy family? With an extremely nervous matriarch.

Peter gave her a slight smile. "How old are your girls?"

"Six and ten," she said.

"Fun ages," said Bella, as if she knew anything about children. Alder was ten. He was fun. That was about the extent of her knowledge of children.

Rawley led them into a sitting room off the foyer. It was decorated in the same vanilla bland as his wife: tan wingback chairs with patterns of pink flowers and a sea grass green couch, pink striped pillows, and dozens of small details obviously designed by a professional. There was not a thing out of place; no one actually lived in this room.

Rawley, unlike the men from their earlier visits, did not offer them a drink. Even Jenkins had offered them a drink, thought Bella. She shivered, thinking of Jenkins's sweaty, fat face leering at her.

"As I said on the phone, we know you've been blackmailed," said Peter, straight away. "And we know by whom."

One eyebrow lifted. "Yes?"

"Tiffany Archer."

"The actress?" He moved his glass from one hand to the other; the ice rattled.

"Correct."

"The dead actress," said Rawley. It was not a question but a statement. "How would she have access to Ms. Zinn's client list?"

"We believe she stole it from Ms. Zinn's home. They were friends. Rehab."

Rawley took a sip of his drink, watching Peter over the rim of the glass. "Rehab. That makes sense."

"Did you have any idea who was blackmailing you?"

He moved his gaze into his drink. "Of course not. If I did, don't you think I'd have turned it over to the police, given my line of work?"

"Not necessarily," said Peter. "Turn it over to the police, everyone knows. Including your wife."

"I am not a man who negotiates with blackmailers."

"What does that mean?"

"It means I didn't pay the bitch a penny of what she asked for."

"How long since you visited your hometown?" asked Peter.

"Pardon me?"

"You heard me."

"Since my mother died. Ten years ago. I'm not fond of River Valley."

"Were you aware Tiffany Archer was filming a movie there?"

"I saw it in the news. Hard to miss since it's been on every news station. Apparently our media isn't interested in real news, instead spending every waking moment detailing the death of a two-bit actress dying in some town no one's ever heard of."

"They've heard of it now," said Bella.

"Where were you Thursday and Friday?"

"Here. I have a big case I'm working on. My family went to the desert."

"So you were here alone?"

"Correct."

Peter's gaze was on his notebook as he scribbled notes. "Do you have anyone to vouch for seeing you Thursday night? Take-out delivery person, housekeeper, that kind of thing?" He looked up, staring at Rawley in a way Bella could only describe as intimidating.

"I stayed in. My wife left food for me so there was no need to go out."

Peter stuffed his notebook back into his pocket. "Thanks for your time. We'll be in touch if we have further questions."

* * *

Outside Rawley's home, Peter drummed his fingers against the steering wheel. Bella swore she could hear him thinking. After a moment, he turned to her. "Surely he has the resources to figure out it was Tiffany, given his position. He went up there to get rid of her."

"He's the only one without an alibi."

"Yeah. And, really, the most to lose of the four of them. The others faced scandals but not losing their positions. And he's not nearly as rich as the others." Peter started the car and pulled out onto the street. "When we get back to your house I'll call Fred and ask him to see if Hough was checked into the lodge over the weekend. He most likely registered under a false name but we might be able to spot him on the security cameras."

They were quiet on the way back to Bella's apartment. It was almost eight o'clock by the time they arrived and Bella's feet hurt as they walked up the three flights of stairs. "Why didn't we take the elevator?" asked Bella, as if she didn't know.

"No reason not to take the stairs. Ever."

"You're starting to get on my nerves."

"I do that to my real partner too. He also likes donuts."

"I haven't eaten any donuts."

"Not today. But I've seen you devour a piece of cake the size of your head. For someone so tiny you eat like crap."

"You sound like my brother."

When they reached her apartment she slid the key into the lock and walked inside, Peter following closely behind her. The temperatures had dropped and they'd left the screen door open. "You cold?" she asked Peter.

"A bit, yeah."

"You want a beer? I'm having one whether you do or not."

"You have any scotch?"

"No. Sorry. I never have any male visitors. Red wine or beer."

"Beer's fine."

After closing the screen door and turning on the fireplace, she fetched them both a beer. Bella sat cross-legged with her head resting on the back of the couch, her thoughts turning to Ben. Was he despairing, sitting in a jail cell? If she concentrated hard enough, might he hear her thoughts? She imagined them traveling up the coastline and then jagging across the Siskiyou mountain range to southern Oregon. *Ben, I'm here. We will get you out of there.*

Peter paced with his beer, which remained untouched, tugging occasionally on his ear. Bella, after spending the last twenty-four hours as his sidekick, knew better than to interrupt or ask him any questions. A few minutes later her cell phone rang and she hopped up to dig for it in the bottom of her purse. It was Annie.

"Annie, what's going on? Was Drake able to bail him out?"

"We have to wait until tomorrow. After the arraignment."

"Were you able to see him?"

"No, honey. We weren't. But the attorney did. He's fine. Will you guys be home tomorrow?"

"Yeah. Around mid-morning. I have to be on set right after lunch. Cleo and Gennie are both filming."

"Drake will go to the arraignment and arrange bail. We'll have him home by tomorrow night."

Bella fought tears. "Is it awful? The place where they're keeping him?"

"The attorney says it's fine. He'll be safe there until we can sort this whole mess out. Did you guys have any luck?"

She filled Annie in on everything, asking her to relay it to Drake, and then they said goodnight.

Peter was outside on the balcony, leaning against the railing with his head down, talking on his phone.

She went to the kitchen and opened another beer, realizing they hadn't eaten since lunch. Peter must be starving. As she was thinking about what to feed him, Peter came inside, closing the glass door behind him. "Talked to Fred," he said. "He's going to look through the hotel security footage for us, see if he can spot Hough in the lobby at any point during the day."

"That's good. That's really good."

"And he's going to show the front desk people Hough's photo. If he was there, surely one of them will remember."

But what if he wasn't in the footage? What if the clerks didn't remember him? Then what?

"You want me to order a pizza or something?" asked Bella.

"How about some hummus and pita bread?"

"Yep, you're officially on my nerves. And just for that I'm going to punish you by taking you to my favorite diner tomorrow for breakfast. Nothing but carbs and grease."

Chapter Fifteen

THE SHOW WENT ON, thought Bella, watching Cleo and Genevieve film their scene for the sixth take. Tiffany Archer's body was still in the morgue and here was her replacement filming the scene she'd filmed less than a week ago.

The scene was the first in several conflict sections between the two sisters. Cleo was holding her own, even playing against Genevieve, who was as good as they came in this business. Bella would have never guessed had she not known that Cleo had never filmed a professional movie in her life. She never missed a line, hit every mark Richard gave her, and adjusted after he gave her direction with every take. Genevieve, at one point, looked over at Bella and mouthed the words, "She's good."

While Richard was setting up for the scene they'd film that evening after it turned dark, Bella hiked along through dead grass, heading toward Ellen White's house. The heavy rains from earlier had ceased but the sky was dark and moody. There was a sliver of gray smoke rising from Ellen's chimney and Bella took in a deep breath, enjoying the scent of wood-burning smoke. When had she smelled that last? Growing up in Seattle, perhaps. In October it would suddenly be in the air. Once, walking hand in hand with her mother, she put her nose up in the air and sniffed. "Mommy, it smells like campfire."

She reached the bank of the river. There was an old oak with a rope swing tied to it. Alder had told her of this; he often used it when he stayed with Ellen. The farmhouse and this swing, they needed children and laughter and the smell of wood smoke in the air. Would she and Ben have the opportunity to do all the living they dreamt of together? Perhaps they could live here in Lee's farmhouse and have babies and teach them to swim in this river with Alder and her new little niece. She went to the swing, held the rough rope between her fingers. When the weather warmed this summer, she would come here with Alder and Ben. They would take turns swinging and she would watch. She could not swing, of course; the height as the rope glided over the water would be too frightening. But she would watch. Maybe she'd have Ben's ring on her finger by then. Maybe there would be a wedding to plan.

She marched toward the ribbon of smoke. The grasses were wet but her boots were high. Warmed from the exercise, she took off her fleece and tucked it under her arm, her breath not exactly labored but increased. Physical exertion after yesterday's sedentary activity and riding on the airplane this morning cleared her mind and buoyed her spirits. Of course they would get Ben out of this. She would have the life she wanted.

Before she knew it, she'd reached Ellen's house. She knocked on the front door and heard footsteps before the door was thrust open, revealing Ellen. She had on an apron covered in flour and carried a rolling pin. "Bella, what a nice surprise. Come on in." She opened the door wider and motioned for Bella to follow her.

It was warm inside and smelled of cinnamon and butter. Ellen's house looked remarkably similar to Lee's house. She said as much to Ellen. "Well sure, Lee's grandfather built this house right after he built the other. We had a tiny one-room shack for a whole year before this house was built. Let me tell you, spending a long rainy season with my husband, well, it wasn't what you'd call a party. He was a drinker, you see, and a mean drunk. Used to get in the whiskey and start beating on me. I'd have to run on over to Rose's and hide out there 'til he sobered up." Without pausing, she cut a piece of apple pie and put it on a plate. "You better go ahead and have a piece of this. I've made plenty." Ellen pointed to the counter. There were six pies lined up in a row. Two more, uncooked, sat by the stove. Two others were in the oven.

"Why so many? Is there a bake sale or something?" River Valley was the type of place to have a bake sale, right? What was a bake sale for? Raising money for something, Bella supposed. Venice Beach did not have bake sales. Maybe she should learn to bake. Then she could participate in bake sales.

Ellen clapped her hands together. "Where did you go there, sugar? Your eyes got all glazed over."

Bella shrugged, feeling sheepish. "Just daydreaming about learning how to bake. Or bake sales." She shook her head. "I don't know what I'm saying. I'm delirious from the last couple of days."

Ellen was now pouring a glass of milk. "I can't ever get Lee and Annie to eat any of my pies. Those two nitwits always worried about their weight, which is ridiculous—don't know why you modern girls think being stick thin is attractive. What I wouldn't have given for Ava Gardner's figure."

Bella dug into the pie. It was heaven: a burst of cinnamon and apple and the crust was flaky and tasted of butter. "I may have to have another piece of this," she said between bites. "What did you say all these were for again? 'Cause if it's a bake sale, I want to buy one."

"You just take whatever you want home. I made these for the crew. Oh, and that director Richard—what a nice man—so polite and intelligent, not at all what I would have expected from someone from Hollywood. You know, I never actually met a Jewish man before. Now don't look at me like that. Around here we don't have any Jews, not that I have one thing against them. Matter of fact, I'm not one much for organized religion or doctrine. Lee's always trying to get me to go to church now she's married to Tommy—he's a Jesus lover, you know." She opened the oven and leaned over, peering at her pies. "Yep, these are done." Using oven mitts with a pattern of roosters, she pulled out the pies. Gooey sauce spilled from the sides and onto the counter. "Shoot, Bella, I never saw such a sight in my life as this movie business right here in River Valley. I hate to admit it, but I'm a little star struck, which is downright embarrassing. But think of it! Filming a movie in the old Tucker place. Oh, Lee's other grandmother, Rose, she was my best friend you know, she'd have gotten such a kick out of this. She practically swooned for the movies. I always thought it was a bit of nonsense but we used to go into town and watch the matinee. We'd wear our hats and our Sunday best and Rose's husband always sent a few extra nickels with us so we could buy a treat. Lord, that Rose loved her candies. She was a plump little thing, always sneaking a cookie even when she told me she'd like to reduce. That's what we called it back then, reduce. I was always skinny as a bone. Lee took after me that way, nothing but a flat board. The amount of cottage cheese poor Rose used to eat. That's what all the magazines back then would tell you. Cottage cheese to reduce. Ridiculous, of course. Well, I guess. Actually, I shouldn't say that, not having ever been on a diet in my life."

"Ellen?"

"What's that now?"

"Do you think Lee would rent me her house when the filming's over?"

"I'm sure she would." Ellen crossed her arms over her chest. "You thinking of moving here?"

Bella flushed with warmth, realizing she hadn't told anyone out loud. "Ben and I want to get married."

Ellen's eyes sparkled. "Well, now, that's a little soon, don't you think?" But Bella could tell by the way she said it that Ellen didn't really think it was too soon.

"Do you think love at first sight's a real thing?"

"I most certainly do. Verle and I are the perfect example."

"Was that how it was for you two?"

"Yes, and think about that. Both of us in our seventies, just minding our own business and boom, there was the other."

"How come you two don't get married?"

Ellen smoothed her apron with her hands. "He wants to. I just don't know if I want some old geezer in my house all the livelong day."

"But you said you love him."

"I surely do. And he stays over most every night. But there's something to be said for us choosing the other every day instead of waking up married, obligated, so to speak. This way the romance never dies. Each day, he calls me up and asks may he come over and I always say yes. We choose the other every time. Does that make sense?"

Bella sighed, making a heart with her fork in the leftover sauce around the empty plate. "It does. So romantic, actually."

"Why Bella Webber, you're nothing but a softie. I had you pegged for a saucy, hard little thing when I first saw you traipsing around in your bikini at Drake's."

"That was before I met Ben. My heart's turned into a bunch of goo."

"Well, now, I don't think you two should live in sin like Verle and me. Don't want to give you that impression one bit."

Bella laughed. "Why not? You just said how romantic it is."

"Yeah, but we're not young. You two need to get married and start making some babies."

"Oh, Ellen, I would love a baby. I mean, not right away. But I saw that swing out there by the river and all I could think of was a little boy and Alder shouting and swinging on Sunday afternoon."

Ellen patted her arm. "That would be something."

Bella glanced at her watch. "Yikes. I have to get back to set. We're filming in a half hour and I have to make sure my beauties are beautiful."

"Run along now. You tell Richard I'll bring the pies over later tonight."

"Los Angeles caterers have nothing on you, Ellen."

"Amen to that."

* * *

Cheered by Ellen's good company, she traipsed back through the grasses, bowed now from her earlier footsteps as if ashamed. The sun had appeared when one of the dark storm clouds moved. Drops of water clung to the grass and glittered in the bright light. The yellow hues of the grasses were as varied as the variety in her eye shadow kits: Dijon mustard, straw, autumn leaves, roasted marshmallow. She could see the farmhouse when her cell phone buzzed with a text. It was from Ben. "Drake posted bail. I'm free. For now anyway. Missing you like crazy. And scared, Bella. Really scared."

She stopped, typing quickly with her thumbs. "I'm scared too. But Peter and I are onto something. I'll be home around nine. Filming until then."

* * *

Bella and Cleo were with Genevieve in her trailer, playing Crazy Eights. As they set cards down, the two actresses ran lines for the scene they would film after dark. Bella kept one eye on the script, prompting them if they stumbled on a line.

"I have to be perfect, Bella," said Gennie. "Not a missing or exchanged word."

"Yeah, I know," said Bella. "I've done this before."

Gennie smiled. "Of course you have. It's just I want to honor the writer by getting every one of her words correct."

"Yeah, I've heard this from you before too." Bella yawned, feeling the effects of yesterday's traveling and the constant worry about Ben.

"Learned this trick in drama school," said Cleo after they'd run the scene through three times without missing a line. "Running lines while doing a meaningless task."

"Whoever says Crazy Eights is meaningless never had to occupy a ten-year-old boy," said Bella, thinking of the many games she'd played with Alder last summer.

"Sometimes I do it jumping rope," said Genevieve.

"Oh, that's a good one," said Cleo. "I need to figure out how to lose a few pounds anyway."

"Can we play poker now?" asked Bella.

"I hate playing poker with you," said Genevieve. "You always win."

Bella grinned. "It's because you have no poker face. I can read you like a book."

"When was the last time you read a book?" said Genevieve.

"Cleo, I have to tell you what Peter said to Madam Zinn." She relayed the story to the two women. "Your husband's a cool cat, as Alder would say. Although his whole health food thing is annoying."

"Tell me about it," said Cleo.

Genevieve's voice was soft, almost wistful. "They don't make many men like Peter Ball."

"Or Ben Fleck," said Cleo to Bella.

"Or Stefan Spencer," said Gennie.

Had she just said that? Bella watched her friend's face carefully. Was there something between them or were they just friends? "What's going on between you two?"

Gennie smiled, her eyes glassy. "He's the most generous actor I've ever worked with." She put her hand on Cleo's forearm. "And by actor, I mean male actor. Most of the women I work with are very generous. Comes with being a woman, I think. We're more apt to give others the spotlight."

"I can't believe I'm actually sitting here talking to Genevieve Banks about acting." Cleo pinched her own arm. "Is this a dream?" She sobered, looking guilty. "Of course, I feel terrible about the way I arrived here."

"Tiffany made poor choices, again and again, and received many second chances," Genevieve said, not unkindly or with judgment, but with the sad tone of inevitability.

There was a light tap on the trailer door and then Peter entered. "Am I interrupting anything?"

"No, we're running lines and waiting for them to call us," said Cleo.

Peter kissed his wife on the cheek and then turned to Bella. "I have news. We were right about Hough. The front desk clerk remembered him. And he's in the footage. Registered under John Miller. Paid cash. But it's him. Which means he was in the lodge the night she was killed."

Hope beat loud in Bella's chest and spread to her limbs. This was the break they needed. He had to be the killer. And Hough's brother had pinned it on Ben to cover it up. "What next?" she asked Peter.

"I'm going to the Echo Grove District Attorney with this. If he has any integrity at all he'll order a DNA test, and if it's Rawley Hough's sperm, they'll start an investigation. My prediction is both brothers will go down."

"Have you told Ben yet?" Bella realized she was still holding her cards. She set them on the table.

"I talked to Annie. Drake and Ben are on their way home from Echo Grove. She said she'd tell them about it when they got there. I'm going to track down the local D.A. Apparently he eats at the Echo Grove Country Club every Tuesday night."

Bella slid her cards across the table. "I'm coming too."

"But what about us?" asked Gennie.

"I'll get the other girl to cover me. But I'll probably be back in time given how slowly they're moving."

Gennie nodded. "All right. Good luck."

"Yeah, good luck," called Cleo as the trailer door shut behind them.

Chapter Sixteen

THE ECHO GROVE COUNTRY CLUB was next to a golf course overlooking the valley below. Peter asked the hostess at the club's restaurant to point him to the District Attorney, Jeremy Hayes, which she did without question, which Bella found odd. No one in Los Angeles would do that. People were so trusting here. It was weird.

Mr. Hayes was dining alone. He was a large man, not overweight but oversized, with shoulders the size of a linebacker and legs that stretched almost the entire length of the table. There was a half-eaten steak and baked potato on his plate and a diet soda with lemon next to it. He looked up from his dinner when they approached, with an expression of curiosity on his square face. Bella guessed he was in his fifties but his skin was dark and unlined. His nose was hawk-like and his eyes the color of bitter coffee next to high, deep cheekbones. Native American, Bella wondered?

"Mr. Hayes, I'm Peter Ball from the Seattle Police Department. I apologize for interrupting your dinner but I need a word with you about a personal matter."

Hayes nodded at him, his thick eyebrows knotting together like two caterpillars kissing. He set aside his plate and indicated for them to sit. "I know who you are. I'll choose to ignore the fact you're clearly working outside your jurisdiction." His voice was low and deep and without inflection.

Peter looked surprised. "You know who I am?"

"My people know you've been looking into the Tiffany Archer murder."

"Oh, well, do you know why?" Peter and Bella both sat.

Hayes ignored the question. "I knew your father back in the day." Peter flinched like Hayes had suddenly moved to strike him. "Oh." Hayes moved his eyes to Bella. Although he spoke to Peter he kept his gaze upon her. "Played football with him at Oregon. Shame what happened to his knee. These are defining moments, I'm afraid. How we react to something catastrophic can determine the path of our lives."

Bella squirmed in her seat. Was it unusually hot in here? She shrugged out of her jacket, slipping it around her waist where it stayed, like a child's inner tube.

"Yeah, well, all indications were he was an asshole even before he blew out his knee." Peter played with the tablecloth, his fingers gathering the material into a bunch before smoothing it with his other hand.

Shocked, Bella turned to look at her new friend. This was not the Peter she knew and had grown so fond of the last several days. His voice had sounded like someone young and petulant but at the same time weary and sour.

Hayes turned his gaze back to Peter. "Ah, well, the sins of the father are evident here."

Peter stared back at him with the eyes of a wounded child but was silent.

Hayes's glittering black eyes moved to her, resting without blinking on her face. "You're Drake Webber's sister." It wasn't a question.

"Yeah. You know him?"

"I know of him. He's a generous man. There are several philanthropic endeavors he's committed to here in Echo Grove very close to my heart." He pushed back his chair slightly from the table and crossed one enormous leg over the other. "You're both here to talk to me about Ben Fleck's innocence. Isn't that right?"

"That's right," said Bella, somewhat alarmed. Did he know everything about them? Hayes was like the male, suit-wearing version of the freaky medicine woman telling fortunes out of her shack in the bayou.

"I'm good at my job, Mr. Hayes," said Peter, sounding again like a child talking to his father.

"I know. I've followed your career."

"You have?" Peter was still now. Was he breathing?

"Yes." Hayes said this simply, as if it were of no consequence and therefore needed no explanation. "You're a man of character." He spread his enormous hands over his chest and took in a deep breath. "Tell me your theory."

Peter did so, telling him what they'd discovered and his suspicions about Hough and Carrot Cop. Hayes kept his gaze focused on Peter's face the entire time but did not react in any discernible way. After he finished, Hayes sat forward and took a sip of his soda. "I've suspected all along Ben Fleck was innocent. And I believed there was something rotten inside our police department. However, I wasn't sure why they would pin it on someone who would surely be cleared the minute a DNA test came back and I could not imagine the motive for doing so. Therefore, I've chosen to let it unfold, hoping the guilty parties would become obvious. My sincerest apologies to Mr. Fleck but up until now, I've had nothing concrete in which to substantiate my suspicions other than an anonymous tip from someone inside the police force. Mr. Ball, you're indeed good at your job. I expect my colleagues in Los Angeles and my Echo Grove team can adequately take it from here. And now, if you'll excuse me, I need to go to the office. Expect all charges against Ben Fleck to be dismissed within the hour." He rose to his feet and it seemed to Bella it must take great strength to heave such a body out of a chair. "Before I go, tell me about young Fred Hughes."

"Green, but a man of character," said Peter.

"Excellent. I'll call you later, Mr. Ball, to apprise you of the situation. Good night, then." He shook both their hands in succession. "The sins of the father, Bella Webber, needn't dictate your life. You're a woman of character, despite it all." He headed toward the exit in long strides, surprisingly graceful for a man his size. And then he was gone. The room seemed smaller, somehow, and dimmer.

And although it would have been normal for them, in elation and relief, to hug or shout or do a cartwheel, they did not. Instead, they stared at one another across the discarded steak and potato dinner in a kind of shock. Finally, Bella spoke. "What the hell just happened?"

"I don't know but I wish he'd adopt me."

"Yeah, me too."

* * *

Peter dropped her off at the set less than thirty minutes later. As she suspected, they hadn't yet started to film. They did only four takes of the scene and the minute they were done, Bella left, leaving Gennie and Cleo behind to watch the dailies. By the time she arrived at her brother's, Ben, Peter, and Drake were sprawled on the couches in the front room with their feet on the coffee table. There was a roaring fire in the stone fireplace and several bottles of wine open. When he saw her, Ben stood, his face twisting with emotion. He came to her and brought her into his arms, lifting her off her feet and holding her tight against him. "Bella, I missed you."

He smelled as he always did; she breathed in his scent, wrapping her arms around his neck. "I missed you too."

Peter motioned for them to sit. "Bella, have a glass of wine. I just heard from Hayes."

After they'd met with the Hayes, Hough, his lawyer at his side, was brought into the LAPD and questioned. He confessed rather quickly to, as he put it, "Sleeping with Tiffany. She liked it rough." And yes, he'd gone to scare her, to put a stop to the blackmail scheme. When she opened the door of her room at a little after one in the morning, disheveled and still somewhat out of it, he'd pushed her inside and told her the reason for his visit. She denied the blackmail, saying she had no idea what he was talking about. She pretended to know nothing about the client book and told him she was broke. "I have the almost-empty bank accounts to prove it. If I'm blackmailing you, then where's the money?"

During questioning, he'd become agitated at this point. "I just wanted the little bitch to own up to what she'd done and I had my ways of getting her to confess. What started out as a little physical intimidation turned into hot, rough sex. She liked it that way and so do I. Is this a crime? Not in my experience."

Given the bruising and tearing, though, there was no doubt in anyone's mind, according to Peter, that it was anything other than rape.

Regardless, Hough would not admit to killing her. He told them he'd torn the room apart looking for the book but adamantly denied murdering her, saying he left her a little before two o'clock in the morning, very much alive.

His brother, Carrot Cop, was also brought in for questioning and immediately admitted to pinning the entire thing on Ben Fleck in order to protect his brother. Peter said Hayes told him it was pitiful the way he gave in so quickly. "I just wanted to help my brother," Carrot Cop said. "So he'd finally respect me."

And just as it had begun in an instant, so it was done. Ben was free of suspicion. "This is really over?" Bella asked Peter.

"At least as far as Ben's concerned. Proving Hough killed her may or may not be easy." Peter smiled. "But it's no longer our problem."

"Ben, it's done." Bella held his hand and put her head on his shoulder. He was home where he belonged.

"Tonight, we celebrate," declared Annie, bringing in a plate of appetizers. "I'll invite everyone over and make whatever you want to eat, Ben."

He didn't hesitate. "Coq au Vin."

"Done," said Annie, hugging him. "I'm so happy this is over."

"So am I," he said, making eye contact with Bella. His eyes were laughing.

* * *

That night, the gang gathered once again around the long table in Drake's dining room. Besides the immediate family and their houseguests, in attendance were: Tommy and Lee, Peter and Cleo, Ellen and Verle, Alder and Ellie-Rose, Mike and Sharon, Linus and his boyfriend John, Cindi, and Gennie and Stefan. Everyone talked and laughed. To Bella it felt as if nothing could possibly ever bother any of them again. Ben was free.

Before they began the first course, Ben rose to his feet, tapping his glass with a spoon. "I don't know what to say in way of thanks, really, to any of you. I'd be facing a long trial if it weren't for you all. I'm not sure why you all believed in my innocence without knowing me better than you do. But I'm grateful. Especially to Peter and Bella, obviously. Knowing how easily I could have lost everything that mattered to me brings everything into crystal clarity. Who I am. What I want. How grateful I am for my life, for freedom, for all of you." He held up his glass. "To freedom. To friends. To life." They all toasted, the table exploding with voices and laughter. Then, Ben set his glass on the table, wiped his eyes with the cloth napkin and reached inside his jacket pocket. "I have one more thing I want to say before we dig into Annie's amazing food." In his hand was a small blue box. Bella stared at him, her heart pounding against the fabric of her blouse.

He went down on one knee. "Bella." He choked, tears filling his eyes. "Dammit, I can get through this."

Bella put her hands to her mouth, afraid to breathe.

"Bella Webber, I feel as if we lived a lifetime together the last week. You proved to me I can count on you during the worst of times. No one has ever gotten me like you have. There is no one I'd rather spend time with. From the moment I met you last summer traipsing around here in your bathing suit I have loved you. Everything's brighter with you in it. My life makes sense with you in it. Will you give me the chance to spend the rest of my life trying to give you the best of times? Will you marry me?"

She couldn't see through her tears. She nodded and whispered, "Yes." He slipped the ring on her finger. The diamond was a blur of light. She leaned into him, wrapping her arms around his neck. Around them the room was loud with shouts and claps but it was nothing but a dull roar in her ears because it was only Ben and this moment. Destiny, she thought. This was her destiny.

"Do you like the diamond?" he said into her ear.

She spoke quietly, wanting the moment to be just between the two of them. "Can't see a thing, you've got me crying so much." She removed her arms from around his neck and held up her hand. It was princess cut and seemed enormous on her small hand. "It's beautiful. But I could care less about the ring as long as I have you."

"I know. But it's important to me. I want the world to know how proud I am you decided to spend your life with a schmuck like me."

"Can we live part of the time in Venice and part of the time here?" She would propose her idea of renting Lee Tucker's farmhouse later.

"I will follow you wherever you go," he said, pulling her close.

By the time they turned back to the rest of the table, Annie and Gennie were already planning the wedding. "I'm thinking here in June. Or do you want a church wedding?" Annie asked them. "Ben, we'll have to invite your parents down for a visit. They should get to know us before the big day."

"We should have a weekend in Portland for the bachelorette party," said Ellen. "You know, stay in a fancy hotel and go out for, what do you call them, the pink drink, you know, Cindi."

"Cosmopolitans?" asked Cindi.

Ellen snapped her fingers. "Yes, that's it."

Gennie waved her salad fork in the air. "We could have the wedding at my place in Malibu. Looks right out to the ocean, which is Bella's special place." She turned to Bella. "How big do you want this to be? Just us?" She indicated the room with a sweep of her hand. "Or big? Ben, what's your family like? Will your mother want to invite a lot of people?"

Ben grimaced. "I think my mother's still scarred from the wedding that never happened. I don't think they'll care one way or another."

"Small," said Bella. "Just us and Ben's family."

Gennie seemed not to hear her, pulling out her cell phone. "I'll text Rico right this minute." She turned back to Annie, holding her phone in the air as if it were evidence. "He's my party planner. An absolute genius. What date should I tell him?" She pushed a button on her phone. "Here's the calendar for June. A Saturday? Like June seventh or fourteenth? Which do you prefer?"

"There's my place up north in B.C., too, Bellalicious," said Stefan. "In the woods. Very quiet and serene." He gazed at Gennie with hooded eyes. "Gennie, you've been to B.C. Isn't it beautiful there?" He said it, Bella could swear, like he was asking her to go there with him. *Oh, Stefan, play it cool*, she told him silently.

Gennie nodded as she texted something into her phone. "I love B.C. Gorgeous place for a wedding. And Rico could plan it anywhere. Whatever Bella wants. I'm paying for everything."

"That's my job," said Drake. "No offense but the one who walks her down the aisle is also the one to pay."

"And sorry, Gennie, but I'm planning this wedding," said Linus, looking uncharacteristically flustered. "Bella belongs to us now. And

I think we should have it at the inn. We could make the lobby into the perfect location for the ceremony. White chairs. Rose petals."

"Me flower girl," said Ellie-Rose, poking into her chest with her thumb.

"How do you know about that?" asked Alder before glancing at Lee. "She's getting way too smart."

"That's what we think about you." Drake chuckled.

"We can have the reception at Riversong," said Lee, her eyes dancing. "Annie, we could do a formal sit-down if it's a small wedding."

"Our band will play, Bella, if that's what you want. Or not." Tommy looked sheepish for a moment. "Whatever you want, of course."

"Me flower girl," repeated Ellie-Rose, biting into a cherry tomato.

Gennie was flushed. "Linus, Bella will always belong with me. She's my best friend. We've known one another for over ten years. I should get to plan her wedding if I want to. Or, if she wants me to." Her eyes brimmed with tears.

Mike, very mayor-like in his diplomacy, cleared his throat and leaned forward in his chair. "Of course she belongs to you, Gennie, just as she belongs to us, and the Webbers here, and to Ben. We all love her, just as we love you and Stefan. Loving one another means we belong to one another. We're like family here and that means sometimes we fight over what we think is best."

"Sorry, Linus," said Gennie, wiping tears from her eyes. "I guess I got carried away."

"No, I'm sorry, sweetheart. I get a little territorial about events." Linus picked up his wine glass. "Truce?"

"Truce," said Gennie. She put her head on Stefan's shoulder for a second before appearing to realize what she'd done and straightening in her chair.

"Bella, honey, whatever you want is what we'll do," said Sharon, with a glance of pure adoration at her husband.

"I think she wants a big wedding. Huge. Major guest list with all of Hollywood invited," said Peter.

"Laugh it up, Ball." Bella gave him the middle finger. He laughed and toasted her with his wineglass. "Ben and I will talk about it and let you all know what we decide. Now, let's eat, drink, and be merry," said Bella.

She hadn't seen Drake leave the table but he'd come back with three bottles of champagne and some sparkling apple cider. "Let's have a toast to my sister's engagement." He handed a bottle each to Ben, Linus, and Tommy. "Open them up, boys."

"Let's get this party started," said Alder, pouring a glass of the cider for Ellie-Rose and then one for Annie. "Sorry, Mom, but you've got to stay off the sauce until the baby comes."

"What did you say?" Annie, mouth slightly open, stared at her son.

"Come on, Mom, I wasn't born yesterday. There's only one reason you wouldn't be imbibing at a dinner party, especially one where your friend has just learned he no longer faces incarceration for a crime he didn't commit. Not to mention you've been tired and sick. Totally knocked up."

"Don't call it that, my goodness," said Lee, trying to look stern, but the sides of her mouth twitched.

Annie continued to stare at him, obviously at a loss for words.

Drake smiled, his eyes darting first to Annie and then to Alder. "Yep, you're going to be a big brother. What do you think of that?"

"I think I already feel like one with munchkin here." He put his hand on top of Ellie-Rose's strawberry blond curls. "So I'm prepared and ready for service."

"What I want to know is how you know the word imbibing," said Tommy.

"From a book, of course," said Alder. "This is why it's important to be well-read. Right, Dad?"

"That's right," said Drake, laughing. "One of the reasons, anyway."

"We'll teach the baby that too," said Alder, looking over at his mother. "Don't worry."

"I'm not worried." Annie was gazing at her son with so much love it caused Bella's chest to ache. The love one felt for their child was like no other. This is how her mother had loved her. Someday she would love her own child this way. She glanced at her brother as he leaned toward his wife, brushing a curl from her forehead. Bella looked away, swallowing the lump in her throat. This ordinary gesture of love was extraordinary given Drake's losses. The unimaginable pain that came from loving a daughter and losing her was too much to bear for any father. And yet he continued forward, choosing to live, to love again, to laugh, to participate in the ordinary cadence of life, eating and drinking and taking a shower and tending roses, despite the gaping hole. Surely this was the greatest act of courage? And to create a new life, a new child, with what remained of your torn, tattered heart? Surely this was the essence of hope. Surely it was a whisper of light in the dark night. Yes, we go on, we live, despite our sufferings.

Bella spoke quietly in her future husband's ear. "I don't want to wait to marry you. I don't want to waste another moment. I'm thinking Vegas. Eloping."

He chuckled. "Really?"

"Maybe."

He sobered, looking into her eyes while holding her chin with the tips of his fingers. "But whatever you want, whenever you want. I'm here. For the rest of your life."

Chapter Seventeen

THE NEXT DAY ON SET Bella was starving. Apparently her appetite had returned intact. She filled her plate with two sandwiches, chips, and a diet soda and grabbed a Caesar with chicken for Genevieve. Holding onto the food with one hand, she knocked on Gennie's trailer door with the other. "Come in," she heard Gennie call.

"I brought you salad." She tossed it all onto the table and looked over at her friend. "And don't tell me no. You need to eat something or you'll never get through the rest of the shoot."

Genevieve was sitting cross-legged on the small bed near the back of the trailer, with the script in her lap. Her makeup was smeared and her eyes were red. Had she been crying? "I'm not hungry."

"I don't care. Just eat some of the chicken at least. You need protein."

Genevieve stood, stretching her arms over her head. "Okay."

Bella pointed to one of the chairs at the small table. "Sit. Eat. Then I'll fix your makeup."

Genevieve picked at the chicken, finally taking several bites before pushing it away. "I'll eat afterward. I feel sick."

"Were you crying?"

"I guess."

"Is it nerves?"

"That, and Tiffany. I know it's silly since I hardly knew her but I can't stop thinking about her last moments. The rape, that is."

Bella sighed. "He's a monster. Sounds like he always was, according to Lee."

"Here's what I don't understand though. If he went up there to kill her, to keep her from blackmailing him, why would he rape her first?"

"Power, maybe? Punishment? I don't know. Who can understand someone like that?"

Genevieve shuddered, as violently as Bella had ever seen someone do. She took her friend's small hands. They were like ice. "Don't think about this right now. You have an intense scene to film. Just focus on that, okay?"

"God, I hate these love scenes."

"But Stefan will take care of you. It'll be all right."

After she coaxed Genevieve to eat a few more bites of chicken, she pulled out her makeup kit and began repairing her face. She reapplied foundation, patting the area around her friend's eyes gently so as not to hurt the area, probably tender after crying.

There was a rap on the trailer door. "You want me to see who it is?" asked Bella.

"That would be nice. I don't really feel like talking to anyone right now. Except you."

It was Stefan. He carried a bouquet of flowers in his arms. "Hey Bellalicious."

"For me?" she teased, motioning for him to follow her back down the steps to the wet ground below.

"Well, I should've gotten you some as well, now you say that," he said, following her. His face was dark, unusually serious.

"I'm just teasing. Walk with me for a minute?"

"Sure."

They strolled toward the house, where the crew was busy setting up for the interior shot. The love scene. Forbidden love. Never goes out of style, thought Bella.

"Stefan, she's having a tough day. She's a wreck over the scene. I found her crying just now."

He flinched. "I figured as much. I've been worried about her. I tried to call her earlier but she didn't answer the phone. It's awful, really, even for me. But she's, well, she's sensitive and hates to be touched. Isn't that right?" He paused, looking Bella in the eyes. "There's something more to it, I know that. Something from her past."

If he only knew what had caused Gennie's marriage to fail. She averted her eyes, lest she give away too much information.

"Bellalicious, I think I'm falling in love with her."

"Oh, no, Stefan, that's not good."

"I know. Right?" He glanced toward the trailer and lowered his voice. "Why is it not good, exactly?"

"Because she's not really available. At least I don't think so."

"The divorce? Too soon?"

Bella shuffled from one foot to the other. What should she say to this sweet man with his heart thumping outside his chest for the world to see? "I'm not sure. But she's fragile and, sweet as she is, closed off."

"So it's hopeless. I guess I should give up." He ran his empty hand through his hair. "But that's not really my way."

"I know. Me either." She pointed at the trailer. "Come on. Give her your flowers."

They found Genevieve inside her trailer, sitting on the bed, turning her phone over and over in her hands. Without looking up, she said, "Bella, my husband called. Again. I mean, my ex-husband." She glanced up and started, like the deer Bella kept seeing in the yard. "Oh, Stefan, hi. What're you doing here?"

He handed her the flowers. "These are for you."

"Why?"

"A gesture of good luck, I suppose. Or something." His voice was low and soft. He set the flowers on the table.

Genevieve stood, holding onto the table with one hand. "Thank you. It's sweet of you. Really. Are you dreading this as much as I am?" Her voluminous eyes shone in the light.

Bella, feeling conspicuous but knowing she needed to finish Genevieve's makeup before the shoot, began searching the cupboards for a vase. She found one in the cabinet above the small refrigerator and stuffed the flowers into it before filling it with water from the sink. "I need to finish you up, Gennie." Bella turned to look at them.

Stefan was holding Genevieve's hands. "We'll just do it quickly. One or two takes. Then I'll take you to dinner at Riversong. You can order the veal or whatever you want. No worries about calories tonight."

Genevieve sighed, her shoulders relaxing. "Veal does sound good."

He hugged her quickly. "It's a movie, not brain surgery."

"Right. Just acting."

"I'll see you in a bit." He turned and walked toward the door. "Later, Bellalicious."

"Later."

After the door shut, Gennie burst into tears. Bella rushed to her. "What is it?"

"Oh, Bella, I think I'm falling in love with Stefan Spencer."

"What?"

"And I have no business falling in love with anyone, given how I am." She sniffed, resting her wet face on Bella's shoulder.

"Gennie, don't you think it's time you figured out what's wrong with you? I mean, like see someone. A therapist, maybe?"

"Maybe." But the way she said it, Bella knew she didn't believe there was anything to be done. "I just have to focus on the work and forget all this." Her tone had changed to being dismissive and final. Bella knew not to push her any further.

"All right, then, get in that chair and let me fix your face."

"Thank you," she whispered.

"For what?"

"For not pushing me."

They made eye contact then and it was understood between them that some things could not be said, even to one's best friend in the world. "You're welcome, my love."

Chapter Eighteen

SABRINA ARCHER OPENED THE DOOR to her room at the lodge a split second after Bella knocked. She held out her arms to Bella and the two women embraced. "It's good to see you, Bella. I've ordered some tea and pastries for us. They should be here in a moment." Behind them, near the window, were four suitcases, open, and half-packed. Several stacks of clothes were folded neatly on the bed. "I'm sorry for the mess. I'm checking out this afternoon."

"Where will you go?"

"Home. To Los Angeles. It'll take me several months to sort through Tiffany's affairs."

"Will you be all right? Financially, I mean."

She nodded. "I plan on selling all four of her houses and her art and jewelry and buying something modest with the proceeds. I can live nicely for what I'll make on them until I figure out what I want to do next. I thought about living on the Oregon coast for a couple of months, let the sea air help me gather myself."

"I think that sounds great. You deserve to take some time. But have you thought about managing another actress? You have the contacts, after all."

Sabrina's eyes clouded over. "I think I'm done with this business. It eats at a person's soul until there's nothing left of you but guts and blood and a thin shell called skin."

The valet came then with the tea service. While he was setting up and Sabrina was signing the bill, Bella heard her cell phone buzzing from her purse.

Picking it up, she saw it was a missed call from Peter. She'd call him later, she thought, not wanting to be rude to Sabrina. A second later, a text came through from Peter.

"Call me asap."

"What sort of tea would you like?" asked Sabrina.

"Green?" She smiled, thinking of Peter.

Sabrina poured them both a cup and motioned for them to sit in the easy chairs by the fireplace. "It's been such a long and sad week. I hated to leave town before they figured out what happened to her but now that we know I feel it's time to go. Nothing but bad memories here." She took a sip of tea. "I will never forgive myself for not hearing her that night. I go through it a hundred times a day. What if I'd just not used my ear plugs that night, would I have heard her screaming out? I guess I'll never know." She touched her scar. "It's the same as the night I got this scar. I keep going over it a hundred times and wishing I'd done something different than I did."

Bella didn't say anything, nodding in a way she hoped translated her sympathies. She didn't want to push the poor woman to talk about something traumatic if she didn't want to and yet she was curious. What had happened?

"Tiffany was driving the car, you know," said Sabrina, her eyes glazed over as if remembering.

"Was it a car accident then? I never knew."

"Tiffany never wanted me to talk about it, afraid if it got out that she was the one who drove the car that killed our parents and left me disfigured it would be bad for her image. Of course I agreed." She cocked her head to the side. "It was always about her career, which fed us both, I suppose."

"She relied on you and trusted you. I hope that gives you some small comfort."

Her eyes flickered. "I wish I could say yes, but I'm afraid not. I've wasted my life giving it to an ungrateful child whose carelessness cost me my dreams. I know it makes me sound terribly bitter but alas, it's where I'm at these days. They say one of the stages of grief is anger, do they not?"

It was the feeling of coming upon an accident, the inability to look away, the hungry need to see, that came over Bella then. What had

Sabrina's dreams been? And suddenly she knew. "Did you want to be an actress?"

"I did." She stood, smiling. "May I show you something?"

"Of course."

She went to one of the drawers in the bureau and yanked it open, pulling out a scrapbook. It was tattered and faded. Sabrina put it on the coffee table and opened it. The first page was a newspaper article. "Local girl wins talent contest." Was it a photo of a very young Tiffany?

As if she read her mind, Sabrina shook her head. "No, it's not Tiffany. That's me." She pointed to a child in the background of the photo, holding onto a woman's hand. "This is her with my mother." She turned the page. There was another article, this time about a high school play. The caption under the photo, "Sabrina Archer, freshman, knocks them dead in a production of *Oklahoma*."

"I was the talented one. She was always in my shadow, too shy to perform. Until the accident and then suddenly she comes up with this idea she wants to act. 'We should go to Los Angeles,' she told me. 'We have nothing here now that Mom and Dad are gone. What do we have to lose?' I told her, 'Nothing. I already lost it all.' But she continued her campaign for weeks. 'It's a chance for us to go somewhere that no one knows our sad story. And Beany,' that's what she called me back then, 'it's our only chance to get out of this town and make a life. If you had the talent, surely that means I do too. Twins share gifts.' Turns out she was right. She was just as good and she was still beautiful, not a freak like me."

Bella couldn't think what to say. How sorry she was for this woman who felt her life had been robbed. "I'm sorry, Sabrina."

Sabrina shook her head as if to dispel the cobwebs of memory. She closed her scrapbook. "Well, no matter. The future is ahead. I just need to figure out what's next for me."

Bella's cell phone buzzed again. "I'm so sorry. Someone wants to talk to me, obviously." She looked at the screen. It was a call with a 310 area code—Los Angeles. "Sabrina, this is a Los Angeles number. I should check my voicemail. It might be a work thing."

"Of course. Take your time. I've tons of time to kill before I leave for the airport."

Bella went to the window. Below, the news trucks and reporters still lurked about. What did they expect to find? Poor Tiffany was dead. It's not like she was about to come out the front door. Idiots.

She listened to the voicemail.

"Hey, Bella, this is Austin Blu. I left a message for Peter Ball as well. I don't know what made me remember this but I started thinking back on when I received the last call from the blackmailer and realized it was the morning *after* Tiffany Archer was killed, which was Friday. I checked my phone just to be sure and it said 8:27 a.m. on Friday. According to the papers she was already dead by then. I don't know if it matters at all in the investigation but I thought I'd mention it, especially given when I read about Rawley Hough being arrested this morning. I had one of my sound guys decode the message so I could hear it without the distortion and I could swear it's Tiffany Archer's voice on the message, which is impossible so then I think maybe I'm crazy? But you know, that's my thing, being able to decipher subtleties of tone and all. Anyway, yeah, well, I guess that's it. Call me back if you need more information."

Bella hung up the phone, still standing at the window, her hands damp from perspiration. *Could swear it's Tiffany Archer's voice.* Tiffany was dead by then. But Sabrina wasn't. They sounded just alike. Was Sabrina the blackmailer? What had Sabrina said the morning after the murder? *My sister can't even get money out of the ATM, let alone figure out how to extort money.* Had Sabrina made the call to Austin before she knew her sister was dead? No, that wasn't possible. Bella had received the call from Gennie with the news closer to 8:00 a.m. She turned to look at Sabrina, feeling her heart pounding between her ears. Was Sabrina thinking only of money hours after getting the news of her sister? Or was Rawley Hough telling the truth? Had he raped her but left her alive? Was it possible for a sister to do the unthinkable?

She typed with shaking hands to Peter. "Got voicemail from Blu. With Sabrina now."

"Everything all right?" asked Sabrina.

"Yes, just Ben wanting to know when I'm coming home. We're so relieved, you know, that he's in the clear. I'm just texting that I'm on my way home after our visit."

Get her to confess. Why this thought came to her next she could not have said. *Get her to confess.* But it was there nonetheless. Prove who did this once and for all. *Screw the haters.* She and Tiffany had agreed the day before she was killed. Yes, she was a flawed woman, like we all are, thought Bella. Regardless, she didn't deserve to die. Each day was a battle against her demons. Who is to say she wouldn't have fought them down had she lived? Had her last thought been the knowledge that her sister wanted her dead? Was it a fight? Had Tiffany gone to her after the visit from Rawley and confronted her? Had she threatened to expose Sabrina? Surely it couldn't have been planned? All these thoughts were roaring in her mind, a jumble of tossed thoughts. And then Peter's voice in her head—*get her to talk.*

She opened the photo application on her phone, changed it to the recording setting and pushed the "on" button. Then she dropped it in the pocket of her sweater.

"You're white as a ghost." Sabrina was watching her carefully. "Come sit."

Bella did so and picked up her cup of tea, trying not to spill it from the shaking in her hands.

"I thought you said it was a Los Angeles number that called." Sabrina's gaze was unflinching, watchful. Suspicious? Yes, suspicious. *Get it together*, thought Bella. *Stay calm.*

"Did I? I must have been looking at the number below. I think Stefan called me yesterday—it was probably his number." *Talk about something that connects you.* "Sabrina, I feel terrible about everything you've just told me. I know how it is to feel like everyone you love is gone. I lost my mother when I was only sixteen, just like you and Tiffany. And, of course, I'm sure you remember what happened to my little niece and her mother. Talking like this brings it all back." She paused, acting as if she just thought of it. "Matter of fact, I could use a drink. Care to join me?" She went to the mini bar and pulled out two vodka bottles. "How does a screwdriver sound?" *Screw the haters.*

"You know, why not?" asked Sabrina. Her face had relaxed back into its usual placid expression. "As callous as it might sound, I'm ready to embrace a new life. Tiffany-free. Which means I can have a drink every once in a while."

"Of course you're ready to embrace a new life. Who could blame you? You've had to babysit your sister for so many years. None of us knew how you did it." Bella glanced behind her. Sabrina had opened the scrapbook and was tracing her finger over the photo in the newspaper article. Bella poured both vodkas into one of the two glasses sitting on the minibar and added orange juice. Into the other she poured only orange juice. She handed the one with vodka to Sabrina.

Sabrina took a sip. "Strong."

"Too strong?"

"Heck no. I have a car to take me to the airport. Might as well enjoy your company and this drink without worry. I'll have enough of those when I get back." She drank from the glass again. "Doesn't taste as strong with the second sip." Sabrina closed the scrapbook and leaned back in her chair, staring at the ceiling. "You know, my mother was the one who asked Tiffany to drive that night. I'd wanted to but our mother insisted Tiffany be the one because I'd had all the spotlight that night and she was always worried about poor, sensitive little Tiffany's feelings." She took another sip of her drink. "It used to disgust me, the way she coddled her."

"I can understand that. Must have been so hard for you."

"It really was. Thank you for saying that. It feels good to talk about it."

"You know what I can't figure out is how someone as unable to function without you figured out how to blackmail those idiots. Not that I blame her for doing it. Those guys deserved everything they got from her. I'm just sorry, of course, that Rawley Hough killed her over it. I mean, what was it to him? A little cash he could probably easily afford to give her. No reason to give up his life for it. But I'm seriously impressed with our little Tiffany. I never knew she had it in her. The scheme was so complicated and well thought out. And the fact that she had the balls to actually steal the client list from Ms. Zinn? Genius and major guts. Don't you think?"

Sabrina's glass was empty. The drink had not seemed to relax her. Instead she was sitting forward in her chair now, twitching her foot and rocking back and forth slightly. Her eyes were piercing. "Yes, it is hard to believe." She placed her hands on her knees. "How about another drink? That one went down very easy."

"Sure. Same?"

Sabrina nodded. "Only make it a double."

Gladly, thought Bella.

"You know what I find odd, though." Bella handed Sabrina the drink. "Is that the client list book is still missing. Where do you think she hid it?"

Sabrina pulled on her ponytail, her eyes darting to her handbag next to the suitcases and then back to her drink. She shifted in her chair. She took another sip of her screwdriver. "It is odd. Guess it doesn't matter now. Excuse me a moment. I need to use the restroom. Then, let's order lunch from room service. Something bad for us. The menu's on the bedside table there."

As soon as the bathroom door closed, Bella jumped from her chair and bolted to the handbag on the floor. Kneeling, she opened it and there, nestled next to a wallet and a Kindle was a black leather book. It had to be the client book. Sabrina was the blackmailer. Had she also killed her sister?

"Find what you were looking for?"

Bella, heart pounding, came to her feet and turned toward Sabrina. She was standing five feet from her, aiming a gun right at the middle of her chest.

Bella took in a deep breath and held up her hands. "Hey now, no reason to get crazy. I won't tell a soul."

"Why is it I don't believe that?" She motioned toward the chair with the gun. "Sit, while I think what to do with you."

Sabrina paced in front of the chair, the gun pointed at Bella. "Did you really think Tiffany was smart enough to blackmail those guys? It was her fault we were broke in the first place, putting it all up her nose as fast as we could make it. I had to swoop in and figure out what to do, how to save us from ruin. She'd told me Zinn kept all her client names in a little black book on her desk, like something out of a bad movie, and I started thinking about it—couldn't stop thinking about it—how this was the answer. I just needed to get my hands on that book and pick a few men who would pay for my silence. So I tagged along one night over to Jocelyn's house and when they snuck into the kitchen to get high, like I didn't know what they were up to, I took advantage of the fact they were totally out of it and snuck into her office. The book was on the desk, plain as day. I figured it was a sign from the universe or something. Boom—my plan was in action. And when Tiffany found out, was she grateful to me? No, the little bitch had the nerve to lie to me that Hough had beaten and raped her over it when God only knows she probably welcomed him into her bed like she did every other man in town. Oh, she loved the married ones. She had that in common with you, I guess. And meanwhile, here I am chaste and pure, uncomplaining when no man will come near me and my horrid face. No man has ever touched me, Bella. Not one."

Bella kept quiet, hoping Sabrina would continue. She did, her eyes ablaze, the words coming fast with little pause between sentences.

"And then that night I woke up and felt like something was wrong—twins do that, you know—so I went to check on her. I found her curled up in the corner of her room, crying. 'Hough came looking for that goddamn book and then he raped me for punishment when he couldn't find it,' is what she said. 'He thinks it's me doing the blackmailing. Do you realize what you've done?' I asked her how she knew and she said the minute Hough accused her of blackmailing her that she realized it had to be me who'd taken Jocelyn's book. She added that I always underestimate her, which isn't true. She always lets me down. I told her that too. I said, 'If you weren't always so out of it with booze and pills we wouldn't be in this mess.' I tried to explain to her that I only did it for her own good since she blew all our money. I told her it was just like it always was—me cleaning up her mess. Well, that made her go crazy. Like certifiable, screaming that I'd gotten her raped and that she never wanted to see me again and that I was the devil. After all I'd done, this is what she says to me? She had the nerve to tell me it was *her* money, she'd earned it and it was hers to lose and I was nothing but a leech. Then she lunged at me. Can you believe that? She came after me. What was I to do but defend myself? We started fighting like when we were kids, rolling around on the ground like a couple of animals. I didn't mean to kill her but my God she wouldn't stop screaming." She paused, tilting her head to the side and her voice was higher-pitched than the moment before, like a plaintive child's. "I'm the victim here. Can't you see that? My mother never could. No matter what I did. It was always Tiffany this and Tiffany that. I was the one who deserved the life she had. Not her. It was not supposed to be her."

Outside came the sound of sirens. Peter had gotten her text and Austin's voicemail. He'd figured it out as well. They were on the way.

Sabrina went to the window. She muttered an expletive and turned back to Bella. "Get up."

There was pounding on the door. "Open up, Sabrina." It was Peter's voice.

Sabrina yanked Bella to her feet. She put the barrel of the gun into the small of Bella's back. "March."

At the door, they stopped. "I have Bella at gunpoint. Let me out of here or she gets it."

Peter's voice was soothing. "No reason to get carried away. We just want to talk to you, that's all."

"Bullshit, I know what you want. Move out of the doorway." She pulled Bella close to her body, holding the gun at her neck now. "Open the door, Bella. Nice and slow."

Bella inched open the door. "Peter, don't shoot. She has a gun on me." She was surprised how calm she sounded. Just keep thinking clearly and calmly, she thought. As long as no one made any sudden moves she might get out of this alive.

Peter and Fred stood in the hallway with their guns pointed at the door. Fred's chest was moving up and down and his forehead glistened with sweat. Peter's clear green eyes were sharp and unblinking. "Let her go, Sabrina," he said.

"Get on the elevator," Sabrina hissed into her ear. "We're going to the roof."

The roof? She'd told Sabrina she was afraid of heights. And she remembered.

Bella couldn't breathe. She gasped for air. Her legs felt as if they might collapse under her. But it didn't matter. Sabrina, probably with adrenaline coursing through her, seemed almost to carry her.

Her daddy had carried her like a sack of potatoes to the roof. Her mother's cries were in the background. "Drake, call the police." Her voice was high-pitched. It didn't sound like her mother. Her voice was like a cold blue wave through the air.

They were at the elevator now. "Don't come any closer," Sabrina said to the men, pushing the gun harder into Bella's neck.

Bella heard a cry of pain. It was her own, she realized. She tried to breathe but it felt as if her windpipe was being crushed. Sabrina shoved her into the elevator and punched the rooftop button. They went up, first to the seventh floor, then the eighth and finally to the button labeled Rooftop Terrace. The doors opened and Sabrina dragged her outside. It was raining; a puddle had formed where the floor dipped slightly and Bella stepped in it. Dampness soaked through her shoes and into her socks. Then they were on the edge of the building. There was a lip and a safety fence. Below, the news people were pointing upward, perhaps calling out to one another.

Everything tilted and swirled. Bella sobbed. She had begged silently when he held her over the edge of the building. *No, no, no, Daddy. I'll be good. Please don't drop me.*

Sabrina's voice near her ear was low and menacing. "You wrecked everything for me." She pushed her against the cold metal of the fence. "All I wanted was to drive that night. I never got one thing I wanted because of you. I should be the star instead of a freak. And now you're going to give the crowd what they want. You're going to jump, Tiffany."

It was raining that day too. She screamed as he dangled her over the crowd, "Mommy, mommy, mommy. Come save me," and the rain had been in her mouth and the smell of her daddy's musty and smoke-infested clothes in her nose. Would she go to heaven to be with Jesus like her grandmother had? Would Grammie be there to greet her?

"Tiffany, climb up the fence, slide your legs over and I'll just give you a little push. It'll be over so quickly."

Bella heard shouting. Was it Drake? Had he come to rescue her? She slid her eyes to the noise. It was Peter and Fred. Below there was the sound of more sirens.

Sirens. The good guys were coming. They would rescue her so she wouldn't have to go to heaven. She could stay with Mommy and Drake.

Peter's voice reached her, loud but still coaxing. "Sabrina, let her go. We can talk things through. Work a deal."

The gun was at her temple now. "Climb up the fence, Tiffany. That's a good girl." She said it like she was encouraging a child down a slide. Bella grasped the top rung of the fence with both hands and put one foot onto the bottom rung. Could she push backward and knock her captor to the ground?

Drake had grabbed them both from behind and pulled them both to safety. Drake, her big brother. He always knew what to do. He always came for her.

Kick the gun out of her hand.

Whose voice was this? It was a woman. Hushed but firm. Mommy.

Do it suddenly. Act like you're going over but suddenly change direction and swing your leg out and knock the gun from her hand.

"Jump, Tiffany. You can do it." Sabrina's breath smelled of alcohol and was sickly sweet from the orange juice.

Honey, you're so strong now. Not like when you were little. You don't have to be afraid any longer.

"Sabrina, put down the gun. We can talk this over." Peter again. He sounded closer now.

Then, she thought, *Ben*. His laughing eyes. The way he always talked about her like she could do anything she wanted. How he turned every negative comment around on her to point out how wonderful she was. And this was love, she thought, how the other person made you feel about yourself.

And Gennie. The sweetness of their friendship was an ache in her chest.

And Annie and Alder. And the baby coming. The family she and Drake both so desperately needed and wanted after Chloe and Esther left them.

And Drake. Her brother who had and would do anything for her.

Draw on that, Bella. You have so much to live for.

And her dreams. They were all within her grasp. If only she had the chance to pursue them. If she escaped this, she would stare fear down.

She had both feet on the bottom rung now. Gripping the top railing with both hands, and using the strength of her core, all those planks and sit-ups over the years, like steel bands around her middle. She took in a deep breath and muttered, "Not today, bitch." She swung her left leg high and aimed toward the gun in Sabrina's hands. It went off as it flew through the air, landing several feet from them. The force of the kick caused Bella to fall forward, landing on all fours. By that time Peter and Fred were upon them. Peter tackled Sabrina to the ground while Fred held the gun on her. Behind them, another group of armed police officers were coming up the stairs. Peter handed a subdued Sabrina over to them and came to help Bella to her feet.

"Peter, I got her to confess and it's all on tape." She pulled out her cell phone, shouting, the adrenaline continuing to rush through her body. "Do you see this? On record the whole time."

He took the phone, shaking his head as if in disbelief. "Holy crap, Bella, you ought to think about going into police work."

"I've had just about enough of this line of work, thank you very much. Plus, I have a business to start." If she could face down a psychopath on the roof of a building, surely she could start the business she'd dreamed of all her life.

"And a wedding to plan."

She groaned and rolled her eyes. "Oh, God. The wedding. Is it too late to jump?"

Peter laughed. "There's something wrong with you. You know that, right?"

She grinned. "Totally." Letting out a yelp, she lunged towards him and hugged him quickly before stepping back and sweeping her arms in a wide circle to indicate the world around them. "Holy shit, it's great to be alive."

"It most certainly is."

* * *

Ben was waiting for her in the lodge's lobby when she and Peter came out of the elevator. He held open his arms and she ran toward him, not caring that she probably looked like the last scene of a bad television movie. He pulled her up into his arms and held her tightly against his chest. "I didn't know if you were going to make it," he whispered in her ear.

"Come on, now. I'm small but scrappy. You know that." She looked into his eyes. "Is it time for wine yet?"

"I'd say you earned the good stuff tonight."

In the car, they drove in silence, Bella holding Ben's hand, running her fingers through the soft hair on his forearm. Rain made a steady pitter patter on the roof and the windshield wipers swayed in a steady rhythm. The car's heater was warm on her feet.

"Bella, are you sure you don't want a wedding?"

She turned to look at him. "Why are you asking me?"

"Well, I just don't want it to be my agenda. I was the one left at the proverbial altar, not you. You sure you don't want a wedding?"

"I can think of nothing worse. All those people looking at us. And us dressed up in monkey suits."

"I think it's just the guy who wears a monkey suit."

"Well, a dress then. Do you know how long it takes to find a dress? It's like a month-long process and you have to go to all these pretentious shops and try on a zillion of them before you find one decent one and then there are fittings and tuckings and other super boring stuff."

"Tuckings?"

She waved her hand in a dismissive gesture, grinning. "Whatever. You know what I mean."

"But every girl wants to wear a wedding dress. Don't they?" He took his eyes from the road for an instant and she saw he was earnest in his question. Her heart fluttered and expanded. She turned to look out the window. They were driving across the valley now. It was dark with a few yellow lights of houses in the distant fields. "Ben, the truth is I don't want a wedding because my mother isn't here. It hurts too much. Especially the finding the dress part."

He brought her hand to his lips and kissed the knuckle of her index finger softly. "Sweetheart, I'm sorry."

"The sad thing is I know Gennie wants to take me shopping for the dress and plan a shower and every detail of the wedding, like my mother would have. And I just want to marry you. Just us. Without anything I can attach pain to. Do you understand?"

"Five-hundred percent." He squeezed her hand. "But you need to tell Gennie tonight, not later. She's going to be crushed but it will be much worse if we elope without her knowing. Annie says she's headed to the house now."

"You're right. Of course. I'll do it tonight." She turned to look at his profile. How had this man who understood something as subtle as this particular dynamic between women appeared so suddenly in her life? It should not be questioned, she thought, just welcomed with gratitude. "I love you, Benjamin Fleck. This is all I can think to say."

He grinned at her, before bringing her hand to his mouth once again and keeping it against his lips as he answered. "I love you, too. And this is all we need to say."

* * *

That night, after Bella was fussed over by Annie, called "badass" by Alder, and given a large glass of one of his finest bottles of Washington wine by Drake, she took Gennie's hand and led her into the sitting room. They sat on the hearth of the stone fireplace, holding glasses of red wine in one hand and clasping one another's hands in the other. Indicating the glass, Bella raised her eyebrows. "So I have to almost get killed for you to risk staining your teeth?"

Gennie smiled but unshed tears made her eyes glassy. "Oh, Bella, I'm so grateful you're all right. If anything happened to you, well, I don't know if I could get through it. You're family to me."

"I know. Me too." She leaned her head on Gennie's shoulder. "Listen, about the wedding."

"Yeah?" Gennie's voice sounded wary, as if she knew what was coming.

"Ben and I want to go to Vegas. Just the two of us."

Gennie sat up straighter, dropping Bella's hand and scooting away several inches to look at her face. "But why? I don't understand why."

Bella took a deep breath. "Because my mother's dead."

Gennie's eyes filled; several tears escaped from the corners of her eyes and ran untethered down her perfect cheeks. "Oh, Bella. Yes, I understand."

"You do?"

"I do." And that was it.

They hugged, in soundless agreement that sometimes nothing more needed to be said between two people who loved one another, who understood one another. Because despite their flaws and demons and expectations that wanted to pull their love asunder, they understood this was not the way of true friendship. No, it grew between the silences, through all the words unsaid, all the ways love could not be expressed except in silent acceptance of the other.

Chapter Nineteen

THE DAY BEFORE THANKSGIVING Bella and Ben sat at the counter of Amanda's newly opened diner. Fred, sitting two seats from them, nibbled on a BLT on wheat and sipped coffee as he told them of his recent transfer over to the Echo Grove police force. "Darnedest thing. From what I can piece together, Peter Ball made some phone calls and next thing I know I'm being called in for an interview."

The diner was cozy, only a dozen tables plus the counter and decorated in shades of blue. The menu was simple: traditional breakfasts served all day and soups and sandwiches starting at eleven. The clientele had been steadily growing, helped enormously by the movie crew, still filming for another two weeks after a short break for the Thanksgiving holiday.

Amanda set a plate of blueberry pancakes in front of Bella and a Denver omelet in front of Ben. "I liked it better when Fred worked out here," she said. "Nothing ever happens in River Valley. Well, I guess that's not true but, you know, for the most part we don't have anything too dangerous, and now I'll be worried about you all the time."

Fred pushed aside his plate, having eaten everything but the crusts. "Honey, it's nothing to worry about. I'm still a small town cop. Not much happens in Echo Grove either."

Bella pointed her fork at Fred. "I, for one, am thrilled to know they'll get an honest cop in Echo Grove considering what Ben went through."

"Amen to that," said Ben.

"You guys really eloped?" asked Amanda.

"Yep," said Bella, sliding her eyes over to her new husband. Would she ever stop feeling so utterly smitten with this man?

Fred wriggled his finger at them as if they were in trouble. "And you two don't look one bit guilty for denying your friends and family the pleasure of a wedding."

"That's because we aren't," said Ben before taking a large bite of omelet. "This is really good, Amanda."

Amanda lowered her voice to just above a whisper. "Don't tell anyone but I hired my cousin to cook for us. He used to cook in prison."

"Really?" asked Bella, intrigued. "What was he in for?"

"Insider trading." Amanda said this like it was a dreaded disease. "He took the fall for his boss."

"That's terrible," said Ben, shuddering. "How long was his sentence?"

"Five years. But he learned how to cook really well in there and now he's here for a second chance," said Amanda, still talking just above a whisper.

"River Valley's the place for that," said Bella.

"Something about the healing powers of the river, according to Annie," said Ben.

"The river will teach you your name, Amanda. Tell your cousin the minute it warms up in the late spring to jump in head first," said Bella.

Amanda put her hands on the counter. What was this? A ring? "Wait a minute, did you guys get engaged?" asked Bella.

Fred grinned; Amanda blushed. "Fred asked me last night under the stars. We haven't told anyone yet."

"I guess this marriage thing is contagious," said Ben, slapping Fred on the back. "Congratulations."

"Maybe the river makes people fall in love too." Bella laughed and stole a bite of Ben's omelet.

"Or the stars," said Amanda.

They spoke for a moment about wedding plans, Bella and Ben assuring them that eloping was the way to go if they could possibly get away with it.

"You've never met my mother if you think that's even close to a possibility," said Fred.

"Same with mine," said Amanda. "That's why we're keeping it to ourselves for a while before all the madness starts."

My mother. Ben squeezed her knee under the counter. He understood.

"I hear from Mike you guys are full-force ahead on your business," said Fred.

"That's right," nodded Ben. "Bella's going to be famous. We have the business plan of all business plans."

"Being married to an MBA is so hot," said Bella, teasing.

"Being married to a makeup mogul is so hot." He leaned over and kissed her lightly on the mouth. "You taste like blueberries." He whispered this in her ear, causing her to shiver with desire. They should finish up lunch and head home for an afternoon nap.

"What're you naming it, Bella?" asked Amanda, pouring more coffee into Ben's cup.

"Bellalicious."

"Sounds delicious," said Amanda, her innocent eyes wide.

Fred glanced at his watch. "Shoot, I've got to get back to work. I'm still on duty here in River Valley for another week and who knows, we might have another big crime."

They said goodbye and congratulations once again before Bella happily took another bite of pancake. *Bellalicious.* She couldn't wait to tell Stefan tomorrow at Annie and Drake's Thanksgiving dinner. Gennie had already given her blessing on the name. She'd actually flushed with pleasure when Bella had told her. She couldn't help but think it had something to do with the fact that Stefan was the originator.

When Amanda left the counter to tend to another customer, Bella leaned close to Ben. "I'm not giving up hope on Stefan and Gennie. You know that, right?"

"I would expect nothing less from my blushing bride." His eyes were laughing as he leaned over to kiss her. *Laughing eyes.* Her husband had laughing eyes. And there were blueberry pancakes to eat and the possibility of Gennie and Stefan falling in love and her gang of misfits joining together in a feast tomorrow and babies and kissing in the rain and honorable work. All of these small and large joys that were love must be gathered close, experienced fully, knowing all the while they were fleeting and elusive. And in that moment she understood it was only this, only love that offered meaning and even possible redemption in a world too often dark, too often difficult. Just this. Just love.

* * *

"You did what?" asked Annie, her eyes as angry and shocked as Bella had ever seen them. She slid forward on her chair, almost knocking over a bowl of yams. "Please tell me I didn't hear you right."

Alder shook his head, sounding resigned to the inevitability of fate. "They eloped." Sitting next to Bella at the long table filled with all their friends, he leaned close enough so only she could hear. "You're in so much trouble."

"Don't sound so happy about it," she whispered back.

Linus, sitting on the other end of the long table, had both of his hands covering his mouth. "Oh, sweetie, what have you done?"

"But I was going to walk you down the aisle," said Drake, looking positively mournful.

"And a dress?" said Annie. "Didn't you want a dress?"

"Hey, it was my idea," said Ben, putting his hand up in protest. "Don't blame Bella."

"Bullshit," said Annie, her eyes wild, scanning the table as if for confirmation. "Everybody knows the woman makes the decision."

"Well, that's not always true," said Tommy. "I decided what kind of wedding we had."

Linus guffawed. "Yeah, but you're not a normal straight guy and Lee could care less about girly stuff."

Lee scowled at him. "That's not true."

"Honey, it kind of is," said Tommy.

"Well, we're staying out of this anyway," said Lee, with a pointed look back at her husband.

"Right. Of course," said Tommy.

Annie was looking almost accusingly at the silent Gennie. "Did you know about this?"

"I'm sorry, Annie. But it was what Bella wanted." Gennie moved her wineglass in a circle, her gaze fixed downward and her voice soft. "Sometimes motherless girls can't pick a wedding dress without pain ripping the whole thing to shreds."

The table went quiet. Finally, Drake reached out across the table and took Bella's hand. "Congratulations." He looked at Ben. "Welcome to the family."

Stefan, sitting next to Gennie, put his arm around the back of her chair. "Maybe we could have a reception. You know, just a party or something."

Her gaze on Gennie, Bella nodded. "That would be wonderful."

Ellen, sitting next to Verle, raised her glass. "Here's to the happy couple."

Verle, nodding vigorously, raised his glass as well. "Mazel tov." Everyone raised their glasses and toasted them. She looked over at Ben, who winked at her.

"If you're all so hellfire determined to have a wedding to plan, Verle and I have decided to go ahead and get hitched." Ellen straightened her dessert fork and sniffed. "So you know, feel free to go crazy on the planning."

"Badass, Momo," said Alder.

Ellie-Rose clapped her hands together. "Yay, Momo."

"You don't even know what we're talking about, Munchkin," said Alder, shaking his head and laughing.

"Thank you, children," said Ellen before looking over at Tommy and Lee. They were staring at her as if she were a stranger that had suddenly come in from the street to join them for dinner. "And I want a big wedding. Huge. Pulling out all the stops." She took a large sip of wine. "What? You two can afford it."

Tommy laughed. "It's not that. Whatever you want, Ellen, I'll give you. We're just surprised."

"Good." She turned to look at Linus and then Gennie. "Feel free to take over the planning if you're so inclined. I'll be much too busy preparing for the big day to bother with all the details. I mean, I *am* almost seventy-five. I may get a little Botox before the big day."

"Do you even know what Botox is?" asked Lee.

"Botulism injected into your skin," said Alder, matter-of-factly.

"You're not getting Botox," said Lee. "It's ridiculous."

"I may or I may not," said Ellen.

"I'm sending you on a honeymoon," said Drake. "Wherever you want to go."

"I've always wanted to go to France," said Verle, who had methodically worked his way through a heaping plate of food, never ceasing except during the toast to Bella and Ben. "I live for bread and cheese, you know."

"Done," said Drake.

"I do not think it's a good idea for you two to go to a foreign country alone at your ages," said Lee. "Absolutely not."

"You're not the boss of me," said Ellen.

"We'll talk about this later," said Lee.

"I'm excited to help plan your wedding, Ellen. I'll get my planner on it right away," said Gennie, already typing something into her phone.

"I don't think so, Missy," said Linus. "I'm doing the planning."

Gennie looked over at him and put up her hands. "Of course. Just let me know if you need anything."

Stefan leaned close to Gennie, whispering something in her ear that made her blush. Bella wondered what he'd said. What was going on between them?

"Bella, could I throw you guys a party? At my house in Malibu," said Gennie. "Nothing fancy. Just however you want it. You can all come and stay at my house. Enjoy the beach."

"Like a big barbeque type of party with tequila shots and chips and guacamole?" asked Bella, blowing her friend a kiss. "And can we have cake? White with raspberry filling?"

Stefan laughed and slapped the table. "That's the spirit, Bellalicious."

"I had my toast prepared and everything," said Annie, sniffing.

"You can give it at the party," said Drake, with an indulgent look at his pregnant wife.

"Fine," said Annie, smiling in her gentle way. "But it won't be the same."

"I'm sorry, Annie. But maybe this will make it up to you." Bella cleared her throat. "We have another announcement."

"Oh God, don't tell me you're not knocked up too?" said Alder.

"Alder!" said Annie. "Completely inappropriate." She turned to Bella, appearing almost hopeful. "That's not it, is it?"

"No, I'm not knocked up. But Ben and I are moving to River Valley. We've bought Lee's house."

"And I'm quitting my job and opening a fly-fishing shop." Ben said it like it was nothing important.

The room, for the second time that night, went silent.

"Cool," said Alder, breaking the tension.

"Yeah, cool," said Stefan. "Can I invest?"

"Dude. Totally," said Ben. "What the hell? Really?"

"I love fly-fishing," said Stefan.

"Can I work there when I get older?" asked Alder.

"Sure." Ben paused, lifting his glass toward the two of them. "You guys get me."

"You sure about this?" asked Drake.

Ben nodded, glancing at Bella. "Life's short and unpredictable. If the last couple of months have taught me anything, it's that."

"Well, maybe keep your job for a while longer," said Lee, with a worried nod of her head. "Just until you get the shop established."

"That's smart," said Ellen, mirroring Lee's expression. "Best to be cautious."

And the room erupted in laughter.

* * *

After dinner Bella stood with Drake on the deck. The temperature had dropped into the 30s and the forecast called for snow. The night sky was inky black. "My sister. Married. Hard to believe." Drake lit a cigar and the unique and pungent scent filled the air. "You realize Annie's going to cry over this for several more days. It's the pregnancy hormones. She's a mess."

She laughed, thinking of the reception and dress in her future for the supposedly casual affair. There was no way that was happening if Gennie and her party-planner-on-steroids were in charge. "She'll have her revenge."

"I'm glad for you, Bella. I love Ben like a brother. You know that. And I'm proud of you. Beyond proud."

"Speaking of which, there's something I want to talk to you about." She hesitated, nervous to say it out loud. From the yard she heard a rustling. It was the doe, her soft brown eyes glimmering in the light from deck. She pointed at the doe and Drake murmured something under his breath she couldn't decipher. A sudden gust of wind came, blowing Bella's curls.

"I miss Mom. Every day." She slipped her hand into Drake's like she had when they were children.

"Me too." He squeezed her hand.

"Someday we'll see her again. All of them. There'll be rose gardens for you and Mom to tend for eternity."

"I want to believe that so very much."

They stood in silence then watching the doe. She remained near the rose garden, steadfast in her gaze. The clouds parted, suddenly, revealing a slender window of stars. Bella took in a deep breath, startled by their unexpected brilliance. Anything was possible if the universe made such a thing as this, she reminded herself.

"I'm ready to start my makeup line. Ben helped me with the business plan. Before I left Los Angeles I found the chemists to do it. They're willing to do it how I want—no preservatives and with natural ingredients and all that. Mike's agreed to help me build a factory where the mill was in exchange for providing jobs for his displaced workers. Gennie said she'd be the face of the product and wants to invest as an equal partner but I'd need the capital in order to match her contribution equally."

"Bella, you know I'll invest. I've told you that for years. What good is my money if I can't do something for people I care about?"

"What if it flops?"

"Gennie's face? Your talent? I don't think so."

"Thanks for always being here for me. I don't say it enough. I love you."

"Jeez, Bella, you're getting soft on me." But his voice was strangled as if he was fighting back tears. "I love you too, kid." He squeezed her hand. "Make it rain, Bella Webber. Make it rain."

Such a thing as this. Surely anything was possible.

The doe moved her head toward the forest as if someone called to her. Then, she bounded across the yard and was swallowed by the thicket of trees.

A bright star, larger than the others, twinkled. "Coming in?" asked Drake.

"No, I'll stay with the stars for a while longer."

"Don't linger too long. It's cold."

"You're so bossy."

"I know. I'm sorry."

"Don't be."

After he was gone, she raised her fingertips to the shards of scattered light. They were made just for her. Of this she was certain. One by one she plucked them from the inky sky, gathering them inside her body until she was satiated and lustrous and courageous and so effervescent the pain and fear diminished to dormancy. Yet, even as the stars filled her they regenerated, perhaps for someone else who stood and watched, who needed and yearned to be nourished with something brighter and grander than their own timorous and desolate heart. And although she could not see it now in this night of silver and black, she knew the currents of the river flowed below her in their undaunted drift to the tumultuous sea and gurgled her name, ever vigilant lest she forget.

THE END

Preview of
Caramel and Magnolias
by Tess Thompson

PROLOGUE

THE WIND OFF THE PACIFIC OCEAN brought the smell of seaweed and saltwater, everything encased in the constant damp and gray so that it seeped in through skin and flesh to bone, impervious to fleece or knit or rain gear. Alicia Johnson trudged across the Legley Bay High School campus on the way to gym class, the September drizzle on her cheeks and hands, her rain hood pulled over her head. She was coming from math class, thinking about the new teacher, Jack Ball, of the angry scars she'd spotted on his wrists. What had made him sad enough to attempt such a thing? Despite all her angst and disappointment, Alicia wanted to live. That above all. To stay alive and somehow make it through to a life outside of the small Oregon coastal town of Legley Bay that was nothing but the smell of fish and sea air that made houses, cars, and people gray before their time. Yes, this was the best she could hope for. And hoping kept her going despite failing grades and worry over her mother and the endless cycle of classes and her job at the minimart after school.

Alicia glanced up from beneath her hood. There was a woman just outside the metal gates, leaning against the fender of a white, four-door Mercedes, holding a bottle of water like a beer, as if she were at a tailgate party. The woman had blue eyes, so light they reminded Alicia of ice cubes, encircled by purple glasses. Unusual color, Alicia thought. And she was short, almost square, and wore a long, black coat and thick-soled shoes, the kind nurses might wear, only brown instead of white. Her hair was short and spiky, standing up despite the rain in a way that indicated wealth. Not from around here, Alicia thought. Anyone could see that.

The woman nodded and their eyes locked, as if they knew one another. Alicia felt the cold, more so than the moment before. Shivering, she pulled the zipper of her raincoat higher, averting her gaze to the muddy path between the main part of the high school campus and the gymnasium.

Later, in the locker room after gym class, Alicia pulled socks over damp feet. Lola was at the mirror, applying blue eyeliner.

"Hey," said Lola, catching her eye in the mirror's reflection.

"Hey," said Alicia, polite but not too friendly. Lola was the type of girl to attach herself to anyone who was kind to her. Like a puppy that followed you home, Alicia often thought. If she were too kind, she'd never be able to get rid of her. Lonely girls recognized one another. Regardless, she couldn't be seen with Lola. It might mean hazing and teasing, torturous taunts in the hallways and maybe even shoving or punching after school. No, it was better to live on the fringe, on the sidelines, skirting between classes, invisible and unknown, rather than caring whether you had friends or not.

"You wanna hit DQ after school?" Lola turned back to the mirror and put a thick coat of mascara on her lashes. "I'm supposed to be on a diet but life's short, right?" She laughed, her lips pulling up to show her gums, and snorted. Alicia turned away. She'd noticed Lola had gained a lot of weight this year. But so had a lot of girls. It happened. Alicia was skinny and never thought much about what she ate but her mother was always on a diet, living on cigarettes and diet soda.

"Can't. Have to work," said Alicia.

"You still at the minimart?"

"Yep." Alicia grabbed her sweatshirt and pulled it over her head.

"Well, tomorrow, maybe? I've got a new car. A Mustang." Alicia knew about the car. She'd heard Lola telling anyone who would listen about it.

"Where you working?" asked Alicia. It must be better than her minimum wage job if Lola could afford a Mustang, even if it was used.

"Nowhere. Nothing around."

"How'd you get the money for your car?" Alicia asked, working on a tangle in her hair with the brush she kept in her backpack. Lola's mother worked down at the Pig-n-Pancake near the entrance to Highway 101 and they lived in an apartment above some old man's house down a long, dirt road.

Lola turned to Alicia, her eyes darting back and forth. "Why? You need money?"

"Thinking about going to masseuse school."

Lola's eyes widened. There was a smear of mascara under her left eyebrow. "You mean drop out of school?"

"I hate it here," Alicia said, surprised by her sudden honesty and the lump at the back of her throat. "Just trying to stay under the radar until I can get out."

Lola joined her on the bench. "You have a plan?" She smelled of cherry lip-gloss.

"Not really. Costs ten grand," said Alicia. "I researched it on the Internet. It's probably just a dream for other people, not someone like me."

Lola glanced behind them. The locker room was nearly empty. "Meet me after school. I'll tell you about a way to get some money." She paused, lowering her voice. "But you have to swear to keep it a secret."

* * *

Later that night she was on the couch with her mother watching her mother's favorite show about rich women who were always fighting with one another. The rain was a steady drum on the tin roof of their mobile home. "You wanna diet pop, Mom?" she said.

"That'd be nice. Thanks, baby," said Jo, playing with a strand of her long, drab hair, her eyes fixed on the television. Jo wore sweats and a loose T-shirt, standard uniform for her one day off from the bar. Alicia recorded all her favorite shows during the week and Jo watched them on her day off, one after the other.

Alicia went to the kitchen and opened the refrigerator. There wasn't much in it, just a half case of diet cola, the generic kind they bought at Walmart, a carton of nonfat milk, and ketchup, mustard, and mayonnaise in the side door. Leftover cardboard boxes were stacked on the counter from dinner. On Tuesdays Alicia always brought them dinner from the minimart - a corndog for her sister Misty, a hamburger for her mother, and chicken strips for herself. They shared a dozen Jojo's between them, fried potatoes that only places like the minimart and deli counters at grocery stores sold. According to Misty, no matter where you bought them, they always tasted the same. "Some kind of secret molecular creation by scientists in plastic suits and face masks," Misty had said tonight, laughing, as she grabbed two more on her way out to her Math Club meeting at school.

Alicia laughed too. "You're such a show-off."

"These fabricated potatoes will probably kill us yet, but what a way to go," Misty added before the door closed behind her, causing the trailer to shudder.

Alicia grabbed two sodas and closed the refrigerator door. At the doorway, she paused. Something was dripping. Her eyes scanned the ceiling. There, to the right of where they kept the trashcan, was a leak – a brown stain the shape of a pineapple in the false-ceiling tile. She sighed and grabbed the bucket from under the sink and set it there, watching the water splash against the plastic. After a moment, she joined her mother back on the couch. "There's another leak."

Jo didn't take her eyes off the television. "Great. That's all we need. Did you put the bucket under it?"

"Yeah. I'll try and fix it tomorrow, Mom, don't worry."

"You're a good girl," said Jo.

"You're a good mommy," said Alicia, snuggling closer.

The women on television were at a spa. An attendant wrapped them in seaweed. "I'd like to work at a spa someday," said Alicia. "Maybe become a masseuse."

"You'd be good at that, baby. Such strong hands."

"Really, Mommy? You think so?"

"Sure. Once things pick up at the bar, maybe we'll send you to one of those schools."

"They cost ten thousand dollars."

"That much?"

Alicia shifted so she was sitting on the far end of the couch. "Give me your feet, Mommy. I'll rub 'em for you."

She held her mother's feet in her hands, listening to rain beat against the roof of the trailer. She thought about Lola's offer. If she did it, she could work in one of those swanky spas in the city and wrap women in seaweed. She could send money to her mother so she could fix the roof. And maybe Misty could go to college when she graduated in three years.

The next day Alicia sat slumped in her seat, watching Mr. Ball explain an equation by scrawling it in messy handwriting on the whiteboard. Jack Ball was a new teacher, young, without the wary defeat of the other teachers. He dropped his whiteboard pen and as he reached for it, his sweater sleeve inched up over his wrist. There was the angry red scar on the inside of his wrist again - this telltale sign of a sad man.

In the row next to her, Josh Wilson doodled a pattern like a checkerboard on his folder. His brown hair was on the long side, cut in the way all the boys wore it now, brushed over their foreheads. He shifted in his seat and glanced over at her, and seeing that she watched him, raised an eyebrow and smiled. He was an athlete and his arm muscles flexed as he tapped his pencil on the side of the desk and his thigh muscles pressed against the fabric of his jeans. He was considered good-looking but wasn't the most popular boy because he was on the sweeter side. Would he be interested enough in her to have sex?

What had Lola said to her? *All boys will do it with you if you let them know you want to.* So she smiled at him, hoping he would understand - *I am available.* It must have worked, she thought, since he grinned at her before he leaned back over his notebook, continuing his doodle.

After school, Alicia walked towards home with her hood pulled tight against the slanted rain, her gaze focused on the tips of her soaked tennis shoes. Large drops of water dripped from the edge of her hood like a mini-waterfall. A car pulled up beside her and stopped. She lifted her rain hood. Water splashed her face and ran down the back of her neck. It was Josh, in his blue Subaru. Leaning across the passenger seat, he rolled down the car window and grinned, his pale face flushed. "You wanna ride?"

She looked to the sky and let the rain fall upon her closed lids and her cheeks. When her gaze returned to Josh, he had one arm draped over the steering wheel, peering at her from under his fringe of hair. "Sure," she said, taking off her backpack and sliding into the bucket seat. Accelerating with a lurch, he pulled out to the highway and turned up the radio. It was playing some kind of hip-hop music she didn't like. Josh tapped his fingers against the steering wheel. She stared out the front window, holding her bag against her chest. "Don't you have cross country practice?" she asked.

"Had it this morning."

She nodded and licked her chapped lips, pulling lip-gloss from the side pocket of her bag and running it over her mouth. "You know where I live?"

"Sure."

"Yeah. I didn't have to work today." She let it dangle out there, knowing he would catch it if he were interested.

His eyes slid to her and back again to the road. "You wanna go down to The Landing, listen to some music in my car?"

She stared out the window. The Landing was the state park. A lot of kids went down there for parties and to hang out, both in the parking lot and on the stretch of flat, sandy beach. "I guess."

"Cool," he said, tapping his finger on the steering wheel.

She played with the zipper on her backpack. Her pants were wet from the rain where her coat hadn't covered them, and her legs were numb from the cold. "Could you turn up the heat?" she asked.

"No problem." They passed the Dairy Queen, heading south. The heater blew hot air onto her lap, and steam began to rise from her thighs.

When they pulled into the lot, Josh parked at the farthest spot from the entrance and turned off the car. She was instantly cold again. Rain pounded on the roof of the car. There was the sound of waves crashing below and the occasional seagull. Josh pulled the parking brake. "You wanna mess around?" She looked up at the firs surrounding the parking lot. They swayed from side to side.

"I guess." She made her mind numb, watching the drops of rain make their way down the passenger side window.

He gestured towards the back. "More room in the backseat."

They both climbed over the front seats to the back. Taking his wallet from his letterman jacket, he pulled out a condom.

"We don't need it," she said. "I'm on the pill." She looked at a rip in the car's ceiling upholstery. She hoped Misty remembered that the key was under the mat on the front porch if she decided to come home early from the library. She tugged at the wet jeans that stuck to her skin.

"Great," he said, grinning.

She kept her eyes fixed on the ripped ceiling. "I've got to get home soon, make sure my sister isn't locked out."

He ran his fingers through his shaggy hair and unzipped his pants. "That's cool."

"This is my first time," she said.

"Shit. Really?" His eyes searched her face. "You sure then?"

"Yeah. I don't want to be a virgin anymore. But you can't tell anyone."

"Totally uncool to kiss and tell, right? But why me?"

"I like the color of your skin," she said, staring at the vein in his neck that bulged near the muscle there.

He grinned and put his hand on her left breast and squeezed. "Good enough reason, I guess."

* * *

Afterwards, he drove her home. The rain had lessened and his windshield wipers were on intermittent. She counted two seconds between each swipe. "It only hurts like that the first time," he said, turning down the radio. "I hope it wasn't too bad."

"Don't worry about it. I figured." One-one thousand, two-one thousand, she counted in her head.

"Wanna try again?" He stopped in front of her house.

Her hand on the car door handle, she looked back at him. "Tomorrow?"

"You bet," he said.

CHAPTER ONE

DRESSED IN HER ONE COCKTAIL DRESS and knock-off Spanx undergarment, Cleo Tanner stood near the bar at the annual fundraiser for scholarships for underprivileged children. The smell of tiger lilies in vases on the dining tables set around the Seattle Art Museum made her eyes water. She dabbed at them with a cocktail napkin, wondering if her eyeliner was smeared. Her dress felt tight, like she was a mouse being ingested by a cobra. Why couldn't she stick with a diet? Really. Five pounds. Did it have to be so hard? It was the Sierra Nevada Pale Ales that did it. She should tell Nick to stop giving her so many free pints during her frequent visits to Cooper's. Who was she kidding? That would never happen.

It was the silent auction portion of the evening. Attendees perused the items displayed—gift baskets and a homemade quilt and weeks at vacation homes—on long tables covered in white cloths, all procured by well-intentioned but slightly frightening mothers of Cleo's little Montessori students. Late May, it was an unusually clear and warm night for Seattle, and the committee of mothers had decorated the room with blue and silver ribbons and sparkly things that hung from the ceiling.

She was about to head to the bathroom to adjust the torturous undergarment when suddenly there was a man standing in front of her, carrying two glasses of red wine. He was handsome, she supposed, if one liked the slick type, which she never had, even before Simon. He had an olive complexion and brown eyes and his hair was perfectly cut and blow-dried so that it gave the impression of being tousled instead of carefully groomed. He wore a well-draped, expensive suit, like Sylvia's husband often wore.

"I saw you were empty handed," he said, holding out the wine with a small bow, like an offering to the gods. "Can't have our best teacher without a drink."

She took the glass from his outstretched hand. His fingernails were manicured to a gleam. *Never trust a man with a manicure,* her father always said. But there was no reason to turn down free wine. "Thank you. Do I have your child this year?"

"No children," he said, sticking out his hand. "I'm Scott Moore."

"Ah," she said, keeping her voice light. "The big donor."

"Guilty," he said.

"Your scholarships are being well-used this year," said Cleo.

He smiled, sipping his wine without taking his eyes off her. "I'm pleased to do it."

"Am I right, remembering you're an attorney, Mr. Moore?"

"Trained as an attorney but I run an adoption agency."

She felt a pang, thinking of Sylvia. "Really? How interesting." Then a lie. "I have a friend contemplating adoption."

He raised his brows, took another sip of his wine. "I should mention the fees at my agency are a bit steep."

"My friend is a professor of music," she said, tugging on the skirt of her dress. "But she's from a wealthy Seattle family. Money is not a problem." She felt defensive. Did he only help rich people?

"Really? Would I know them?"

"You would," she said, keeping her voice cold.

"I see," he said. He was trying to hide his curiosity, she thought, watching his eyes glitter.

Everyone in Seattle was familiar with the Holm family and their business enterprises that ranged from oil to timber to technology during a span of 100 years. Sylvia's father was one of five sons, all of them successful in one venture or another, having inherited mass wealth from their oil tycoon grandfather, which they subsequently used to start ventures of their own. Her father was in biochemical engineering.

Scott Moore smiled and tapped his fingers on her bare wrist. "Come to my office sometime. I can explain how we do things. You can decide then if you want to pass the information on to your friend." This was the kind of man who made deals, who was skilled in the art of negotiating, Cleo thought. Someone who got what he wanted.

"I'll think about it," she said.

"Or I'd love to take you to lunch," he said. "Or drinks."

"I don't date," she said, keeping her voice light, without emotion, merely stating a fact. Just then a photographer came over to them, a "Press" I.D. around his neck.

"Pose for a photo, Mr. Moore?"

Scott Moore put his arm around Cleo's shoulder. "Sure."

The photographer snapped several photos of them before thanking them and moving across the room to a different couple.

She shrugged away from his embrace, trying not to shiver. There was something disturbing about this man. Despite her aversion to him, she paused, remembering Sylvia's puffy eyes two nights ago, after the fourth failed in-vitro procedure. "My friend would consider adoption. Her husband isn't so sure."

"What's his hesitancy?"

"I'm not sure."

"But you say she'll consider it. What's holding her back? Besides her husband?"

"She's afraid she'll be disappointed. Have a birth mother change her mind. It happened to other friends of ours."

"It never happens in my agency," said Moore.

"How is that possible?"

"We have ways of making sure a birth mother is certain before we commit to the adoptive parents."

"Is there a long waiting list?" asked Cleo.

He smiled. "You go out with me, I'll put your friend on the top of the list."

She felt her mouth fall open. She stared at him. Surely he was kidding? She laughed. "Very funny."

He smiled and shrugged his shoulders, his voice low. "I'm actually not kidding. I know it seems a bit unorthodox, but I want you to let me take you out. It won't hurt, I promise."

"I hardly know what to say."

He raised an eyebrow, his voice calm, like she was the crazy one for even questioning it. "I mean no harm. And I'm happy to help your friends, regardless. She just won't go to the top of the list."

"Thank you for the wine, but I should join my teacher friends at our table."

"I understand," he said. He handed her his card. "But call me if you change your mind."

* * *

PREVIEW OF
CARAMEL AND MAGNOLIAS

She left the auction before dessert, slipping out the back after a quick goodbye to her table. Driving home, the pounding rain seemed to come out of nowhere just as she exited the West Seattle Bridge onto Admiral Way. Although she tried to dismiss it, the thought of Scott Moore would not leave her mind. What kind of man was he? Obviously, he was controlling and demanding, a man accustomed to getting his own way. But he had another thing coming if he thought he could manipulate her. And yet, she wanted nothing more than for her best friend to be a mother. It begged the question - how many times would she have to go out with him before he'd arrange an adoption? Would Sylvia and Malcolm even consider it? She didn't know. But it was worth asking. If it was something Sylvia wanted and would ease her pain, what were a few dates?

She set the wipers on high. But they had almost no effect against the Seattle downpour, and her shoulders tensed as she drove up the hill, winding up and around, past the main street of West Seattle before turning onto a side street where her apartment building was located.

She waited for the parking garage gate to open and then drove in slowly, her tires squealing on the wet cement. She parked in her designated spot and climbed out of the car, exhausted, anticipating her favorite jeans and a soft T-shirt. What kind of music was she in the mood for? A little Nanci Griffith, circa 1989?

As she exited the elevator, she saw Mrs. Lombardi from 3C going into her apartment, her white hair plastered against her pink scalp. She wore a flimsy raincoat dripping with water, which soaked the cheap carpeting that lined the hallway. "Mrs. Lombardi, why are you so wet?"

"Oh hello, Cleo," she said. "I couldn't find a parking space close to the front at the grocery store and I'm chilled to the bone."

"I wish you'd let me pick things up for you when you need them," said Cleo. "You know I'm happy to get whatever you want when I shop for my dad."

"You're a good girl, but I was out of cat food and you know how Stewie needs his food."

Stewie was the meanest cat ever born, and also one of the fattest. Going a day without food surely wouldn't cause him much harm, Cleo thought, stifling a smile. Sweet Mrs. Lombardi kept shrinking while her cat grew fatter with each passing day. It reminded Cleo of the Danish folktale she often read to her Montessori students, about the cat who ate all the people in the village and grew so fat he couldn't move.

Mrs. Lombardi wiped under her eyes, scrutinizing Cleo. "You look so nice. Did you go out with a man?" she asked in a hopeful tone.

"You know I don't date."

"Cleo, ten years without a man is too long. And thirty years old is so young. You know what I would give to go back and do it all over again? You should be out living it up."

Cleo didn't say anything. She heard this quite often from Mrs. Lombardi. And Sylvia. And, of course, there was Nick. He probably lectured her the most, which was ironic, given that he'd pined for Sylvia in secret for four years, never having the courage to tell her his true feelings. And now it was too late. Four years ago Sylvia had married arrogant and distant Malcolm, whom both Cleo and Nick hated, without ever knowing Nick's feelings. *I'm not good enough for her*, he always said to Cleo. Which, in Cleo's opinion, was absolutely not true. But he saw only that he was a poor bartender trying to make a living as a glass blower. *It wouldn't be enough for her*, he said, time and time again. *She wouldn't respect me.*

"And you're so pretty," Mrs. Lombardi said now. "Men should be lined up around the block for you."

"I'm not interested. You know that."

"Maybe you should get a cat."

"Very funny," said Cleo.

"You want to turn out like me? Alone at sixty living with a cat that only loves me when I feed him?"

Cleo ignored her. "I'm making chicken cacciatore for Dad tomorrow. I'll drop some off for you before I go over there. But only if you promise not to give any to Stewie."

Mrs. Lombardi opened her door wider and stepped inside. "You know I can't promise that." They both laughed. Just then, Stewie came running to the door, leaping into the hallway and sitting back on his hind legs, hissing at Cleo while holding his front paws like a boxer.

"Stewie, nice to see you," said Cleo. He hissed again, this time with even more venom. "I'll check on you tomorrow," said Cleo, backing away. The cat scared her. No question.

"Goodnight, dear."

PREVIEW OF
CARAMEL AND MAGNOLIAS

Cleo crossed the hall to her apartment, 3D. Living alone, she kept it tidy, her familiar objects pleasing during long, rainy afternoons and evenings. It was only 900 square feet - just one bedroom and a front room divided by a counter into a sitting area and kitchen. She'd decorated it in white and blues, replicating photos she found in a beach house magazine she'd purchased standing in the grocery store line. There was an attractive off-white couch, which she kept spotless by almost never sitting on it, and two soft reading chairs in light blue. She'd hung white, filmy curtains over the front windows along with various Impressionist prints and Ansel Adams photos on the walls. Between the two front windows was her one prized possession: her mother's old turntable, set inside a white cabinet and surrounded by books and several photos.

She paused, gazing at the photo of her mother and father on their wedding day, the other of she and Sylvia, arms linked in front of their dormitory room at USC the second week of freshman year. They'd already been best friends by then. She picked up the frame, peering into their eighteen-year-old faces. *So young.* Their cheeks were rounded with youth, eyes sparkling with the possibility of everything. It was before Simon then, before she even knew him and loved him, before the empty space left when he was gone. And the years since for Sylvia? She felt trapped in a loveless marriage, Cleo suspected, although her friend never confessed to it. And maybe she didn't even know herself because all Sylvia wanted was a baby. So much so that all other dreams had faded.

If someone took their photo today, what would they see? Cleo knew the lens would not lie. It would capture two women living on the edges of life, waiting and yearning for that which they could not have.

In her bedroom, she kicked off her dress and slipped into her favorite jeans and T-shirt, which were draped over the reading chair near the window. Then she padded to the kitchen and poured a glass of red wine from an open bottle on the counter.

She took one sip before going to the hall closet and pulling a purple hatbox from the top shelf, next to an umbrella and a Mariners baseball cap. She carried the box and her wine to the bedroom, placed the glass on the bedside table near her mother's high school portrait, and settled cross-legged on the bed. Then she emptied the contents of the hatbox: two photos, a slip of paper with one sentence scribbled on it, a DVD labeled *The Soup Kitchen*, and a typed manuscript entitled *Cleo*, held together with a large, black clasp.

The first of the photos was of her and Simon lounging on the fountain outside of Bing Theater on the USC campus. Each morning before their ten o'clock classes they would spend fifteen minutes together, either chatting or dozing or practicing Cleo's lines for scene class, before Cleo headed into the theater and Simon went to the film school for his graduate level screenwriting class. How they had gloried in the symmetry of that one small thing: class at the same time. It indicated to them that they were meant to be, that the future they envisioned would come to fruition because of that small aligning of the universe: a writer and his muse - an actress and her filmmaker.

The second photo she'd taken of Simon was on the set of *The Soup Kitchen*. He was behind the camera, setting a shot, his shoulders slightly curved, his face focused. She allowed herself to stare at this one for several minutes. But tonight the tears didn't come. She hadn't had enough wine. Instead the cavern in her chest opened wider until all that was left was the terrible emptiness that had once been him.

Next, she held the manuscript to her chest, knowing the story of the Seattle girl and her young mother dying of cancer not only because she'd read it so many times but because she'd lived it once. It was her story before Simon captured it so beautifully in his manuscript. And now it was nothing but these sheets of fading pages in her hands.

Lastly, she picked up the slip of paper. The last words he'd ever written to her. *Gone for donuts*. Gone. Never to return.

She put everything carefully back into the box and returned it to the closet, next to her ordinary things - this Pandora's box of another time and place.

Then she went to her stereo, kneeling on the floor as she rifled through her old LP's for music to suit her mood. There was every type of music, much of it from her mother's collection but some added in the last several years because of the resurgent interest in old LP's as collectors' items. She was embarrassed to say how many hours she spent on the Internet finding and ordering from vinyl sellers all over the world.

She chose Pink Floyd. As the lyrics to *Wish You Were Here* engulfed her as only music could, she grabbed her wine and curled up in the blue chair closest to the stereo. The rain continued outside, cascading down the window in sheets.

From her purse by the door, her cell phone rang. She uncurled from the chair and reached into the bottom of her bag. What was this number? Should she answer?

Against her better judgment, she answered.

"Hi, Cleo. Scott Moore here."

"Hi, Scott. How did you get my number?"

"One of your teacher friends gave it to me. Hope you don't mind? I promise I'm not calling to ask you out."

"All right." What was wrong with this man?

"That's a lie. Actually I am." He sounded amused, which annoyed her further. "No, I'm calling because I just talked with someone from my office and it turns out we have several birth mothers who specifically put in their profiles that they wanted musical adoptive parents. I couldn't help but remember you said your friend is a music professor."

She shivered. The hair on the back of her neck stood up. What did this mean? Was it a sign? Just then her phone buzzed in her hand, indicating another call. She held it away from her ear and looked at the small screen. It was Sylvia. Was it another sign? She looked out the window. The rain still pounded against the pane. "I'll let her know," Cleo said. "I'll have her contact you if she's interested."

"Does this mean you'll agree to go out with me?"

She hesitated. "Let's not get ahead of ourselves. Let's see what she says first." She said goodbye and clicked over to Sylvia.

"Can you meet me at Cooper's?" asked Sylvia.

"I'll be there in thirty minutes," she said, already heading towards the bedroom to find her favorite sweater.

ALSO BY TESS THOMPSON

RIVERSONG

Sometimes we must face our deepest fears to find hope again. A redemptive story of forgiveness and friendship.

RIVERBEND

A woman finds her life in danger when her abusive ex-boyfriend gets out on parole, leaving her no choice but to accept help from a cold and wealthy recluse hiding a dark history of his own.

CARAMEL AND MAGNOLIAS

A former actress goes undercover to help a Seattle police detective expose an adoption fraud in this story of friendship, mended hearts, and new beginnings.

MORE GREAT READS FROM BOOKTROPE

A Tainted Mind by **Tamsen Schultz** (Romantic Suspense) Vivi DeMarco is a woman running from her demons, but now she's facing the worst demon of all: a twisted mind that leaves behind a string of corpses that look suspiciously like Vivi.

Fool's Game by **Heather Huffman** (Romantic Suspense) Targeted for assassination, government agent Caitlyn O'Rourke finds herself working alongside the man who broke her heart and betrayed her long ago.

Work in Progress by **Christina Esdon** (Romance) Psychologist Reese Morgan refuses to let go of a childhood trauma. When she meets a handsome contractor, Josh Montgomery, she wonders if the walls around her heart can be knocked down to let love in.

Blogger Girl by **Meredith Schorr** (Contemporary Romance) Kimberly Long has two passions: her successful chick lit blog and Nicholas, her handsome colleague down the hall. But when her high school nemesis pops onto the chick lit scene with a hot new book and eyes for Nicholas, Kim has to make some quick revisions to her own life story.

Discover more books and learn about our
new approach to publishing at **booktrope.com**.